GINGER, YOU'RE BARMY

David Lodge's novels include *Changing Places*, *Small World*, *Nice Work*, *Thinks . . .* , *Author, Author*, *Deaf Sentence* and, most recently, *A Man of Parts*. He has also written stage plays and screenplays, and several books of literary criticism, including *The Art of Fiction*, *Consciousness and the Novel* and *The Year of Henry James*.

ALSO BY DAVID LODGE

Fiction

The Picturegoers
The British Museum is Falling Down
Out of the Shelter
Changing Places
How Far Can You Go?
Small World
Nice Work
Paradise News
Therapy
Home Truths
Thinks . . .
Author, Author
Deaf Sentence
A Man of Parts

Criticism

Language of Fiction
The Novelist at the Crossroads
The Modes of Modern Writing
Working with Structuralism
After Bakhtin

Essays

Write On
The Art of Fiction
The Practice of Writing
Consciousness and the Novel
The Year of Henry James

Drama

The Writing Game
Home Truths

DAVID LODGE

Ginger, You're Barmy

VINTAGE BOOKS
London

Published by Vintage 2011

6 8 10 9 7 5

Copyright © David Lodge, 1962, 1982

David Lodge has asserted his right under the Copyright, Designs
and Patents Act 1988 to be identified as the author of this work

First published in Great Britain by MacGibbon & Kee in 1962
This edition first published by Martin Secker & Warburg Ltd 1982

Vintage
Random House, 20 Vauxhall Bridge Road,
London SW1V 2SA

www.vintage-books.co.uk

Addresses for companies within The Random House Group Limited
can be found at: www.randomhouse.co.uk/offices.htm

The Random House Group Limited Reg. No. 954009

A CIP catalogue record for this book
is available from the British Library

ISBN 9780099554134

Penguin Random House is committed to a sustainable future for
our business, our readers and our planet. This book is made from
Forest Stewardship Council® certified paper.

Printed and bound in Great Britain by Clays Ltd, St Ives plc

FOR MARY

AUTHOR'S NOTE

The coarseness of soldiers' speech and behaviour is a well-known fact, the representation of which I found necessary to my purpose in this novel. Readers likely to find such representation disturbing or distasteful are warned.

I am very grateful for the assistance, on points of information, of Dr G. Billington, Arthur Harris, John Jordan, Marcus Lefebure, and a Regular Army officer who would, I am sure, prefer to remain nameless. None of these gentlemen is responsible for any errors or improbabilities which remain in the book.

The characters (including the narrator) and the action of the story are fictitious; but in the reference to the Lane Bequest picture I have associated my fictitious characters with an actual event, the true details of which are unknown to me.

D.L.

Ginger, you're barmy,
You'll never join the Army,
You'll never be a scout,
With your shirt hanging out,
Ginger, you're barmy.

PROLOGUE

It is strange to read what I wrote three years ago. It is like reading another man's writing. Things have certainly not worked out as I expected. Or did I deliberately prevent them from so working out? I suppose my present circumstances derive, ultimately, from that visit to the w.c. on the train to London; but I am still not sure what I meant by it. I only remember that I felt I had to do something. At any rate, I take no credit for the action, for I regretted it bitterly later. If I take any credit at all, if I think any better of myself now, than I now think of myself *then*,—as I portray myself in these pages,—it is because I think I have realized that a deterministic conception of character and individual destiny is the subtlest of temptations that dissuade a man conscious of his own defects and others' needs from doing anything about them. I don't think I am a better person, or even a happier one; but perhaps there has been a small advance. I could never again write so unflattering an account of myself as the following, because it would open up so many awful possibilities of amendment. The whole story reeks of a curiously inverted, inviolable conceit.

It reeks too, for me, of the sweet, sickly smell of seaweed which hung about the Mediterranean resort where, in its original, shorter, unpolished version, it was written. Written in a confessional outpouring, at every moment that could be spared,—and at many that could not be spared without impoliteness. Written on beaches where the sun curled the paper and dried the ink as it flowed from the nib; written in the stifling bedroom of the *pension* while the rest of the world slumbered through the siesta; written far into the night by the erratic light of a naked bulb that swung from the impact of bulky moths.

I say 'confessional' because, though there was little contrition about it, the impulse that drove me on to write, which welded the pen to my aching fingers for so many hours, was not a literary one. It was only when I returned to England, and re-read the sweat-stained, sand-dusted pages, that the demon Form began to whisper in my ear about certain alterations and revisions, particularly the aesthetic advantages of concentrating my time at Badmore into a few days, and recounting my weeks at Catterick in a series of flash-backs. And so, what had started out as an attempt to record and confront my own experience subtly changed into an agreeable exercise in the manipulation of bits of observed life. I became a *voyeur* spying on my own experience.

Even now, it seems, I am not immune from the insinuations of Form. It occurs to me that these notes, which I am jotting down on this momentous morning, might usefully form a prologue and epilogue to the main story. . . .

ONE

'I FEEL worn out. I think I'll get ready for bed,' said Pauline.
'O.K.'

This was the ritual. Ostensibly it meant that she could go to bed as soon as I left to catch the 12.15 coach back to Badmore. In fact it lent an added intimacy and excitement to our regular necking sessions last thing on Sunday nights. She took her nightclothes into the kitchenette, and I heard the taps running and the flare of the gas jet under the kettle. Pauline was very hygienic. Because there was only one bathroom to the whole house she could only have two baths a week. But on the other nights she washed herself from the waist up at the kitchen sink. I knew the extent of her ablutions because, a few weeks before, I had squinted into the kitchen through the narrow aperture between the door and the upright.

I got up from the divan and wandered over to the door. But I did not peer through the aperture. It had been too disturbing last time. I had only seen her bare back, but that was enough to set the mechanism of desire lurching into motion. It was only a back; but a nice, shapely back. And I had never seen her back completely bare before. Even the narrow straps of a bathing-suit top made all the difference, I discovered. If I looked now I might see more. But I did not want to see more, unless I could touch more.

'What are you doing, Jonathan?' said Pauline, her voice slightly muffled by a towel. 'Not peeping I hope?'

'Just looking for a match.'

'My lighter's in your jewellery box.'

I had given her the green tooled-leather jewellery case for her last birthday. Rummaging amongst the ceramic earrings and glass beads I found the little heart-shaped lighter. Then my eyes fell on an imprinted metal tab, at the bottom of the case, of the kind that you get from machines on railway stations. I took it out and read the inscription. It said: 'M.B. LUVS P.V.' A door in my mind I usually kept bolted suddenly gave way, and a wind of memories howled through me.

I was still holding the tab, mentally dazed and breathless, when Pauline came back into the bed-sitting room in her dressing-gown, brushing her hair. 'Would you like some coffee?' she was saying. Then, as I did not reply, she stopped brushing and looked at me.

'What on earth have you got there?'

I showed her, and she flushed slightly.

'I didn't know I still had it. Michael gave it to me as a joke once.'

'I know, I was there.'

'Were you? I don't remember.'

'I was watching from the train. And I didn't think it was a joke.'

Pauline was silent, a little sulky. 'Well it's all over now, anyway.'

'Is it?'

'Of course it is.'

'I wonder where he is now?'

'Who, Michael? I expect he's all right. He usually managed to fall on his feet.'

'That's just about the last thing you could say about him. He usually fell on his head.'

'Well, don't let's make ourselves miserable thinking about him now, just before you've got to leave. Come and sit down on the divan.'

This was usually my suggestion, and 'sit down' was a euphemism for 'lie down'. But I obeyed the summons sluggishly, and retained an upright posture. Pauline said:

'Darling, I believe you're jealous.'

'Not jealous. The opposite really. What's the word for feeling you don't deserve to be better off than somebody else? I don't think there is one.'

'Why should you feel like that?' asked Pauline, resuming her hair-brushing.

'I mean I've got you, and he hasn't, for one thing.'

'But darling, we suit each other so much better. Michael and I were never really suited. I was very fond of him—he was my first regular boy-friend. But I never had a moment free from worry. And with us . . . it's been so much fun. I mean, for instance, Michael never took me to a single serious play.'

'And I've never taken you to a dance.'

'Well I agree with you that going to the theatre is more worth while.'

Yes, I had indoctrinated Pauline very successfully. I had not only made her do what I wanted: I had persuaded her to like it. I was silent, and Pauline put down her hairbrush.

'You know, you *are* jealous, whether you admit it or not. I suppose you think I've kept that bit of tin for a souvenir. Well I haven't, and to prove it,'—she rose to her feet—'I'll throw it away.'

She looked round the room, with somewhat comic puzzlement, for some way of disposing of the tab in a sufficiently decisive fashion. The fire, which would have been the obvious place, was a gas-fire. Finally she dropped the tab into a wastepaper basket.

'How do I know you won't ferret it out when I've gone?' I teased her.

'All right.' Her lips pursed in vexation, she retrieved the tab from the basket, opened the window above the divan, and flung the strip of metal into the garden.

'You could still look for it tomorrow morning,' I observed.

'Well, I don't intend to,' she replied crossly.

I laughed, and pulled her down on to the divan. After a token struggle she first submitted, and then responded to my caresses.

She always seemed to get more out of it than I did. At the first touch of my hand, which I slipped under her dressing-gown and pyjama-top, on her stomach, she lapsed into a kind of sensual trance. I enjoyed it all right, and my flesh signalled its response in the usual way, but I never stopped *thinking*, as she seemed to. Perhaps when it came to the real thing I too would stop thinking. Meanwhile my chief pleasure was in a sense of power over her body. There was also a certain academic curiosity in seeing how far I could go.

This time I seemed to be climbing higher up her rib-cage than usual, until my fingers met the soft protuberance of her breast. I held my breath like a thief who has trodden on a creaking floorboard, and then my hand closed over her breast. It felt good, but almost at once I was a little sad. This established a precedent, and yet no subsequent contact would be as exquisite as this. Pauline moaned faintly, 'Better not, darling,' and I withdrew my hand. But I continued to kiss her, guiding her back to the ground.

We lay together and smoked in silence for a while. Pauline yawned and stretched happily.

'Darling, it doesn't seem possible that you're going back to camp for the last time.'

'No, it doesn't.'

For nearly two years, the same hundred miles between Badmore and London covered in each direction, every week-end. Well, nearly every week-end. I had only missed two: once before the General Inspection, and once when I was inevitably kept back with the Rear Party at last Easter's Block Leave (having wangled my way out of every previous Rear Party). It annoyed me slightly that I had missed those two week-ends, but even so it must have been something of a record. It was fortunate of course that at Badmore week-end guard duties were done by visiting N.C.O.s who were on courses. Before I was made up I had paid impecunious troopers to do my week-end guards for me. Expensive, at fifteen shillings a time, but worth it.

'It certainly doesn't,' I repeated. 'I'm sure that next Sunday I'll board the coach to Badmore out of sheer habit.'

'No you won't, darling,' said Pauline gleefully, 'because we'll be in Majorca!'

'So we shall! I'd forgotten that delightful fact for a moment. What time is it again?'

'Six-fifteen in the morning at the terminus.'

'It's a good job they let us out a day early at Badmore.'

The following Thursday morning, the day after I was released from the Army, we were flying to Palma, on a cheap charter-flight, for a holiday. The prospect gave me great pleasure. To throw off my khaki and fly into the sun: it seemed a symbol and a celebration of my release from two years' curtailment of liberty. It would also eliminate that treacherous feeling of faint regret and nostalgia with which we part from any familiar environment, however uncongenial it has been. I had already planned to send to the 'A' Squadron staff from Majorca some glossy, glamorous picture-postcard with a gloating, jubilant message on the back. Perhaps not after all. It would only be a gesture towards that arbitrary, illusory 'comradeship' people talked about so glibly. Better cut off all connections with the Army at once. Except perhaps—for memory is like a sieve that lets the unhappy bits through—to set aside an occasional few minutes for meditation on how boring and tedious and exasperating it all was. And at times really miserable. The first few weeks at Catterick particularly. Catterick. That brought back Mike.

'What about that coffee?' I said.

MY FRIENDSHIP with Mike Brady began on a platform of Darlington station on a Thursday late in August in the mid-fifties. I have forgotten what day of August it was, but I know it was a Thursday because all new intakes of National Servicemen were required to report to their training regiments on Thursdays, at fortnightly intervals. All over England that morning trains had drawn out of stations, out of great termini, out of village halts, with their cargoes of callow youths in varying moods of confidence, apprehension and fear: public schoolboys wondering if they would get a commission in father's old regiment (they needn't have worried, father had written to the Colonel); grammar school boys making resolutions to keep studying in preparation for the university (they scarcely opened a book for the next two years); office boys and factory workers and young fellows of every kind wondering how they could keep their girls or pay the H.P. on their motor-bikes or generally enjoy the prosperity the newspapers accused them of (they soon found they couldn't).

I had come up to Darlington from King's Cross with a pretty fair cross-section. There was the ex-public schoolboy (a minor public school I guessed) who took command of the situation, and of the conversation once it started. He had flat, blond hair and a handsome face, and I took an instant dislike to him. He had been, we swiftly learned, a sergeant in his school O.T.C., and he remarked that he had brought his brasses with him. The significance of this observation escaped me at the time, but I envied him later. After he had succeeded in undermining the morale of the two West Country lads who sat opposite him, grinning awkwardly and twisting their hands, he turned to me and addressed me through my newspaper.

'Are you going to Catterick, too?'

He was a born officer; I was forced to lower my paper, and to reply.

'Yes. Isn't everybody on this train?'

'Not necessarily,' he said humourlessly. 'Which unit?'

'Eh?'

'Which regiment are you going to?'

I fished in my pocket, under his disapproving gaze, for my draft notice. 'Twenty-first Royal Tank Regiment,' I read.

'So am I. Did you apply for the R.A.C.?'

'R.A.C.?'

'The Royal Armoured Corps,' he explained testily. 'The R.T.R. is part of the R.A.C.'

'All these initials make me dizzy. No, I applied for the Education Corps. I'm hoping that this is just preliminary training.'

'Want a cushy time, eh? Well it's not a bad idea if you don't mind giving up the chance of a commission. You get made up to Sergeant automatically in the Education Corps. But I don't think you'll get in. Education Corps chaps usually do their Basic Training with the Infantry.'

I cursed his air of knowledgeability, the more heartily because I thought he might be right. What the hell would I do in the Armoured Corps for two years?

'Got your G.C.E.?' he asked.

'I've just taken my B.A.,' I said, hoping this would deflate him.

'Oh! Where?'

'London.'

He nodded, reassured. 'I'm going up to Oxford myself after the Army.'

Yes, you would, I thought. P.P.E. and hockey Blue. I flipped my paper up to my face. He turned to the remaining member of our little group, a rather slovenly, oafish sort of person, who had got into our compartment at Grantham.

'Are you going to Catterick?'

'Me? Naw.' He guffawed. 'Naw. Ah've 'ad Catterick.' He guffawed again. 'Ah've 'ad the Army.'

'You've done your National Service, have you?' I asked.

'Aye! T'day!'

We all laughed, a trifle edgily. Even the public schoolboy was a little taken aback, displeased to find himself a tenderfoot after all. Actually it wasn't such an ironical coincidence as we all imagined, for, as I afterwards discovered, intake day was also, officially, release day. One of us was taking the place vacated by this released soldier. I looked at him with curiosity. He didn't look very soldierly. His hair was long and his clothes were cheaply flashy—that North of England flashiness that is always about two years behind the South. His pimply brows were creased in some kind of mental effort. Finally his forehead cleared, and he said with a grin:

'Well, you've only got seven hundred and thirty days t' push!'

The train was slowing as it drew into Doncaster. He stood up and looked eagerly out of the window, took his bag from the rack and disappeared into the corridor.

'*His* unit must have been a shower,' said the public schoolboy, re-asserting himself.

I refused to make any further contribution to the conversation. The jubilation of the released soldier had disturbed me slightly. I realized how little thought I had given to the Army. It had been merely an irritating idea which I had brushed aside in the intensive study for Finals, and the anxiety of waiting for results. I realized that I knew nothing about the thing that I was to be for the next two years. I was glad when we reached Darlington, where I was able to shake off the public schoolboy. I was quite delighted when I saw Mike fiddling with an automatic machine on the platform.

'Mike!' I cried, 'Fancy seeing you here!'

'Hallo, Jon,' he replied, more calmly. 'Don't tell me what you're doing here. I can guess.'

'Catterick?'

He nodded.

'Which unit?'

'Eh?'

'Which regiment?'

'Oh . . . Twenty-first something or other.'

'So am I.' I was delighted. 'Come and have something to eat. We've got half an hour.'

He turned back to the automatic machine, and gave it a kick. 'This thing's got my last sixpence and it won't even give me a bar of chocolate.'

'Oh, have something on me.'

We went into the buffet, and I bought a couple of glossy pork pies and two cups of tea.

'Well, this is a coincidence,' I said. As with the released soldier, however, I was wrong. It wasn't really a coincidence. The number of forms you filled in might have led you to believe that some thought and discrimination went into the allocation of National Servicemen to particular branches of the Services. In fact it became quite clear that nobody paid the slightest attention to the forms, bundles of which were pushed into whatever pigeonhole happened to be empty. Mike and I had both come down from the same college of the same university at the same time, and it was not really surprising that we were destined for the same training regiment. However we were both pleased to find a friend amid the alien crowd of bewildered and unhappy youths shambling about Darlington station.

Our greeting was warmer under these circumstances than it might otherwise have been. For though Mike and I had both studied the same subject, English, and had both been in the same year, we had had very little contact with each other at college. Neither of us had been very typical undergraduates. I had lived at home, and devoted myself almost exclusively to study. But even had I participated more fully in 'Union activities' I doubt whether I would have been any more intimate with Mike, who had taken as little interest in the extra-curricular activities of the college as he had taken in the curriculum itself. I knew him mainly as a curiously aimless individual who could be seen at most hours of the day in the Union Bar, drinking beer and playing darts with a group of cronies who seemed hell-bent on occupying their time at the university as unprofitably as possible. He contributed some violent and obscure poems to the college literary magazine from time to time, and on one occasion had delivered in a debate what was said to be a striking speech against birth control. ('Mr Brady said that the people who advocated birth control always waited until they were born before doing so,' the college newspaper had reported.) That was the sum total of Mike's contribution to university life, as far as I knew.

I looked across the marble-topped table at Mike, and speculated, with some amusement, as to what the Army would make of him. In his soiled and neglected clothing he had always stood out from the calculated and self-conscious bohemianism of college like an authentic cowboy on a dude ranch. He wore now a dirty sports shirt open to the lower chest for want of buttons, and revealing the absence of a vest; an old brown sports jacket frayed at the cuffs and button-holes; a pair of shapeless, stained corduroy trousers; and black shoes that had never been polished since he walked out of the shop in them, leaving their disintegrating predecessors, no doubt, in the hands of a scandalized salesman. His vivid ginger hair was longer than I had ever seen it, hanging shaggily down over his white, freckled forehead and neck.

'Hanging on to your hair till the last minute?' I joked.

'Is it very long?' he asked innocently. 'I meant to have it cut, but I couldn't afford it.'

A topic of some embarrassment hung between us, and I was relieved when he acknowledged it.

'Congratulations on your First.'

'Thanks,' I replied. 'It was bad luck for you.' Mike had failed. I didn't really mean what I said. Mike hadn't been unlucky. He hadn't done a stroke of work, and the only surprise was that the Department had let him carry on at college after his first year.

'Yes,' he said, 'It was a nuisance. My mother got rather worked up.' He shook his head like a horse in summer, as if to rid himself of unpleasant memories. I was sorry for purely selfish reasons that Mike had failed. My First was still recent enough to give me a pleasant glow whenever I thought of it, and I would have welcomed the chance to gossip about the papers and other people's results. But this would have been tactless in the circumstances.

'Couldn't you have stayed on to do research?' he asked.

'I'm going back afterwards. I wanted to get this thing over first.'

'I'd have kept out of it, if I were you; they might abolish it soon.'

'Yes, that *would* be rather sickening. But I didn't want to start studying again so soon. I think it might do me good to have a break.'

God knows where I had got this idea from, that the Army might 'do me good', that two years of tedious serfdom would be 'a break'. I suppose I had concocted it as some kind of re-assurance.

'Our train goes in a few minutes,' I said, glancing at the clock above us. 'We'd better move.'

Darlington was never for me anything more than a railway station, a junction on the route to London, a frontier post. One could almost trace the line of the frontier through the station. Where the London expresses pulled in the platforms were wide and spacious, with buffets, bookstalls, prosperous-looking travellers and smart girls. Mike and I now left this sector and crossed over to the smaller, bleaker, dirtier part which was the terminus for the branch line to Richmond. We got into a compartment of a train full of conscripts. The air was thick with Woodbine smoke and confused accents from every quarter of the British Isles. There was a constant restless activity in and about the train: doors were opened and slammed shut, faces were thrust in at the window, and abruptly withdrawn. People changed seats and sometimes compartments, charged past at a gallop, and rushed back again, leaned out of the windows, shouted gutturally to each other. There was a strange nervous hilarity in the air, as if a Clacton Excursion had got mixed up with the Siberian Special, and no one quite knew whether they would end up at Butlin's or a concentration camp.

Our first weeks in the Army were to lean towards the latter. We had an indication of this as soon as our train, after wheezing and creaking through the soggy Yorkshire countryside for three-quarters of an hour, reached Richmond. In the station yard were several lorries drawn up to take us to our various units, each lorry with an N.C.O., and each N.C.O. with a mill-board.

'Twenty-first R.T.R. over here,' called out a tall, tense

corporal with a thin, fair moustache. Mike and I clambered into the back of the awkwardly high vehicle. Finding the interior dark and dank, we stayed near the tailboard. Other conscripts scrambled in. One lit a cigarette.

'Put that cigarette out!' rapped the corporal sternly. There was a nervous tittering from the rest of the passengers as the offender hurriedly dropped his cigarette on to the floor, and stamped on it.

'And we don't want your dog-ends in the truck,' continued the corporal. The dog-end was duly picked up and ejected from the truck. The episode seemed such a naïve act of military assertiveness that Mike and I instinctively looked at each other and grinned.

'What are you two grinning at?' the corporal barked at us. 'The first thing you nigs can learn is that you don't smoke in army vehicles.'

We learned more than that from this brief episode: a new word, 'nig', meaning new conscript, an item in the weird philological tangle of army slang; and the realization that for the first time since childhood we were to be subjected to abuse and criticism without any appeal to the written and unwritten laws which control conduct in civilized life.

'Well, you're in the Army now,' I said to Mike, as the corporal called 'Roll it', and the truck jerked into motion.

'A rather unpleasant individual,' he remarked. 'I hope they're not all like that.'

Richmond is a lovely town blighted by the Army. Through it, in it and round it, Catterick Camp has spread like a pox, defacing the antique beauty of the town and the fine contours of the Yorkshire hills with its squalid architectural improvisation. The size of the camp is appalling. Our truck ground and whined through a seemingly endless expanse of squat huts huddled together round bleak parade grounds, forbidding barrack blocks, dejected rows of married quarters, and everywhere obtrusive military notice boards, with their strident colours and barbaric language of abbreviations.

Amiens Camp (the name was pronounced phonetically), the home of the Twenty-first Royal Tank Regiment, lay on the outskirts of Catterick. In one sense this was a disadvantage since one was at some distance from such amenities as Richmond offered, and in particular from the railway station. On the other hand, one looked from the slopes of Amiens Camp on to a noble landscape as yet unspoiled by the Army. There was something peculiarly oppressive about the older, inner part of the camp, where a military slum had grown up with the haphazard ugliness of an industrial town in the nineteenth century. Not that Amiens Camp was by any means new. Most of the huts had been condemned in 1939. But it suggested rural rather than urban decay: grass grew thick and rank around derelict huts, and a few sheep were allowed to graze on various parts of the camp to keep the vegetation under control.

We jumped down from the truck and were fed into the machine that dealt with new intakes. Clerks behind trestle tables took down details we had already given on various forms to various officials before being called up: name, address, occupation, education, sports, religion.

'Catholic,' said Mike, who was just beside me.

'R.C.,' muttered the clerk, penning the letters laboriously. 'Hobbies or special interests?'

'Red Indians,' replied Mike. The clerk looked up, startled.

'Now don't be funny . . .' he began.

'I'm perfectly serious. I'm very interested in Red Indians. My great-grandmother was raped by one. She was a pioneer in the Wild West. *I* may have Red Indian——'

'All right, all right.'

I was so absorbed by this exchange that I missed the question my own clerk was asking me.

'Religion?' he repeated.

'Eh? Oh, Agnostic.'

'What's that?'

'I don't subscribe to any religion.'

'Atheist,' he said.

'No, Agnostic. They're quite different.'

'You've got to be C. of E., R.C., O.D. or Atheist.'

'What's O.D.?' I asked, interested.

'Other denominations.'

'Put down Agnostic. I'll explain if necessary.'

He hesitated.

'How d'you spell it?'

Next we had a medical examination. We sat round the walls of a warm, stuffy room which smelled of perspiration, wearing only jackets and trousers, waiting to be called in to the Medical Officer. Three soldiers in denims were making some adjustments to the lights. We sat, quiet and depressed, hoping perhaps that the medical might result in a last-minute reprieve, while the three soldiers conducted at the tops of their voices, as if oblivious of our presence, the most obscene conversation I had ever heard in my life. It might almost have been laid on by the authorities as an introduction course in Army language. It was obscene not only in its liberal and often ingenious use of the standard expletive that lingers like a persistent echo throughout any conversation in the Army, but also in its use of words whose obscenity, at that stage, I could only guess at, and in its content: sexual encounters experienced at the last week-end, or anticipated at the next, the merits and demerits ('too messy') of virgins as sexual prey, the dangers of intercourse with menstruating women ('my mate said 'is bollocks turned blue') *et cetera*.

I listened with a kind of furtive fascination, furtive because I thought Mike might disapprove. But he seemed lost in thought.

'Very select company,' I said at last.

'Hmm? Oh, them. Yes they are rather tiresome. But you'll get used to it.'

Meditating on this remark, I realized that Mike had had far more acquaintance with this kind of thing than I. At school and at college I had lived a protected life. Unlike most students I had never worked during my vacations, but had prudently conserved my grant to be able to study. Mike, on the other hand, had taken all kinds of temporary jobs, in factories, on building sites, often, unknown to the college authorities, during term. He had, therefore, already a broad experimental knowledge of the manners and conversation of the vast, uncouth British proletariat which were to me, in my first weeks in the Army, a revelation.

One of the things I shall always associate with Basic Training is the exertion and indignity of carrying large, heavy objects. We always seemed to be moving our belongings at

Catterick from one part of the camp to another. It started on that first afternoon when, after the cursory medical, we were issued with knife, fork, spoon, mug and bedding. A mattress, I found, was a peculiarly awkward thing to carry, since it was impossible to get one's arms round it in any way. Eventually, after dropping the mattress once, and smashing my mug in the process, I stumbled into a hut and flung my burden down on a vacant bed. I quickly tossed my blankets on to the next bed to keep it for Mike.

I sat on the bed and inspected the inhospitable interior of the hut. The floor was of uncovered stone flags. Several panes were missing from the windows. There was a low, battered tin locker beside each bed. Two deal tables and a few chairs made up the rest of the furniture. In the middle of the hut, at some distance from my bed, was a small, ineffective-looking stove. I was glad it was still August.

The hut was already partly occupied by new Regular recruits. It was the practice to train these with the National Servicemen, but to receive them a few days earlier. If this was intended to give the Regulars a certain superiority of status, it was partially successful. For in Basic Training one lost one's sense of proportion, as regards time. A fortnight later I looked upon a newly arrived intake, long-haired and civilian-clothed, with the jaundiced relish of an old lag seeing the prison gates open to admit some bewildered new detainee. So it was that we felt somewhat ill at ease before these Regulars of three days' seniority, who lay on their beds with an air of composure and familiarity, directing rhetorical questions at us and exchanging jokes with each other in coarse, harsh voices.

But their supremacy was not to last long. When training started in earnest we were all on equal terms, and soon the National Servicemen had the upper hand. The Army blundered, in fact, in training Regulars with National Servicemen. In any argument or exchange of abuse every National Service-man could rely on the unanswerable riposte of 'Well, at least I haven't got three [or six, or twenty-two] years to push.' Ironically the Regular soldiers, who had voluntarily enlisted, were quickly infected by the National Serviceman's habit of 'counting the days'.

When Mike came in and deposited his bedding, we followed a bunch of Regulars to the cookhouse, a dark, high-roofed cavern, echoing with the clash of cutlery and the noisy mastication of sausages, mashed potatoes and gravy. It was a meal I found peculiarly repulsive at that hour, particularly the gravy, which I was too slow to intercept as it was splashed on to my plate. Mike ate his food mechanically, without discernible pleasure or distaste.

'Did you put down for the R.A.C.?' I asked him.

'No. I didn't put down for anything.'

'I put down for the Education Corps. I said that it was the only Corps in which I thought I could be of any use. Do you think they sent me here out of spite?'

'I doubt if they have the intelligence,' replied Mike. 'I doubt if they see anything inappropriate about putting you in the Armoured Corps. I expect they think they're honouring you.'

'I hope to hell I can get transferred,' I said, looking round at the dismal scene.

An officer in a black dress uniform, with highly polished belt and buckles, moved among the weary conscripts as they sat shovelling sausages and mash down their gullets. A sergeant with a black sash paced watchfully at his heels, as if he were conducting the officer through some zoo of cowed but potentially dangerous animals.

'Any complaints?' inquired the officer briskly as he came up to us.

The others at our table muttered 'No, sir'. I couldn't find the courage to complain, but Mike said in his soft, distinct voice:

'The potatoes are watery.'

The officer checked himself in the act of turning away. One could almost see the mechanism of his training grinding laboriously into motion. He appropriated my spoon and tasted a morsel of the potato with a rigid control of his facial muscles. Swallowing hard, he said:

'Nothing wrong with that.'

The sergeant lingered behind after the officer had walked off.

'Just arrived?' he asked, in a tone of ironically affected doubt.

'Yes,' replied Mike.

'Uhuh. . . . You'd better change your attitude quick, sonny, or you'll be in trouble. And just remember to address an officer as "Sir" and a sergeant as "Sergeant".'

The others at our table regarded Mike curiously.

'Pom,' said one of them, digging his fork into the potato.

'Eh?' said Mike.

'Pom. That's why it's watery.'

'Oh. Yes, I see.'

'What's Pom?' I asked Mike.

'Dehydrated potatoes. They mix it with water.'

I pushed my plate back in disgust.

'No wonder it's so vile. What's the object? Potatoes are cheap enough.'

'They're probably still using up stocks from the last war.'

We rose from the table and went over to the waste-food bin, into which I scraped most of my meal. I learned to avert my eyes while performing this task in future. As we moved towards the door I saw a face which I seemed to recognize.

'Just a minute, Mike, who's that over there? My God, surely it isn't——'

But it was: Gordon Kemp, another member of our department who had graduated that summer. My surprise was due partly to the fact that all three of us should be in the same place, but more to the change in his appearance, which had caused me to falter in recognizing him. His clumsily-cropped hair stuck up in tufts above a white, haggard face; his neck, always rather long and thin, sprouted like a sickly stalk from the gaping collar of his drab denims, which seemed to contact no part of his anatomy between his shoulders and ankles. He was eating greedily, and spluttered when we clapped him on the back.

'Oh hello,' he said finally. Then, with a grin, observing our civilian clothes, 'Just arrived?'

'Yes,' answered Mike. 'How's life?'

'Pretty grim at the moment. Bags of bull. But we pass out on Thursday, thank God.'

'Bull, what's that?' I asked him.

He grinned again. 'You'll soon find out.' He looked up at

me as he sluiced down the last of his gravy-sodden potato with a gulp of the sweet amber-coloured tea. 'Congratulations,' he said, laying down his mug.

'Thanks,' I replied, taking the reference to my First with more alacrity than was perhaps consistent with modesty. 'You were unlucky not to get a First yourself.' Gordon had plodded his way to a deserved Upper Second.

'No, I was quite satisfied. I'd never have got a First in a thousand years. Mike here would have, if he'd done a stroke of work.'

Mike shrugged his shoulders. It was true, and the honesty of the remark was typical of Gordon. But it seemed to disqualify Gordon from membership of the small cell of cultured resistance to the Army which I was already subconsciously forming with Mike. Despite his gaunt appearance Gordon seemed to be almost enjoying the rigours of Basic Training; or at least applying himself to mastering them with the same dogged persistence he had brought to the study of Anglo-Saxon sound-changes and textual variants in *Love's Labour Lost*.

'Must dash now,' he said, scrambling to his feet. 'Full kit layout tomorrow.'

'We're just going too.'

We followed him out to the tank of murky, lukewarm water in which we rinsed our plates and cutlery. Gordon's hut was in the same direction as ours, and we accompanied him for a while. We learned the reason for his zeal : he was set on getting a commission.

'Why d'you want one?' asked Mike.

He seemed somewhat taken aback by the question.

'Don't *you* want one?'

'I don't know. I haven't thought about it.'

'Well you get better living conditions for one thing. And it's always useful for getting jobs afterwards.'

'What sort of jobs?'

'Oh, industry, Civil Service, that sort of thing.'

We parted from him, and wandered back to our hut, which was chill and damp in the evening air. Mike threw himself down on his bed and smoked a cigarette. We exchanged a few desultory remarks about Gordon as I dusted the inside of my locker and unpacked my grip. I took out the Pelican translation of the *Inferno* by Dorothy Sayers, but found it difficult to concentrate. A few National Servicemen sat glumly on their beds, writing letters or watching the boisterous pranks of the Regulars. The dominant personality among the latter was an individual called Norman, squat and powerfully built, with short legs and a great pear-shaped head ravaged by what I took to be the legacies of venereal disease: he had what the Elizabethans called a 'French crown'. He spoke a thick, harsh dialect of the East Midlands. His favourite exclamation was 'a French letter wi' a patch in it', and his favourite threat 'I'll ride ya'. This last, when carried into action, consisted in his throwing himself on one of his mates who was lying on his bed and pretending to rape his victim by bouncing violently up and down on top of him. This had evidently become quite a sport among the group, and often half a dozen of them would pile on top of one man and pound the breath out of him, shouting and laughing. After the third such demonstration I closed my book in despair.

'Isn't there somewhere else we can go?' I asked Mike.

'I think there's a Naafi somewhere,' he replied, sitting up. 'Let's go and look for it.'

'Our friend Norman is rather like Caliban, don't you think.' he observed as we walked through the dusk. ' "A very land-fish".'

'That's Ajax, in *Troilus and Cressida*, actually,' I said. '*He's grown a very land-fish, languageless, a monster*. Thersites, Act Three scene three, I think.' Catching the flicker of a grimace on his face I added hastily. 'But it fits him all right. So does Caliban.'

The Naafi canteen was a large, high room with round Formica-topped tables screwed to the floor at regular intervals and a long bar which supported two urns, some wizened doughnuts under a plastic cover and the breasts of a pasty-faced girl who surveyed us listlessly as we approached her. The canteen was almost empty except for a group of seasoned-looking veterans who were sitting round a table littered with beer bottles. Mike's eyes brightened as he saw the latter.

'Can you lend me a pound, Jon?'

'Sure.'

'I feel like a drink. In fact I feel like a whisky.' He asked the girl for a whisky.

'What d'you think this is, the Officer's Mess?' she replied, without lifting her breasts from the counter.

'Oh all right, I'll have a beer. What have you got on draught?'

'Only bottled.'

Mike sighed. 'Bass?'

'Yes.'

'Red Triangle then.'

I was glad to see that there was a better selection of food behind the bar than on it. I bought a ham roll and a cup of coffee. We occupied one of the corner tables. Mike swallowed a third of his beer and lit a cigarette.

'Penny for your thoughts,' I said.

'Not worth it. I've just taken a pound off you.' He added: 'I must write off for some money.'

'Don't worry, I've plenty.'

After a pause Mike said:

'Actually, I was thinking that if I had had any sense I wouldn't be in this place.'

I was pleased to hear this. I had been trying to disguise from Mike my own increasing dismay at the prospects opening up on all sides, fearing that he might consider me rather weak.

'Where would you be then?'

'In Ireland.'

'*Are* you Irish, Mike?'

I had been wondering about this. His name and physical appearance seemed to suggest that he was Irish, but his speech was distinguishable from standard Southern English only by a certain melodic softness of the vowels.

'No, unfortunately. Otherwise I wouldn't be here. My parents are Irish, but I was born in England.'

He told me something about his family background, which was a vivid miniature of recent Irish political history. The Bradys were a politically conscious clan, fervently nationalist and anti-clerical. Mike's great-uncle had been a friend of Parnell. His father, a medical student at the time, had been closely associated with the Easter Rising of 1916. He still treasured a piece of rusty thread with which he had stitched a flesh-wound of Pearse's. Mr Brady had escaped the reprisals after the failure of the Rising, but he had continued to support the Nationalist movement until, disgusted by the betrayal of Partition, he had emigrated with his wife, paradoxically to England, in 1924. He re-qualified as a doctor and set up practice in Hastings. Mike had been born there in 1934.

'Has your father ever been back to Ireland?'

'Never.'

'Have you?'

'Oh yes. I go there nearly every summer. I was in Dublin this summer, actually. I got my call-up papers there. I burned them, and took a job as a guide to American tourists.'

'Why did you come back?'

'My mother sent me a telegram saying my father was seriously ill.'

'Oh, I'm sorry Mike. Is he all right now?'

He smiled wryly. 'It was only a cold. The telegram was a trick, to get me back to England. My mother didn't want the disgrace of having a deserter in the family.'

I groped unsuccessfully for a reply. Mike's laconic words opened a door on a violent, dramatic family life quite beyond my experience or comprehension. Ever since I had won my scholarship to a grammar school I had never encountered or expected any objection to my conduct from my parents. They were both over forty when I, their only child, was born, and they still seemed somewhat dazed by surprise. Sometimes I wondered if they had stumbled on the trick of procreation by accident; at other times I wondered if I were their child at all. They behaved towards me like an honest peasant couple in an old myth, entrusted with the care of some divine changeling. My by no means exceptional academic success had awed them into a timid submission to my will. Since my own temperament leaned naturally towards a tranquil, prudent, industrious existence, our relationship was an untroubled one.

I was beginning to feel tired, and had heard that we would be woken at some impossible hour the next morning, so I suggested that we should return to the hut. Most of the occupants were in bed, some sitting up reading or writing letters, some asleep, despite the noise and chatter of the Regulars, some just staring vacantly at the ceiling, dreaming perhaps of the girls, suits and record-players they had left behind them. One—a married man with a family, as I later discovered—was reading a child's comic, *Beano* I think it was.

I changed into the pyjamas my mother had packed for me, and got into bed. Mike, like most of the others, slept in his underpants, and, like most of the others, continued to do so after pyjamas had been issued. This curious distaste for pyjamas among a large section of the male population of Great Britain, was another of those small, interesting discoveries I was constantly making in the first weeks of National Service.

Just as the hut was settling down for the night, a lance-corporal came in, followed by a young fellow entirely hidden behind a mattress. The lance-corporal dropped a bag on a vacant bed, and guided the new recruit towards it.

'Here you are,' he said.

A muffled 'Thank you' was heard from behind the mattress, which dropped on to the bed to reveal the latest and unhappiest addition to our ranks. He was a slender, willowy boy whose physical appearance suggested that he was a product of aristocratic inbreeding. The refinement implied in his fine, white skin and delicate bony fingers was qualified by a certain foolishness and even decadence suggested by his weak mouth, receding chin and pale, alarmed eyes. And even in those first few minutes I noticed that all his limbs were just perceptibly out of control. He fumbled awkwardly with the straps of his bag, dropped several objects several times, and his rather large feet were constantly getting entangled with the legs of his bed. At the time I put this down to nervousness. For he was unfortunate in that the only vacant bed was in the midst of the Regular camp at the far end of the hut. The Regulars welcomed the diversion afforded by his late arrival.

'Miss yer train mate?' asked one of them.

'Yes, I did actually,' replied the newcomer, blushing. There was a general laugh. Someone echoed the 'actually'.

'Yer wanner watch it mate. Yer'll be in the guardroom before yer've got yer uniform on.' More laughs and cat-calls.

'Don't listen to them, youth,' said Norman, with mock sympathy. 'They're as thick as a cow's c——t.'

'I beg your pardon?' said the young boy, plainly uncomprehending, but hoping that this misshapen creature might be friendly.

' 'E don't understand you, Norman,' someone shouted. 'You're too ignorant.'

'Shut up or I'll ride ya.'

'Why don't you ride 'm. 'E's got a nice arse.'

The young boy flushed violently.

'What's your name, youth?' inquired Norman.

'Higgins.'

'No, your first name.'

'Percy.'

Norman turned his head away, grinning with triumph at the information he had extracted. His pals crowed with delight, tossing the name to each other on gales of laughter. Percy's name gave them a kind of purchase on him, and he was assailed with questions from all sides. If he had had any sense he would have remained silent and got into bed as quickly as possible. But he took a painfully long time over his unpacking, and answered all the questions he understood with instinctive politeness. Those he didn't understand were answered for him.

'Where d'you come from, Percy?'

'I was born in Lincoln, but I've been at school in Hampshire.'

'Was it a girls' school, Percy?'

'No, it was a boys' school.'

'Percy, 'ave you ever shagged a girl?'

'No, Percy shagged the other boys.'

When Percy asked where the w.c. was there was a cry of 'Norman, take Percy to the shit-'ouse, 'e wants a piss.' And when the unfortunate boy took off his trousers preparatory to going to bed, the noise grew to a crescendo. One Regular writhed in his bed, vividly simulating uncontrollable sexual excitement. We National Servicemen at the other end of the hut sympathized with Percy, but made no protest. There was in fact nothing really malicious about the ragging; the pain was all in Percy's acute sensitivity, the tenderness of which none of us appreciated until he began to go very red in the face, and puffy around the eyes.

'Christ, I think the poor fellow's going to cry.' Mike said to me.

The poor fellow was evidently a glutton for punishment, because he proceeded to kneel down and say his prayers. This took his tormentors by surprise. A certain atavistic respect for religion enforced a lull, but they soon recovered themselves. Since he no longer answered their questions they were obliged to use him as a kind of reflector for their own exchange of insults. Norman was begged not to take advantage of Percy's posture. This inspired one of his pals to get out of bed and stand in an obscene attitude behind Percy. At this, Mike tossed back his blankets and stepped over to the Regular, tip-toeing on the cold stone flags. His white, muscular body was covered with fine, red hair.

'Why don't you leave the poor fellow alone,' he said quietly. There was a sudden, expectant hush. Percy remained kneeling, but looked up wonderingly at his rescuer.

'It's only a joke, mate.'

'Well, the joke's over. I should get back into bed if I were you.'

'Who are you ordering about? I'll do what I fugging well like,' blustered the other.

This tense situation was resolved by the re-entrance of the lance-corporal who had originally escorted Percy to the hut.

'What the fugging hell's going on in here,' he roared. 'I could hear the row half a mile away.' His eye took in the little tableau around Percy's bed. 'Get back into bed you three,' he said sharply. Percy crossed himself and got between the blankets. The other two returned to their beds in silence. The lance-corporal stood at the door with his hand on the light-switch.

'If I hear another squeak out of this hut tonight I'll have you all on fatigues every night for the next five weeks,' he said. Then he put out the light.

TWO

I LEFT Pauline's flat at the usual time, 11.35. It was my practice to propose leaving at 11.20, so that I could enjoy her pleas to stay a little longer without worrying about missing the coach. Even if I did miss it there was the 1.30 milk-train from Waterloo, but it was a slow journey and meant a long, cold walk from the station. I took the tube to Waterloo, changing at Leicester Square almost unconsciously: I had done it so often.

The car park opposite the Old Vic was full of coaches, though already several were leaving, packed with soldiers, sailors and airmen. The hot-dog stall and the coffee-stall were doing a good trade. A lot of people are going to be sorry to see the end of National Service, I reflected. Ben Hardy for instance. I caught sight of him beside his big grey Bedford Duple, talking to another driver. Ben nodded as I came up to the coach door.

'Nice week-end, Corporal.?'

'Fine thanks. Last time you'll be seeing me, Ben.'

'What! Getting demobbed?'

'Next Wednesday.'

'Bet you're sorry.'

'Oh sure! I'm going to sign on.'

'Get out!' said a voice from behind. 'There's only one thing worse than a Regular and that's a National Serviceman what signs on.'

I looked round and saw Chalky White, who worked in the Q.M.'s Stores. He was a curious creature, by turns witty, naïve, boastful and timid. His long chin, hunched shoulders and the limping, hopping movement of his spindly legs always put me in mind of a wounded heron. We climbed into the coach.

'After you,' I said, motioning him into the inside of the seat.

My action was prompted not by politeness but by self-interest: it was easier to sleep sitting on the outside, with one's feet in the aisle.

'Nice week-end, Chalky?'

'Fair. Very fair. We played at this pub see. Got thirty bob each. Not bad eh? *Oh I never felt more like singin' the blues . . .*' Chalky drummed on the window ledge with his finger-tips. He played the washboard in a skiffle-group.

'How about you, Jon? Good week-end?'

'Very pleasant. I completed my plans for my holiday.'

'What, after your release?'

'That's right.'

'When's that then?'

'Next Wednesday.'

'Next *Wednesday*!' His voice rose several octaves. 'I thought it wasn't for three or four weeks yet.'

'Wednesday's the day, Chalky. On Tuesday I'll be handing you my boots and uniform and the rest of the junk with the greatest of pleasure.'

It was difficult to refrain from this ceremony of rubbing your imminent release into everyone you spoke to, when for two years you had suffered the same thing from others.

'How long have you got to push, Chalky?'

'Nine bloody months,' he replied gloomily.

'Get some service in, youth,' said a flat Midland voice. Lance-Corporal Boon, Orderly Room clerk, carefully placed his grip on the luggage rack, and sat down beside me on the other side of the aisle, spreading his hands over his fat khaki-clad thighs. Since being made up he wore uniform on leave—in order to show off his stripe at home, according to Chalky. As Chalky said, 'It must be a pretty crummy place if they get worked up over a lousy stripe.'

'I see they've got you down for a guard tomorrow night,' observed Boon, looking at me.

'Bollocks! First I've heard of it,' I exclaimed.

'It was on Squadron Orders on Friday,' said Boon smugly. 'But I suppose you didn't see it, seeing you scived off at lunch-time.'

I had wangled permission from my superior, Captain Pirie,

to leave early on Friday, on the pretext that I had to see the Prof. at college about my research. I had gone up by train and booked a coach ticket for the return journey only.

'That bastard Fotherby, I bet,' I said venomously. 'I'll fix that tomorrow morning.'

'You're due for a guard, aren't you?' said Boon. He took a proprietary interest in Squadron Orders, which he rolled off on a duplicator. He always enjoyed telling people that they were down for a duty, before they read it for themselves. 'I noticed you haven't done one for some time.'

'Christ, Boon,' I said. 'Do you memorize every bloody guard anybody does? Haven't you got something better to think about?'

'Keep your hair on. I thought you'd like to know.'

'That's 'ard, that is,' interposed Chalky, 'Doin' a guard in your last week.'

'Hard?' I muttered. 'It's bloody ridiculous. I know who it is. Sergeant-Major Fotherby, the new-broom boy. I'll soon settle *him*.'

But inwardly I was not so confident. My whole strategy at Badmore had been directed towards securing my own comfort and convenience by ingratiating myself with key figures of authority. To my immediate superior, Captain Pirie, I was indispensable, and there was a tacit agreement between myself and the senior officers of the unit that I would contain Pirie's innate tendency to commit acts of disastrous folly. But Captain Pirie, besides being President of the Regimental Institutes (that is, in charge of the welfare and recreational side of unit life) was also the Officer Commanding 'A' Squadron. And while I held sovereign sway over his activities as P.R.I., being myself the P.R.I. clerk, in his capacity as O.C. 'A' Squadron he was under the influence of the Squadron Sergeant-Major. For most of my time at Badmore this post had been filled by a bored veteran of the North African war, whose goodwill I had experienced no difficulty in enlisting, since I was able to get him sports equipment for his son at a considerable discount. A month before, however, he had departed, to be replaced by Sergeant-Major Fotherby, a sour, sardonic individual, whose most eloquent comment on Badmore was a harsh, contemp-tous laugh. I had lacked the time and—as my release was imminent—the inclination to win him over. And although Captain Pirie was in some ways frightened of me, he was even more frightened of Sergeant-Major Fotherby. I began, therefore, unwillingly to resign myself to doing the guard the following evening.

The coach was now full. Ben climbed into his seat and started the motor. We lurched into motion, and I settled back into my seat. The long, familiar journey was beginning,—for the last time in this direction.

As we passed London Airport a plane roared over our heads, lights winking from tail and wing-tips. Usually I felt a pang of envy at this sight. It always seemed a kind of travelling— exciting, adventurous, purposeful—essentially different from my wasteful shuttling backwards and forwards between London and Badmore. I nudged Chalky and remarked:

'That's me in four days' time.' But he was asleep.

Chalky slept until we swung off the A30 into the car park of the 'Alnite Kaff'. We climbed out of the coach and walked stiffly into the hot, smoky café, blinking in the light. Chalky moved like a homing pigeon to the gaudy juke-box and selected a tune.

> Bye bye love
> Bye bye happiness
> Hello loneliness
> I think I'm gonna die
> Bye bye my love bye bye.

I got two cups of tea and took them back to a table. The café, as always at this time, was full of soldiers returning to camp by car, motor-cycle or coach. They sat at the greasy tables, staring vacantly, exchanging few words, tapping their feet gratefully to the music, nourishing the memory of the leave just spent, planning the next one. There was an atmosphere of defeat in the air, the dejection of a retreating army. But for once it did not touch me. I was leaving the battle shortly. This was the last time I should visit the 'Alnite'. I looked round me with a new attentiveness. Recently I had found myself registering the dull repetitive actions of my service life with this detached precision. It was a strange interior ritual, a litany to which the constant response was 'This is the last time.'

As the coach drew away from the café Ben extinguished the lights inside. This was illegal, but was a welcome aid to sleep. At the back of the coach a quartet of Regulars were trying to prolong the beery euphoria of their week-end's leave by singing bawdy songs.

> *We are from Green Street, good girls are we,*
> *We take a pride in our virginitee.*

But the majority of the passengers were, like myself, respectable week-end commuters, who preferred to pass the journey in a decent silence and, if possible, sleep. After several remonstrations the singers quietened down, and I dozed uneasily. Chalky's head, the hair of which was almost solidified with Brylcreem and dirt, fell on to my shoulder. I shrugged it off, but it kept lolling back. I stood up on the pretext of getting something from the rack, and Chalky overbalanced. He woke up and swore at me.

'You shouldn't put your head on my shoulder,' I explained. 'I'm not your tart you know.'

'Nah,' he replied, 'She's got bigger tits for one thing.'

'How d'you know they're real, Chalky?' asked a voice from the darkness. A little ripple of laughter spread round us.

'Wouldn't you like to know,' said Chalky sourly, settling himself to sleep again, this time inclining his head towards the window.

But I found it difficult to sleep. The little exchange about Chalky's girl brought back the moment on Pauline's divan a few hours before. Our relationship was approaching a critical point. There was a ratchet on love-making: you couldn't go back, you could only go on, or stay put. And there was a time-limit on staying put. Looking back over the last few weeks it seemed to me that the ratchet had been clicking over faster than usual lately. At Palma, anything might happen. I forced myself to be more exact: what might happen was that Pauline would be ready for me, would want me to take her. It was essential to decide in advance what course of action I would adopt in such a situation. Otherwise it might be awkward and embarrassing and spoil our holiday.

I considered the matter coolly. I had more or less decided that I would marry Pauline,—I couldn't think of anyone who would be more suitable,—and I was slightly hesitant about applying the have-now-pay-later principle to her virginity. If I did deflower her it would not affect my intention to marry her, but it might blunt the edge of pleasurable anticipation. I have always tried to avoid occasion for regret, the most lingering of all the unpleasant emotions, by prudent foresight. This, then, was a consideration to be weighed carefully. On the other hand I had no intention of marrying till I had completed my research and obtained a satisfactory post. That would be at least two years from now. It seemed unlikely that our self-control would stretch over such a long period : and if it had to give way, would not our holiday in Palma be an appropriate time and place? And at the same time I could propose that we get engaged. Such a sizeable deposit would go a long way towards overcoming my reservations about the hire-purchase system.

The remaining problem was how to provide myself with contraceptives. I regretted the fact that I had not considered these matters before. For it was one of my duties as P.R.I. clerk to indent, from time to time, for contraceptive sheaths (10 per cent discount) which were distributed by the regimental barber. They arrived regularly at the office, wrapped in plain brown paper parcels with a slip enclosed trusting that the goods would meet our requirements for planned parenthood. With a little more time at my disposal I could have obtained what I wanted through the comfortable anonymity of the post. But delivery usually took four or five days, and I couldn't risk not having them when I left Badmore. I had little enough time to play with between leaving the camp and boarding the plane ; and I couldn't have a potentially embarrassing brown paper package following me around in the post. I would have to get them from Henry the barber.

At this point I must have dozed off. The next minute, as it seemed, I was woken by the lights which came on in the coach. We were back. I gave Chalky, hunched up against the window, a rough shake. He swore, and opened his eyes, blinking in the light. We stepped down from the coach, and stood for a moment buttoning our coats as Ben drove away to drop the rest of the passengers at another part of the camp.

The shape of a gutted tank of the First World War, which stood outside the camp on a grass mound, loomed up above us. Chalky cast a nervous glance at it as we moved away. The story went that it was haunted by a German soldier who had been burned alive inside it. The tank had been captured by the Germans and used by them, until a British patrol had recaptured it by setting fire to it. Two of the crew had escaped, but one had been trapped inside. I had never met anyone who had seen the ghost, but the story was widely believed, and many soldiers would make a long detour rather than enter the camp by this entrance when alone, late at night. Guards responsible for this part of the camp studiously avoided even getting the tank in sight.

As we turned the corner of one of the hangars a guard came towards us, his pick-shaft tapping on the ground like a wooden leg. He was a friend of Chalky's, and asked him for a cigarette. Chalky gave him a bent Woodbine. At the Q.M.'s Stores Chalky and I separated.

I pushed open the door of number 4 hut and inhaled the familiar sweet-sour odour of dust, bad breath and perspiration. I switched on the light to plot a course across the hut which would avoid chairs and tables. Huts were not inspected on Sundays, and there was the usual squalid disorder. Tattered Sunday newspapers littered the floor: the pin-ups leered up at me with a jaded, ravished air. Mugs half-full of stagnant tea stood on tables marked with sticky rings. The windows were all shut. I opened two. Someone groaned and cursed. I switched off the light and felt my way across the floor to the far end of the hut where I had a small, partitioned-off cubicle known as a 'bunk'. I switched on my bedside lamp, which illuminated a shelf of books, and the Toulouse-Lautrec poster I had pinned to the wall. Slipping gratefully into bed, I glanced at my watch. Three-thirty. Ben had done quite good time. Soon the autumn fogs would be holding him up. But not me.

As I waited for sleep I thought about Pauline, Palma, and my errand at the barber's. A fragment of a poem by Mike, printed in the college magazine (the editor of which was subsequently forced to resign), floated into my mind. Something about *The rubber-gloves of lechery*. No, *The rubber-gloves of* prudent *lechery*, that was it. And there was an echo of Blake. After about ten minutes' strenuous effort I had assembled seven lines:

> *It's not the harlot's cry,*
> *But the contraceptive sheath*
> *From street to street*
> *Will weave old England's winding sheet ;*
> *The rubber gloves of prudent lechery*
> *Leave no traces*
> *Rifling the virgin's bottom drawer . . .*

The lines didn't scan or rhyme very well, but, recalling the general nature of Mike's poetry, this was not necessarily an indication that my memory was at fault. Pleased with my success, I relaxed and fell swiftly asleep.

'STAND up, Brady, Browne, Fallowfield, Higgins, Peterson.'

Mike and I, the first two named, stood up with the others. On the Monday after our arrival at Catterick, 'C' Squad was addressed by its N.C.O.—Corporal Baker, the tall, moustached corporal who had greeted us at the station. Corporal Baker was not, unfortunately for us, typical of the R.T.R. soldier. The Tanks (as distinct from the cavalry, who were burdened with an older tradition), tended to produce a particular type of trooper and N.C.O.: squat, stooped and grimy, with a healthy contempt for the wilder excesses of 'bull'. Corporal Baker had somewhere acquired that fanatical reverence for meticulous turn-out and drill which made him, in the Army's eyes, so admirably suited to the training of raw recruits. He was tall, thin and wiry; his skin was stretched tightly over the bones of his cheeks and jaw, and shone from the closeness of his shaves. His uniform was impeccably pressed and pleated, and his belt bit cruelly into his narrow waist. Every ounce of surplus flesh seemed to have been burned away by his energy and bad temper.

He looked at the six of us who were standing. The other members of the squad, National Servicemen and Regulars, also regarded us curiously.

'The Personnel Officer,' he began, with a faint sneer, 'has seen fit to class you lot as Potential Officers. I want to get a few things straight before we start. You've been called Potential Officers because you're supposed to be educated. Though Christ knows why, seeing that one of you failed his degree and another couldn't even pass his School Certificate.' He looked at Mike and Percy. 'But even if some of you *are* supposed to be educated, even if you have degrees in every subject under the bleeding sun, that doesn't mean you're any better as soldiers.

In my experience it makes you worse. You needn't think that because you're Potential Officers you've got a cushy time in front of you. You haven't. Even if you manage to pass Uzbee and Wozbee, which I very much doubt, you've got several months of training at Mons which will make the next five weeks seem like a kindergarten. And they won't be a kindergarten, I'll see to that. As Potential Officers I shall expect your conduct and turnout to be outstanding. And if they aren't, I'll want to know the reason why.'

He surveyed us with a thin-lipped, malicious smile, displaying two rows of regular, sharply-pointed teeth. His cold blue eyes rested on each of us in turn. First me.

'Name?'

'Browne.'

'Browne, *Corporal*.'

'Browne, Corporal.'

His eyes flickered to the papers in front of him. 'You've been writing a lot of letters to the Army, Browne.' (I had written once, as requested, to inform the authorities of my Finals result, and had taken the opportunity to reiterate my desire to go into the Education Corps. Evidently the letter had been forwarded to the 21st R.T.R.)

'Only one.'

'*Corporal!*'

'Corporal.'

'Wanted to go in the Education Corps, eh? That's where all the scivers want to go. Sitting on your arse all day teaching a lot of nigs their ABC. Well you're unlucky this time.' His eyes wandered to Mike.

'Name?'

'Brady, Corporal.'

'Well it's nice to see you now you've had your hair cut. When you arrived I thought we'd called up a ginger rug.' He waited for, and got his laugh. Mike presented a very altered appearance; deciding to go the whole hog he had directed the regimental barber to give him a crew-cut, which conformed to regulations, but enabled him to retain a certain grotesque individuality.

Baker dealt cursorily with Fallowfield and Peterson. Fallowfield was the blond ex-public schoolboy I had come up with in the train. Fortunately he was not in our hut. Peterson was also from a public school, but was separated from Fallowfield if not by a social abyss, at least by a pretty sizeable trench. Peterson was an Etonian, and carried about with him an almost tangible aura of nonchalant charm and confidence. His father had been in the Greys, and there was little doubt that if he conducted himself with a mere token show of enthusiasm he would get his commission. Fallowfield's school, on the other hand, had only just crept into the Headmasters' Conference. Although he might easily obtain a commission in one of the less exclusive infantry regiments, or in the Service Corps, it would not be easy for him to become an officer in the R.A.C., which still, as regards its officers, retained something of the traditional and entirely unjustified sense of superiority of the old cavalry. And it was such a commission that Fallowfield desired. He knew what efforts it would require, and in contrast to Peterson he was tense, anxious, and deadly serious. One could be sure that if the unthinkable happened, and neither got his commission, Peterson would adapt himself with cheerful amusement to life in the ranks, while Fallowfield would fret and pine.

Finally Baker turned on Percy.

'Higgins?'

'Yes, sir?'

'You don't call me sir, you fool. My name's Corporal Baker.'

'I beg your pardon, Corporal.'

'Why in Christ's name did they make you a P.O.?'

'I don't know, Corporal. The officer said he'd give me a chance.'

'How old are you?'

'Eighteen, Corporal.'

'Eighteen, and you haven't passed your School Certificate?'

'I was rather backward in Latin and Greek, Corporal.'

There was a general laugh. Baker closed the proceeding by saying, 'Thank Christ we've got a Navy.' We rose to our feet with a clatter of boots and capsized benches, and lined up outside the hut for our first drill instruction.

That Fallowfield and Peterson were P.O.s was of course in the nature of things. Mike, Percy and myself had drifted into this category without premeditation. On the second day in Amiens Camp my already enfeebled hopes of eventually getting into the Education Corps had been crushed. Between being issued with boots and having my hair cut I had a brief, unprofitable interview with an irritable and overworked Personnel Officer. My immediate resentment of his manner was evidently reciprocated, for later I had the opportunity of reading the comments he made that day on my training record sheet: *Educated up to university level: thinks too much of himself.* What I read later only confirmed the impression I received during the interview itself. It was then that I first began to realize how uncongenial the Army was going to be.

I dimly perceived that I had been wrenched out of a meritocracy, for success in which I was well qualified, and thrust into a small archaic world of privilege, for success in which I was singularly ill-endowed. I was brusquely told to forget about the Education Corps. Even if there were a vacancy in the latter I could not be transferred because the R.A.C. was senior in the line to the Education Corps, and a man could not be transferred from a corps of greater seniority to one of lesser. All my arguments broke on this granite wall of irrationality. Because I had been arbitrarily allocated, contrary to my wish, to the R.A.C., which aroused in me neither loyalty nor interest, I was to be barred, by a meaningless convention, from the one occupation in which I might have been of some use to the Army and to myself, and to be retained in a position which promised to be equally unprofitable to us both. I put this, as politely as I could, to the Personnel Officer. He flushed and made a visible effort to control himself.

'Look . . .' (he glanced at his papers to remind himself of my name) 'Browne. You've only been in the Army for two days, so I'll make allowances. I'll just tell you that you could be put in the guard-house for what you've just said. Forget about the university. Forget about the Education Corps. You're in the R.A.C. for two years, and you might as well make the best of it.

'Let me make the situation quite clear to you. On Monday

you begin your Basic Training, which lasts for five weeks. You will then receive trade-training, unless you are a Potential Officer. The four trades open to you are: Signaller/Gunner, Gunner/Driver, Driver, or Clerk. If you wish I can put you down as a Potential Officer, since your educational qualifications warrant it. In that case you will have a short P.O. Course here, at the end of which you will go before Uzbee, or Unit Selection Board. If you pass that you will go to Wozbee, or War Office Selection Board. If you pass that you will go to Cadet School, and if you are successful there you should receive a commission in about ten months' time, though it is extremely doubtful whether you would get a commission in the R.A.C. Probably an infantry regiment, or the Service Corps.'

'Excuse me, sir, but you just said that I couldn't be transferred from the R.A.C.'

He reddened and looked at me sharply. 'The situation is different for officers. There aren't enough places for all the cadets who would like commissions in the R.A.C. Now do I put you down as a P.O. or not?'

Disheartened and demoralized, I pondered dully.

'Come on, Browne, I haven't all day.'

I told him to put me down as a P.O.

Mike was interviewed immediately after me. While the Personnel Officer was committing his unfavourable impressions of me to paper, we had a moment in which I told Mike the unsatisfactory result of my interview. Then his name was called, and I sat and sulked in the ante-room while I waited for him.

It was depressing to find myself in a situation in which all the possibilities were equally unpalatable. I did not want to be an officer. I did not want to be a Signaller/Gunner. I did not want to be a soldier, period. However I thought in my innocence that a P.O. might have an easier time, and I had therefore elected to be one. Even then I felt a certain uneasiness at having entered for a competition I did not particularly want to win. But my main anxiety was that Mike should make a similar choice, and so bear me company. I was relieved to find my hopes fulfilled. His interview had gone more easily than mine, perhaps because he seemed utterly indifferent to what might happen to him. Or perhaps the Personnel Officer was disarmed by his failure to pass his Finals. At any rate the officer had at once suggested that he should try for a commission.

It was immediately obvious from that first drill-instruction that Percy was in for a bad time. We did only simple marching and the halt, but Percy was always out of step, always colliding with the man in front of him on the halt. As, in the succeeding weeks, the drill became more complex, Percy's blunders became more outrageous. At the turn or about-turn, he was sure to go stumbling off at a tangent to the rest of the squad. In arms drill he frequently dropped his rifle, and was a menace to himself and anyone within two yards radius. In his hand the weapon had more offensive possibilities than Lee-Enfield ever dreamed of.

Actually I myself was surprised and somewhat vexed to find that drill was quite difficult, and that it extended my concentration and mental alertness to the full. Arms drill I found particularly irksome, for the rifle was heavy to my meagre muscles, and bruised my collar-bone painfully. Most of us felt the spiteful edge of Baker's tongue at one time or another, but Percy rapidly established himself as Baker's chief butt. Watching Percy inevitably bungling the simplest order and agonizing under Baker's coarse sarcasm, was a painful experience, an army farce in bad taste. Of course there was plenty of laughter from the squad, which Baker made only a token effort to suppress. Sometimes he would stand the rest of us at ease and make Percy perform solo for the general diversion. Once he stopped a fellow instructor who was passing, and showed off Percy's paces like a circus animal's. The other N.C.O. grinned uncomfortably, and I suspected that he didn't really approve. Perhaps the cruellest thing Baker inflicted on Percy was to punish the whole squad because of his ineptitude. Often we would be left pounding the vast, arid barrack square after the other squads had been dismissed, because Percy couldn't master the about-turn on the march, while the precious minutes of Naafi-break or lunch-hour ticked away. Even I, a friend of Percy's in a way, found myself cursing him under my breath at such times; while the resentment of the others, needless to say, was more vocal.

But I was not really a friend of Percy's. I found him pathetic, touching, but dull. However, since Mike's heroic defence of Percy on the first evening, their relationship had followed an archetypal school-yarn pattern and a curious friendship had sprung up between them. I therefore saw more of Percy than I might otherwise have done.

Gradually I filled in his background—partly by what he told me himself, but mainly from what Mike passed on to me, for Percy was far less reticent when he was alone with Mike. He came from down-at-heel gentlefolk in Lincolnshire, but his parents had died when he was young, and he had been brought up by an uncle and aunt. His family were 'Old Catholics' which, Mike explained to me, meant that they belonged to the small minority of English Catholics who had kept their Faith through the Penal days. I gathered that they were a tightly-knit, conservative, clannish group, who regarded Irish and convert Catholics with rather more suspicion than they did Protestants. Percy's guardian had sent him to a seminary school in Hampshire, a boarding school which was attached to a seminary. The education there had a decidedly ecclesiastical slant, and likely boys were groomed for the priesthood from an early age. This was thought to be an appropriate destiny for Percy, and one that his parents would have approved of. Percy, with his usual obligingness, had happily accepted the idea. When he failed to pass his 'O' level G.C.E. at the third attempt, however, his masters regretfully informed his guardian that there was no point in encouraging him to study for the priesthood any more. This slightly surprised me. The life of a priest seemed so unattractive and uncomfortable that I thought the ecclesiastical authorities would have hung on to anybody who was foolish enough to put himself into their hands.

'Agnostic be damned!' snorted Mike, when I expressed this opinion. 'Maria Monk dies hard. I bet you think the Inquisition carries on in dark cellars under presbyteries in Basingstoke and Camden Town. Seriously, I agree with you that it's surprising how difficult it is to become a priest when you consider the shortage of vocations. It's good policy though. In Spain and

Italy, where it's much easier, you find the worst ecclesiastical scandals.'

This conversation took place on the Saturday at the end of our first week of Basic Training. That morning we had received a lethal three-in-one injection against tetanus, typhoid and some other scourge whose name I forget, plus vaccination against smallpox. The effects were highly unpleasant, and we had been put on 'light duties' for the week-end. Some of the lads had violent fever, and lay shivering and sweating under blankets. I had a headache, but the main effect of the injections on me was an indescribable mental depression. Mike and I lay prone on our beds, too wretched and ill to move.

'Was Percy disappointed when he was turned down?' I asked.

'I don't think so. Except that he didn't like his guardians to be disappointed. They sound rather grim. But the Army must be a nasty shock to him.'

'He's not the only one,' I replied with feeling.

'Yes, but it's different for us, Jon. In some ways Percy led a more Spartan life in the seminary school than this. He's used to lousy food, sleeping in dormitories, getting up early for mass, the lack of freedom and so on. That doesn't worry him as it worries us. What worries him is the way people shout and swear at him, no matter how hard he tries to please. Seminarians can be pretty bloody, but at least they keep up the appearances of decency. There's a respect for peace and privacy. It's bad enough leaving a seminary and going out into the world,—my brother did it. But to go straight out of the seminary into the Army—it must be like taking a wrong turning in Paradise and plunging down into the Pit.'

I didn't admit it to Mike, but his simile fitted my feelings as well. Paradise: London, the dull suburb where I lived; college, the cramped lecture-rooms in the converted warehouse block, the dingy, stale-smelling lounge. That was Paradise. And the Army,—yes, I thought, as I looked down the cheerless hut, at its iron beds on which the grey-faced youths writhed and groaned in the grip of their ague, yes, this was the Pit. I closed my eyes.

One thing everyone acquires in the Army is a gluttonous appetite for sleep. To normal young people sleep is just an irritating demand of nature's, confiscating hours of possible enjoyment and study. Sleep is the opium of the soldier, the cheap universal drug, the anaesthetic against boredom and homesickness. The experience of missing sleep,—on guard or on the journey back to camp after leave,—teaches him the value of sleep, makes him greedy for sleep, so that he begins to sleep even when he is not tired. When he hasn't got a leave pass or money, the soldier will customarily spend Sunday in bed, even after a lazy and idle week. But during Basic Training we slept at every opportunity because we were exhausted after square-bashing all day and cleaning equipment half the night.

The day began at 5.30. Groaning and cursing we wrenched ourselves from sleep's narcotic embrace as the orderly corporal slammed in and out of the hut leaving his harsh summons lingering on the air. We reacted in different ways: some hopped straight out of bed; some twisted under the blankets, trying futilely to corkscrew their way back into oblivion; some sat up in bed, yawning, scratching, farting. Mike reached out automatically for the half-smoked cigarette he had extinguished the night before. I lay as I had woken, motionless, as if with practice I might be able to will the world into immobility for a few extra minutes. When Mike had finished his dog-end he swung his legs to the ground, and I followed suit as if our limbs were connected by invisible wires. The more wretched I felt, the less I liked to let him out of my sight. We pulled on our boots and denims, and shuffled out, speechless, to the wash-house, shivering slightly in the chill morning air. If we were lucky there was still hot water in the taps; if not, there was the rasping agony of a cold-water shave and the sting of styptic pencil on ghastly wounds along the jaw bone.

Then, articulate at last, to breakfast: flaccid bacon and tinned tomatoes in a pool of red juice on a cold plate, like the leftovers of a nasty operation, served by surly, white-faced cooks who had already been up for two hours. Back to the huts. We emptied our bowels as quickly as possible: the lavatories never flushed, and each one could be used exactly once without offence. But often there was not time. There were the various jobs to be done in and around the hut: sweeping the floor, polishing the windows, and, if one were unlucky, 'ablutions'. This last meant hurling buckets of water down the clogged pans so that the inspecting officer wouldn't be reminded that the plumbing didn't work. In the hut there was feverish activity as the time of first parade approached. We made up our beds, folding up the blankets to regulation measurements; laid out whatever pieces of equipment were required for inspection; struggled into our webbing and polished our boots.

At five to eight Corporal Baker arrived on his bicycle, dismounting by numbers, to goad us out of the hut with his carefully chosen insults. He marched us off to the barrack square to parade with the rest of the Intake. Then commenced the solemn pantomime of inspection: standing to attention in the brisk air, bowels uncomfortably heavy if one had not had time to visit the lavatory, while the leathery-faced Sergeant Box moved slowly along the line, Baker a pace behind, his needle-sharp pencil poised to inscribe the sergeant's inevitable condemnation of our turnout. Box pored over our brasses like an archaeologist examining some rare bronze medallion. 'What's all this shit?' he would inquire, pointing at a minute smear on a buckle.

It was the special delight of the N.C.O.s to ask questions which could only be answered to one's disadvantage within the framework of military discipline. In the following illustration the words in italics represent possible truthful replies which had to be suppressed for obvious reasons.

'What's all this shit?'
I don't see any shit.
'I don't know, Sergeant.'
'Well, I'm telling you, it's shit. See?'
No.
'Yes, Sergeant.'
'Did you clean your kit last night?'
Of course I did as you very well know.
'Yes, Sergeant.'

'Well you didn't clean it properly, did you?'

Yes.

'No, Sergeant.'

'Why not?'

Firstly, I don't accept that my equipment isn't properly cleaned. Secondly, if it isn't cleaned to your satisfaction, that's because you are not to be satisfied. Thirdly, you know and I know that it's a question of no importance. that you have to pick on something to establish your authority, and that we are going through an elaborate and meaningless ritual to create the illusion that I am being made a soldier of.

'I don't know, Sergeant.'

'You don't know! Well you'd better find out before to-morrow morning. Your trouble is that you're idle. What are you?'

A bloody sight more intelligent than you, for a start.

'Idle, Sergeant.'

Actually Mike developed quite a successful technique for dealing with the 'You're-idle-what-are-you?' formula. He would innocently reply: 'What you said, Sergeant.' Then the N.C.O. would ask with a smirk, sure of getting the admission he wanted: 'And what was that?'

'You said I was idle.'

This would usually satisfy the bone-headed interrogator, but even he would be dimly aware that 'you said I was idle' was not the same thing as '[*I'm*] idle'. I regret that I never had the nerve to imitate Mike.

The inspection was a farce of course, but it was depressing to find how quickly one came to treat it seriously, to observe the approach of Sergeant Box almost with anxiety. A least *I* did, and Percy could be seen visibly trembling. I'm sure Mike never treated the business with anything other than contempt.

After the inspection there was a brief drill period followed by P.T.,—the most hateful hour of the day as far as I was concerned. We changed into singlets and shorts, and trotted to the gymnasium in boots, carrying our plimsolls. We made a grotesque spectacle, with our baggy shorts, knobbly knees, hairy legs, all terminating in clumsy black boots. But then the whole object of the exercise was to destroy one's dignity. At the

gym we were handed over to the tender mercies of the P.T.
instructors, who were typical of their tribe: lounging bullies in
soiled white sweaters, who kept up an appearance of muscular
fitness and agility thinly disguising a profound laziness and
perceptible homosexual proclivities. Everything was done
relentlessly at the double. 'Last one into the gym is on fatigues.'
And so there was always a stupid scramble to get off one's
boots, with one of the instructors playfully wielding a rubber
slipper. 'If he tries any of *le vice anglais* on me he's looking for
trouble,' Mike muttered to me one day. But the instructors
were wary with the older conscripts, and made up for it by
being particularly vindictive in the gym. This was the usual
hygienic torture chamber with wall bars for racking limbs,
horses for rupturing abdomens, ropes for skinning hands, and
bristly mats laughably supposed to soften one's falls. Having
been to a school equipped with a gym, I was able to acquit
myself just well enough to avoid censure. Some of the other
lads, however, were obviously experiencing it all for the first
time. Percy was in pure misery.

I had quickly developed a bruised heel from marching
which made P.T. very painful, and I debated inwardly
whether to go sick and get excused P.T. But this would also
mean being excused all training, and if that went on for more
than a few days I would be 'back-squadded', the most dreaded
sentence of all: it meant joining a fresh Intake, and starting
Basic Training all over again. It was worth any pain to avoid
that, and very few of us went sick during Basic Training.

After P.T. the day was occupied mainly by drill, relieved by
the odd lecture on fire-arms or V.D. We squatted on the grass
in a circle round an oily-fingered N.C.O., who took a Sten gun
to pieces with the dexterity of a magician, and sneered at our
attempts to reassemble it. 'The object of war,' he said, 'is to
kill the enemy.' He paused to let the words sink in. 'Don't aim
at his head: you may miss. Don't aim at his legs: you may not
kill him. Aim at his body.' A little tremor of blood-lust rippled
through his audience. A young medical officer stared at a
point on the wall at the back of the lecture-room and said:
'The best way to avoid getting V.D. is to refrain from sexual
intercourse.' There was more interest in his description of other

ways. On camps overseas, contraceptives and carbolic soap could be obtained at the guardroom, we learned.

These lectures were welcome opportunities for resting aching muscles, but Mike and I most looked forward to the Education periods, when those of us who were P.O.s were left in the library. We were supposed to study Current Affairs. Mike and I sat around chatting and reading the Arts pages of the weekly reviews,—the latter an almost painfully nostalgic occupation. News of the latest books and plays seemed to come from a great distance, from a bright, unattainable world thousands of miles away. Sometimes its controversies and talking-points seemed trivial and frivolous compared to the more concrete world of our present discontents; but I longed to return to those trivialities and frivolities.

Mail was distributed after lunch. I received few letters, and those few from my parents. Regular food parcels from my mother, exquisitely selected and packed in fond memory of my special tastes, were very welcome, but did not appease my hunger for letters, for communion with the outside world. For the first time in my life I realized how few friends I had, and for the first time I regretted the fact. One felt a great need for the kind of sympathy parents could not supply,—particularly my parents, since I could never bring myself to tell them how miserable I was. I had no girl-friend, and found myself almost coveting the letters the other lads received, their contents flamboyantly advertised by lipstick imprints and cryptograms like SWALK (Sealed With A Loving Kiss) over the seals. To receive a letter, however, could be more unpleasant than not receiving one. Letters from girl-friends 'breaking it off' were common. Usually the girl had found another admirer, or was tired of being tied to a soldier who was absent most of the time, and penniless when he was at home.

I was curious about the letters in long, pale mauve envelopes which Mike received every other day. They looked feminine in origin, but I had never seen him with a girl at college, and he never mentioned one. He rarely wrote letters himself. For some reason I refrained from questioning him on this point. If Mike proved to have a girl, I felt obscurely, she would come between us in some way.

There was no such thing as 'free' time in Basic Training. The evenings and week-ends were fully occupied, mainly by cleaning and polishing equipment, or in army jargon 'bull'. Someone had obviously given considerable thought to this part of our training. First of all we were issued with brasses that were green and deeply corroded, and therefore had to be rubbed for hours with emery paper before the application of 'Brasso' produced any effect. Our boots had a dull, orange-peel surface, which is of course a characteristic feature of good waterproof foot-wear, but we had to eradicate the dimples and produce a patent-leather shine. The approved method was to heat a spoon handle over a candle and to rub the boots with it, squeezing out the oil and smoothing out the surface. This process naturally ruined the boots *qua* boots, but such functional considerations were irrelevant within the mystique of 'bull'. Some of the lads used more drastic methods, such as rubbing a hot iron over the boots, or even covering them with polish and setting fire to them. In addition to brasses and boots, there was webbing to be blancoed and clothing to be pressed. When we were first issued with webbing Baker ordered us to scrub off the existing, deeply ingrained khaki blanco. 'I want them white,' he said. Four hours' scrubbing with cold water produced a dirty grey. The next day we were instructed to blanco the webbing again in exactly the same colour as that in which it had been issued. The 21st tanks themselves, like all battalions of the R.T.R., wore black webbing, which gave them a peculiarly brutal and sombre appearance. Until we were allocated to particular regiments at the end of our training we wore khaki webbing. 'I hope I'm not put in the Tanks,' Mike observed to me once, 'I'd feel like a bloody Black-and-Tan.' But the black webbing, which was treated with shoe-polish, seemed to me to be much easier to keep clean.

Pressing was somewhat difficult for me at first, because I had never pressed a single garment in my life before I was called up. The usual pressing technique was to use the iron over a sheet of brown paper which had been wetted with a shaving brush. The hiss of steam and the pungent odour of scorched brown paper are still inextricably connected with the Army in my mind, like the whine of shells and the smell of cordite in the memories of war-veterans. I minimized the pressing by using my own pyjamas and underpants. I pressed the Army's issue once, according to the regulation measurements, and kept them undisturbed for kit layouts throughout my service, carrying them carefully from place to place in polythene bags.

The amount of equipment that was required to be laid out for inspection in the mornings was subtly increased during the period of Basic Training, starting with a few items and culminating in a series of full kit-layouts which kept us working late into the night. An additional vexation was the occasional 'Fire Picquet', a quaintly-named duty which consisted in parading with the guard in steel helmets and peeling potatoes for two hours in a small annexe to the cookhouse, awash with freezing water and potato peel. One had heard of this sort of thing of course,—peeling potatoes was more or less a cartoonist's cliché for depicting the Army—but it came as a shock, to me at least, to find myself doing it. I had supposed that it was some kind of punishment, and probably obsolete, like flogging. I felt the same, only more strongly, about cookhouse fatigues.

One Sunday we had a Church parade. I presumed that even the Army would not compel me to attend church, and said so to Baker, with a certain challenging note in my voice which was probably my undoing.

'You can presume what you fugging well like,' he replied. 'You'll parade with the rest of the squad. After the inspection, fall out and report to me. We'll find you something to do while the others are saying their prayers.'

When I reported to him he sent me over to the cookhouse. If there is a God, and if, as some say, He whiles away the long light evenings of eternity devising choice punishments for His creatures, He need not hesitate over selecting my particular hell. It would be an everlasting cookhouse fatigue. By the end of that Sunday I was almost weeping with misery and a sense of injustice. Whereas those on the Church parade were free (relatively speaking) by noon, I slaved all day in that stinking, greasy cookhouse. It was an old building, irremediably dirty: platoons of soldiers could not have scrubbed it clean, though the Cook Sergeant nearly drove me and my companions into the tiled floor in the attempt. I remember kicking a hot water pipe in sheer wretchedness and frustration, and the shudder of disgust that shook me as a swarm of cockroaches scuttled out over the wall. I kicked and kicked at the pipes in a masochistic frenzy until the wall was alive with the repulsive vermin. Then I retched into a nearby sink. I went over to the Cook Sergeant and said pleadingly: 'I've just been sick. I feel ill. Can I leave?' He looked at my white face and gave permission with a contemptuous jerk of his head. Blessing him, I staggered weakly back to the hut, and collapsed on to my bed. Mike was less sympathetic than I had expected. 'You can now count yourself one of the glorious martyrs for Agnosticism,' he said. Percy, sitting on the same bed, laughed. Their visit to church seemed to have put them in good spirits.

'At the moment I'd cheerfully become a Jehovah's Witness, if it would get me out of cookhouse fatigues,' I said savagely.

'A very good idea,' he replied. 'Being a Jehovah's Witness would get you out of the Army altogether. They're conscientious objectors.'

'That's the religion for me,' I said.

'My brother-in-law was a Jehovah's Witness, but it didn't get him out of the Army,' observed the soldier on the bed opposite to mine. He was an odd, though pleasant little chap called Barnes, with a quaint Leicestershire accent. He had seen me reading the *Inferno* one evening. 'What you reading? Po'try? Here's some good po'try.' And he had thrust a tattered second-hand copy of *The Lady Of The Lake* into my hand. Encouraged by this evidence of literacy, though by no means sympathetic to his tastes, I had attempted to extend the discussion. 'Do you like Scott?' I had asked him. But he hadn't seemed to realize that the poem was by Scott. 'That's good po'try' was all he would say; and taking the volume from me, he had returned it carefully to his locker.

'What happened to your brother-in-law then?' inquired Mike.

'Well, it was in the war, like. And they wouldn't let our Ernie be a conscious objector. But Ernie said he weren't going to put on a bloody uniform no matter what they did. So they sent him to this training depot, and he wouldn't put on his uniform.

So they put him in this cell in his underclothes, and threw in his uniform. It were winter, like, and they reckoned he'd be so cold he'd have to put the uniform on.' Barnes paused.

'And did he?'

'Did he fugg. When they opened the cell next morning our Ernie were still in his underclothes; and on the table were his uniform,—all in pieces.'

'What d'you mean, all in pieces?'

'He'd spent the whole night taking his uniform to pieces. He never tore nothing mind you. He bit through the seams with his teeth. His socks were two balls of wool. He said with a bit more time he could have taken his boots to pieces. He could've too. He was in the boot trade.'

The story pleased us immensely.

'They should put up a statue to that man,' said Mike reverently.

'What happened to him eventually?' I asked.

'A few days after they came and told him his ma had been killed by a Jerry bomb. Went fuggin mad he did. Couldn't get his uniform on quick enough. Joined the paratroops and finished the war with thirteen medals.'

We laughed ruefully.

'The traitor,' said Mike.

'God, is there no way of getting out of this Army?' I wailed.

'Roberts told me he's going to buy himself out,' said Percy. 'Is that possible?'

'Christ!' I exclaimed. 'How much does it cost? I'd sell my birthright to get out of the Army.'

'Calm down, Trooper,' said Mike. 'Only Regulars can buy themselves out. Anyway, he'll only be called up again to do National Service.'

'He says he won't,' answered Percy. 'Because he works in the mines. He said he joined the Army to get out of the mines, but now he can't wait to get back.'

'Well, Jon,' said Mike, 'there's only one thing you can do now. Shoot your trigger finger off, like they used to do in the Great War.'

'My bulling-finger you mean,' I replied, inspecting my forefinger, red and sore from rubbing brasses and boots.

THREE

'WAKEY-WAKEY!'

The call of the Orderly Corporal scratched the surface of my sleep without penetrating it. I turned over and dozed, until the sound of someone whistling off-key woke me at seven. Leaning from my bed I pulled back the curtain over the door of my cubicle and held out a mug to the nearest soldier.

'Get me a cup of tea when you go to breakfast, Scouse,' I said. 'Send it back with one of the other lads.'

'Right, Corporal,' he replied, taking the mug from my hand. He was a new arrival to Badmore, who treated me with flattering deference. He added: 'Ah'm a Geordie, not a Scouse.'

'Oh well, I never know the difference between those little villages up north,' I countered mechanically. One must never let slip an opportunity of teasing the next man about his geographical origins. Geordie, Scouse, Taff, Paddy, Jock. Shakespeare knew what he was doing when he made the comedy in his army play, *Henry V*, a comedy of dialects.

At 7.30, refreshed by the tea, I got up, washed and shaved. I then supervised the cleaning of the hut. There was a Monday-morning gloom in the air, but I felt cheerful. My last Monday. Dust-motes glittered prettily in the bright sunlight.

'Come on! come on! Get that shit swept up,' I said briskly to a group leaning on their broom handles.

'Don't be like that, Corp. You've not got long to push. Why worry?'

'See they've got you on guard tonight, Corporal,' said Jock Gordonstone. 'Will you want me to do your boots for you?'

My mood darkened. 'Fuggit, yes. I'd forgotten about that.' I pondered. 'Yes, do them for me will you, Jock, unless I tell you not to at Naafi-break.'

61

Jock was always broke, because every month he took a forty-eight home to Paisley. Deducting the time he spent travelling, he only had about twelve hours at home, and his fares cost him nearly four pounds, but he always took the forty-eight. When I was on guard I usually gave him half a crown to clean my boots.

Morning parade was at 8.15. I called the roster for my troop, and handed the sheet to Sergeant-Major Fotherby. His predecessor had rarely bothered to take the morning parade, but Sergeant-Major Fotherby was keen. Or, rather, he had been keen: already there were signs that he was realizing the impossibility of mending the ways of Badmore. On his first morning parade he had taken an hour over his inspection. Now he surveyed my troop with pained resignation, and broke his silence only once, to observe to Jock Gordonstone that his hair was long enough for him to wipe his arse with it.

Badmore was, and always would be, the despair of any sergeant-major, because the sergeant-major is a man who works in the medium of outward appearance. His object is to make every man look identical, because if all men look alike, they will act alike, and eventually think, or, rather, not-think alike. But the sergeant-major must have a basic structure of uniformity to work on. Without this he is like a theologian without dogma. The analogy is not inapposite. A regiment is like a religion. Its dogma governs the way its members wear their lanyards, the angle they wear their berets, the manner in which they perform the movements of drill. As in Newman's theory of religious doctrine, developments may occur. It is the responsibility of the sergeant-major, as of the theologian, to control and rationalize such developments, to distinguish genuine developments from heresies, and ruthlessly to suppress the latter. In fact, in the Guards, the regimental sergeant-majors of each battalion have an annual conference, a sort of General Council, in which such matters are discussed and regularized.

Badmore, however, was not a regiment. Known officially as the R.A.C. Special Training Establishment, its function was to train officers and N.C.O.s in the use of new technical developments in armoured vehicles. Its courses were attended by personnel from all the regiments of the R.A.C., and it was staffed with soldiers from as many regiments. When the entire unit paraded for the Queen's Birthday Parade it looked as if remnants of a whole defeated army had met up and banded together. There were cap-badges of every description: the antique tank of the R.T.R., the skull and crossbones of the Dragoon Guards, the wreath of the Bays, the harp of the Irish Guards, the crossed lances of the Lancers. The R.T.R. wore black berets and black webbing; the cavalry wore navy-blue berets and khaki webbing. The R.T.R. wore plain black lanyards; the cavalry wore white or yellow plaited lanyards. Insignia on shoulder tabs and lapels varied similarly. Even from a long distance the 11th Hussars or 'Cherry Pickers' disturbed any impression of uniformity with their curious brown, badgeless berets ringed with a band of crimson, the stigma of some ancient disgrace, when the regiment had stopped to pick cherries on the way to a battle. Soldiers belonging to R.E.M.E., the Signals, the Catering Corps and the Royal Artillery, only added to the confusion. It was enough to break a sergeant-major's heart.

Beneath the surface Badmore resembled a regiment even less. It was more like a sort of military Narkover. The ranks were composed largely of National Servicemen under twenty; the N.C.O.s of aged and decrepit Regulars. The former had been sent to Badmore because they had flat feet, or compassionate reasons for a home posting, or were unemployable elsewhere; the latter because they had varicose veins, or had been involved in some scandal in their regiments, or were unemployable elsewhere. The relationship between the two groups resembled that between the boys and masters of Narkover. National Service N.C.O.s like myself occupied the position of prefects. It was impossible to think of the ranks as anything but boys. Once, Captain Pirie, searching for something to say to Fotherby before a big parade, had asked him: 'Are the men in good heart, Sergeant-Major?' The inquiry was kindly meant, and not without relevance: 'A' Squadron was sufficiently apprehensive about being inspected by a visiting Brigadier. But the contrast between the image summoned up by the words, of grim Tommies with blackened faces, waiting to go 'over the top', and the reality—an irregular file of pimply youths fidgeting in their best uniforms,—was richly comic.

I snorted at the recollection. Fotherby eyed me suspiciously before bringing us to attention.

' 'A' Squadron, dis . . . miss !'

We dispersed to our various tasks in offices, stores, messes, stables. The unit was divided into two squadrons: 'B' Squadron was responsible for the cleaning and maintenance of vehicles used in training. The rest of the unit's activities were controlled by 'A' Squadron, which included the Orderly Room staff. In fact the 'A' Squadron offices were in the same low, rambling building as the Orderly Room.

Captain Pirie's office had three doors: one connected with my office, another with Fotherby's office, and the third with a corridor. Captain Pirie usually sat cowering in a corner of his room waiting for one of the doors to open: Fotherby urging him to inspect the huts, the Second-in-Command or the Adjutant complaining about sports equipment, or me, with ledgers to be balanced. He was usually least worried to see me, since I pencilled in all the figures, and he had only to ink them over.

I shared my office with Mr Fry, a civilian. He was responsible for the pay and insurance of the civilians who worked on the camp, mainly as gardeners, groundsmen and storekeepers. There were quite a lot of them, but one rarely saw them except on Wednesday afternoons, when they crept out of their holes and crannies, and shuffled into the office to receive their pay, grinning and coughing and touching their forelocks like a gang of Hardy's rustics. Mr Fry was a conscientious man, but, however slowly and meticulously he did his work, he could not stretch it over a forty-two-hour week. As usual, therefore, he had the *Daily Express* spread out over his desk when I entered.

'Good morning, Corporal Browne.'

'Good morning, Mr Fry.'

'Did you have a pleasant week-end?'

'Yes thank you. Very pleasant. And you?'

'Quiet you know, quiet.' It would be sensational when Mr

Fry had a noisy week-end. 'Got some weeding done in the garden. Lovely weather.'

'Lovely.' I went to the window, and looked out over the playing-fields. A mechanical mower droned and circled in the middle distance, throwing up a fine spray of cut grass. I opened the window and the smell floated in.

'Won't be long now, eh, Corporal Browne?'

'No, Mr Fry.'

'Wednesday, isn't it?'

'That's right.'

'I'll be sorry to see you go, Corporal Browne.'

'It's very nice of you to say so, Mr Fry. I can't honestly say *I* shall be sorry to go.'

'Of course not. Of course not. The Army's a waste of time for a young man like you. You'll be going back to the university then?'

'Not at once. I'm taking a holiday first.'

'Ah yes, of course. Stupid of me to forget. Spain, isn't it?'

'Majorca. An island off the coast of Spain.'

'You'll send us a post-card I hope?'

'I'll send *you* one, Mr Fry.'

In the distance a door banged, and a pair of boots clumped thunderously up the corridor to the accompaniment of a pop-song, piercingly whistled. Mr Fry winced. The chief reason why he would be sorry to see me go was that he did not find my replacement, Trooper Ludlow, congenial. The door crashed open and Ludlow lurched into the room.

'Ullo, Jonny-boy! Ullo, Mr Fry,' he cried boisterously in the accent of Brum. ' 'Ave a good week-end?' he asked me, and without waiting for an answer jerked his head in my direction and observed to Mr Fry: 'Bloody 'ard man i'n 'e? Takin' a forty-eight just before 'e's released.'

Mr Fry forced a smile, but offered no comment.

'How about you, Roy? Nice week-end?' I inquired.

'Fair. Got pissed on Saturday night,' he replied. 'Got a fag?'

'Only cork-tipped.' Filtered cigarettes were not popular, and I had adopted them as a partial protection against cadging. 'Ask Boon, I heard him just come in.'

'That bastard? 'E's as tight as a crab's arse-'ole. Give us one of your tipped ones then.' He broke off the tip, lit the mutilated cigarette, and strode across to the window to throw out the match. To a soldier who was passing he called out 'Git yer 'air cut, Connolly,' imitating the grating timbre of Fotherby's voice with considerable success. Connolly looked round apprehensively, grinned and made a V-sign. At that moment one of the typists from the Orderly Room passed with her nose in the air. Connolly hastily converted the gesture into a scratch behind his ear. Ludlow responded to this pantomime with ear-splitting laughter. Recovering his breath, he observed that the typist would make a good grind. 'Maybe I can knock 'er off when I've got a stripe, eh, Jonny? When d'you think the Major'll make me up?'

'After the next audit I should think. If the books balance you'll get your stripe. If they don't you'll probably both be court-martialled.'

'Don't you worry, Jonny-boy. I could do them books with me 'ands tied behind me back.'

To do Ludlow justice, he was better at figures than I was, having been a bookie's clerk in civilian life.

'Here comes the Captain,' said Mr Fry, folding up his newspaper. We gathered at the window. It was always worth watching Captain Pirie's arrival, on the off-chance of his hitting something expensive. The green vintage Bentley swept into the camp in a fast four-wheel drift, passed behind a long row of buildings, and, after a strangely long interval, emerged at the other end going slowly, and disconcertingly, backwards.

'Must've 'it an oil-patch,' observed Ludlow knowledgeably.

After much audible wrestling with the gears Captain Pirie pointed the car in our direction and drove furiously towards us, clinging to the great, string-bound steering wheel, and peering myopically through the yellowing windscreen. He swung into the parking bay outside the office, and drew up, missing the Adjutant's Jaguar by inches. The great car seemed to go on shuddering and panting for several seconds after he had switched off the ignition. Captain Pirie prised his great bulk out of the cockpit and climbed down. Two cocker spaniels leapt out, and followed him as he puffed his way towards the office, apparently connected to his heels by invisible elastic threads which plucked them back whenever they roamed more than three yards from him. We heard the dogs snuffling in the corridor as he passed the door and entered his office. I gathered up a sheaf of bills and, knocking perfunctorily at the door, entered the office.

'Good morning, sir,' I said, saluting.

Captain Pirie was filling his pipe. ' 'Morning, Corporal Browne.' He sketched a vague gesture in the air which was his approximation to a salute. Unfortunately he was still holding his tobacco pouch in his right hand, and some of the contents fell on to the floor. One of the spaniels sprawling under the desk instantly retrieved the tobacco, and offered it to his master, who took the soggy tangle from the dog's mouth with a proud smile. Shreds of tobacco still adhered to the mouth of the animal, who licked his chops meditatively.

'A few bills to be paid, sir,' I said firmly, putting them on his desk.

'Oh. Ah. Hmm,' he muttered. 'Couldn't they wait? I think Sergeant-Major Fotherby . . .'

'Two of them are over-due already, sir.'

'Are they? *Are* they? Hmm. Oh well, we'd better pay them then, eh?'

'Yes, sir.'

'Now where's that damned cheque-book?'

'Top left-hand drawer, sir.'

'What? Oh yes. Thank you.'

As he was writing out the cheques, a knock sounded at the door leading to the Sergeant-Major's office. Captain Pirie pretended not to have heard it, but Fotherby came in un-invited. He thudded over the lino in his heavy boots and saluted with precision.

'Can I see you for a moment, sir?'

'Got some urgent P.R.I. business on hand here. I'm afraid, Sergeant-Major. Haven't we, Corporal?' He gave me a sly, conspiratorial glance from under his bushy eye-brows.

'Yes, sir,' I replied, but added to Fotherby: 'It won't take very long, sir.' I was trying to soften up Fotherby, but he wasn't responsive.

'There are two men for orders, sir.'

'Oh. Hmm. Remand to C.O.?' asked the Captain hopefully.

'I think you can deal with it yourself, sir.'

The Captain looked glum. He was a kind-hearted man, and disliked administering punishments. No doubt this was one reason why, at forty-five, he had not yet been promoted to Major, and had few prospects of such promotion.

'I'll get the charge-sheets,' said Fotherby, and left the room.

'It should be ten shillings, sir, instead of ten pounds,' I observed, pointing to the cheque the Captain was signing.

'Oh. Ah. Yes.' He panicked a little, and made a blot as he crossed out the figures.

'What shall I do?'

'Put in the ten shillings and initial the correction, sir.'

He put away the cheque-book with a sigh of relief.

'Well, Corporal Browne, it won't be long before you leave us.'

'No, sir.'

'When do you go?'

'Wednesday, sir.'

'*Wednesday*. Is it really? Will Ludlow be all right? Have you shown him the ropes?'

'He'll be all right, sir. You needn't worry. I'm handing over the inventory and the petty cash to him today.'

'Good, good.'

He rummaged through the paper slum that covered his desk, and produced a pink booklet. It was my release book.

'I've written your testimonial, Corporal Browne,' he said, handing me the document with a shy smile. 'I hope it's all right.'

He seemed to want me to read it, so I did.

> 'An honest, Trustworthy and efficient N.C.O. who is very much above the Average in Intelligence. He is a good Organizer and very thorough at Clerking and accounts. He likes Games, plays a good game of Hockey and gets on well with Others in the Squadron.'

Captain Pirie's weakness for capitals gave his writing an oddly archaic air. It was nevertheless the most coherent piece of prose he had ever composed, and it must have cost him a great effort. I was touched. I hadn't the heart to tell him that I loathed games and had never played hockey in my life.

'Thank you, sir. That's very nice . . .' As I gave the booklet back to him, Fotherby re-entered the office. I saluted and left.

While orders were in progress I handed over the contents of the cupboard behind my desk to Ludlow: 137 jars of blanco. 23 assorted regimental lapel-badges. 961 Badmore Christmas cards (tank and holly motif). 8 paper hats. 1 Father Christmas beard. 1 camera (broken). 15 books of cloakroom tickets. 1 egg-poacher. . . .

'One *what*?' exclaimed Ludlow.

'One egg-poacher.'

'What the fugg's that for?'

'For poaching eggs.'

'I *know* its for poaching eggs you funny bastard. What's it doing in the P.R.I. cupboard?'

'Look, if you're going to start asking why things are in the P.R.I. cupboard I'm not going to get out on Wednesday. If you look at the inventory you'll see that that egg-poacher has been handed on to P.R.I. clerk after P.R.I. clerk. Surely you don't want to break a splendid old tradition like that?'

'I dunno what the fugg you're talking about. All right, let's get on.'

After we had finished I went into Fotherby's office. He was writing out Squadron Orders.

'Excuse me, sir.'

'Well.'

'I see that I'm down for a guard tonight.'

He looked up for the first time. 'That's right.'

'Well, sir, you may remember that on Friday I got the Captain's permission to leave early because——'

'You scived off at twelve. I know that much. Well?'

'Well, sir, I didn't see Orders. So I didn't know I was on guard till this morning.'

'Well?'

'I was wondering whether in view of the circumstances I could be excused guard.'

'You've got a bleeding nerve, Corporal Browne. What bleeding circumstances?'

'Well, sir, I haven't had time to get my kit ready.'

'You've got the lunch hour.' He added with heavy sarcasm: 'And if you're so worried about the state of your kit, I'll ask the Captain if you can dismiss early this afternoon.' There was a brief silence.

'Anything else, Corporal?'

'No, sir.'

I left the room seething with rage. It was a defeat, such as I had rarely received at Badmore. Tubby Hughes from the Pay Office was chatting with Ludlow when I returned to my office.

'Another guard to push then?' he greeted me.

'Oh fugg off.'

Ludlow chortled. 'You didn't get out of it then?'

'No I didn't,' I snapped sourly.

'Corporal Browne!'

Captain Pirie's voice was muffled by the door, but there was a note of urgency in it. I didn't feel like coping with him.

'You go,' I said to Ludlow. 'Get some practice. Tell him I'm not here.'

Ludlow came back looking red and baffled.

'His bloody dog has been sick. He wants me to wipe it up.'

Now Hughes and I laughed together at Ludlow's expense. Unsympathetic laughter was always circulating in this way, making new alliances and dissolving the old ones.

'It must be the tobacco,' I gasped.

'What bloody tobacco?'

'The dog was eating his tobacco.'

'Then he can clean up the shit himself.'

'You'll have to do it, Roy, if you want that stripe,' I said, taking my beret off a hook. 'Coming over to the Naafi, Tubby?'

Roy's misfortune, and a belated breakfast of hot sausage rolls and coffee, made it easier to resign myself to the guard. I saw Jock Gordonstone in the canteen and told him to go ahead and bull my boots.

'Only a few more days to push then?' said Tubby, stirring his coffee.

'Yes. I hope you're working on my demob pay.'

'It'll be ready lad, don't worry. What does it feel like?'

'What? Only having a few days to push? Sort of an anti-climax.'

That wasn't true, but how could you answer such a question, without telling the questioner the story of your life?

'What the fugg's that?'

'You know, when you feel let down. I've waited too long.'

'You're an educated bastard, aren't you, Jonny. Why didn't they make you an officer?'

'Because I didn't want to be one, Tubby. Would *you* want to be one?'

'I wouldn't mind. I wouldn't mind getting pissed in the Officers' Mess instead of pushing the stags.'

'That reminds me. Who's Orderly Officer tonight?'

'The Adjutant.'

'Christ,' I groaned. 'Just my luck.' The Adjutant was a keen young careerist who could be relied upon to be a nuisance on guard. He occasionally came round in the middle of the night to see that everything was in order. Such conduct was considered rather unsporting at Badmore.

I lingered on in the canteen after Tubby had gone, smoking and musing contentedly. I reflected with satisfaction that I had no reason to regret not having been made an officer.

THE Army, it soon became clear to Mike and myself at Catterick, was the last surviving relic of feudalism in English society. The Sovereign was the nominal head of a hierarchy which descended in carefully differentiated grades of privilege to the serf,—the ordinary private soldier. Lip-service was paid to the Divine Right of the Sovereign (on the Queen's birthday we lifted our hats by numbers and gave three compulsory cheers in the general direction of a Union Jack fluttering above the barrack square). The upper ranks of the hierarchy were riddled with jealous intrigue and administrative inefficiency, though corporately they regarded their right to authority and power as natural and unchallengable. They preserved their position by a farcically unjust system of discipline which they called Military Law. The serfs had no rights and did all the work.

Mike and I were now among the serfs, and agreed in finding it unpleasant. But the opportunity offered to us, as Potential Officers, of rising in the hierarchy, did not arouse our enthusiasm. There were advantages in being a P.O. during Basic Training in that we were occasionally released from drill to attend some special lecture or interview. But these activities, though welcome as a relief from square-bashing, produced in us a growing uneasiness.

In my own case this uneasiness was compounded of several different intuitions and responses. I did not like the officers I encountered at Catterick, and my subsequent experience did little to modify my opinion that the officer class was on the whole arrogant, stupid and snobbish, with a grotesquely inflated sense of its own importance. To get a Regular commission in the R.A.C. was no great personal achievement,—any mediocrity with the right background could do it. Yet the officers strutting about Catterick, with their noses fastidiously averted from the more noisome aspects of serf-life, plainly regarded themselves as an élite.

Somehow this superstition, that to be an officer was to belong to an élite, was conveyed to the majority of the P.O.s, amongst whom an oppressive competitiveness developed, as to who could manifest the most keenness and enthusiasm. When we went over to the P.O. Wing they pestered the N.C.O.s there with questions about their prospective training as officers. The descriptions of the latter filled me with gloom. It sounded like a more prolonged and intensive version of Basic Training. Was it worth it? I began to ask myself. Even if one succeeded, one would be at the very bottom of a higher section of the hierarchy: a Second Lieutenant with a National Service Commission. And would I succeed in any case?

This was the crucial question. All through my life I had succeeded in every competition for which I had chosen to enter, because I had restricted my entries to the field of academic study, in which I had some ability. I did not want to experience failure, and I did not want to give the Army the satisfaction of failing me. This competition was one for which I was ill-equipped: intelligence, critical judgment, culture—all the benefits of a liberal education, were of course liabilities rather than assets in applying for a commission. What exactly *was* required in order to pass the successive hurdles of Uzbee, Wozbee and Mons (the cadet school) I never really discovered. It seemed to be enshrined in the mystique of 'leadership'. 'You don't have to be particularly brainy to be an officer,' the Captain in charge of the P.O. Wing would tell us proudly. 'We don't need long-haired geniuses in the Army. (Ha! ha!) But there's one thing you must have. And that's *leadership*.' Whatever this mysterious quality might be, I was fairly certain that I did not possess it. At Wozbee it was apparently assessed by one's ability to handle a knife and fork and to cross a seven-foot ditch with two three-foot planks. I did not see myself excelling in either of these tests.

My growing uneasiness about my status as P.O. was exacerbated by Corporal Baker's continual taunts. We had discovered the reason for his particular spite towards P.O.s: he himself had tried and failed to get a commission. In a way, much as I disliked him, I understood his grievance. He was a cruel, foul-mouthed individual, but he was considerably more intelligent than most N.C.O.s, and by the Army's standards a 'good soldier'. He had been rejected after getting as far as Mons. I could imagine him at Mons, a very different Baker, subdued, anxious, insecure, mixing uncomfortably with the other cadets, speaking as little as possible, and then very deliberately, to disguise his plebeian accent; excelling at drill, initiative tests and map-reading, but fluffing his five-minute talk, and using the wrong spoon for soup. I could understand why he resented us P.O.s who, by benefit of class or education, might soon obtain the commission that had eluded him. But, as I smarted under his insults, powerless to reply, I hated him. And I think that of all the P.O.s, he hated me most. Fallow-field and Peterson he treated with a kind of grudging defer-ence, like the boxing pro. at a public school licking the young gentlemen into shape. His hostility to Mike was tempered by a certain respect for Mike's physical and mental ruggedness. Percy he tormented as a cruel child torments a helpless animal. But in me he found a victim worthy of his spleen. I was from the same class as him, but boosted by educational advantages he had missed. I was bumptious and cocksure. I was physically unimpressive. I exerted myself in all departments of Basic Training to the bare minimum necessary to avoid serious trouble. I did not disguise my personal dislike of him, and I did not laugh at his jokes. And so he reserved his most spiteful abuse for me, usually centring on my pretensions to be a P.O.

All these considerations were accumulating throughout the first weeks of Basic Training, but they did not reach critical proportions until the fourth week when Mike compelled me into a decision. One afternoon that week, all the P.O.s were interviewed by the officer in charge of the Intake, Second Lieutenant Booth-Henderson. He was himself the worst possible advertisement for the desirability of a commission. He was pudgy, flabby, pimply, stupid, nervous and pompous. We discovered his history—how I'm not quite sure, but I think Baker, who shared our contempt for him, had leaked it to a few of his toadies in the squad. Booth-Henderson had tried unsuccessfully three times to get a National Service commission, and since he belonged to a social class where such failure was a slur, had in desperation signed on for a third year and had been rewarded with a Regular commission. When I marched into Booth-Henderson's office I found that I simply could not make the effort to create the right impression.

'Well, Browne,' he began, 'I suppose you think it's going to be easy to become an officer?'

'No, sir,' I replied.

'Well I can tell you it isn't,' he continued, undeterred. 'It's jolly difficult. Now I have Corporal Baker's report on you here. I must tell you that it's very unsatisfactory. Have you any explanation?'

'The only one I can think of is that Corporal Baker happens to dislike me.' His jaw sagged slightly.

'You can't say that, Browne. I mean, it's ridiculous. It's Corporal Baker's job to, er, to . . . to knock you into shape' (he fell upon the phrase with obvious relief), 'to knock you into shape. There's nothing personal about it. It's all a part of, er, knocking you into shape. Now he says here that your brasses are usually dirty. Now that's not good enough, Browne. It really isn't. You must improve.'

'It's not just me, sir. It's all the P.O.s. He seemed to have a grudge against us. He's always trying to make us look fools in front of the other lads.'

'Now that's enough, Browne! I'm not here to discuss Corporal Baker. I'm here to . . . Now what about these brasses?'

'They're as clean as anyone else's,' I replied.

'Ah!' he cried triumphantly. 'That's just the point, Browne. As a P.O. we expect a higher standard of turn-out from you than from the others. Now next week you'll be going before the C.O. for interview before you move over to the P.O. Wing at the end of your Basic Training. I advise you to pull your socks up and get your finger out if you want to have a chance of passing Uzbee. Now have you got any questions you would like to ask me?'

'Yes, sir. Is it true that P.O.s have to report back to camp twelve hours before the others at the end of our seventy-two?'

I was referring to the three days' leave which we were to get at the end of our basic training, and to which we looked forward with an eagerness that is difficult to describe. Booth-Henderson seemed somewhat taken aback by my question.

'Yes, I believe that's the form. Why do you ask?'

'Well, I think it's rather unfair, sir. It means leaving home on Sunday morning. It cuts your leave down to a forty-eight.'

He paused portentously before delivering his reply.

'Browne, I must say I don't think you're approaching this thing in the right spirit at all. Surely the loss of a few hours' leave is a small thing compared to the honour of becoming an officer?'

I was silent, and as he could not apparently think of anything else to say, he dismissed me. In the corridor outside his room, Mike who had already been interviewed was waiting for me.

'Well, how did you make out with the White Hope of the British Army?'

'Pretty badly, I should think. I asked him about having our leave cut short. I think he took a dim view of it.'

'The man's a cretin. I could scarcely keep a straight face.'

We walked towards the huts to collect our eating-irons for tea. A fine drizzle was falling, and we slithered on the muddy paths. Groups of tired soldiers moved like shadows through the rain towards the cookhouse. Mike said:

'Jon, d'you really want to be an officer?'

'I suppose not.'

'Neither do I. All along I've felt in a false position, being a P.O. I detest the Army—the discipline, the snobbery, the idea of doing what you're told and asking no questions. The rest of it doesn't worry *me* so much, but some of the other lads,—I don't mean the tough nuts, they're all right; but the slightly dumb ones, the married ones, the nervous ones, the ones like Percy—they look so bloody miserable, as if they don't know what's hit them. It seems so unjust to me. And I feel that if I became an officer I'd be participating in that injustice. D'you know what I mean?'

'Yes. I feel exactly the same.'

'We'd have to pretend to be like that cretin Booth-

Henderson. We'd have to cultivate a whole new set of attitudes: other ranks are animals; officers are gentlemen. Other ranks are dirty; officers have batmen. Other ranks must only have beer in the canteen, or they get drunk; officers can pig themselves with whisky. Other ranks are issued with French letters at the guardroom; officers pride themselves on getting an exclusive form of pox from Madame Marie's.'

I laughed. Madame Marie, according to Mike, who had a curious fund of anecdote, was a lady who ran a select call-girl agency for officers on leave in London. A young R.A.S.C. officer of Mike's acquaintance had telephoned the establishment and had been informed by a shocked voice: 'We only cater for the *best* regiments.'

'It's all true, Trooper.'

'Well I've decided to withdraw my application for a commission. How about you?'

'Mmm. It's a bit drastic.'

I thought it over as we approached the hut. Mike's altruistic scruples scarcely touched me. It came down to this as far as I was concerned: did I want a commission badly enough to take the considerable risk of failing to get it? Outside the hut we met Fallowfield.

'Well?' he said abruptly.

'Well?' Mike returned.

'How did you two get on?'

'Not very well. I pulled his hat over his eyes and beat him over the head with his swagger stick,' replied Mike with a straight face. 'How about you, Jon?'

'Oh I just told him to stop picking at his pimples.'

Fallowfield turned away with an irritable shrug. He threw back over his shoulder: 'Full kit lay-out tomorrow.'

'We know,' retorted Mike, though we didn't. 'Why do people like Fallowfield take such a pleasure in spreading bad news?' he muttered.

As we plodded over to the cookhouse, it occurred to me that if Mike withdrew his application for a commission, and I didn't, we would be separated.

'I've decided, Mike,' I said. 'I'll withdraw my application, too. How do we set about it?'

77

With typical perversity the Army, having consistently impressed upon us the unlikelihood of our obtaining commissions, made it almost impossible for us to withdraw our applications. We were reluctantly obliged to approach Baker first.

'Frightened you off have I?' he said with a sneer. 'Thought you had more guts in you, Brady.'

'It's got nothing to do with guts,' replied Mike, reddening. 'It's just that we don't want to be officers. What do we do?'

'You'll have to see Lieutenant Henderson,' said Baker. He always deliberately shortened Booth-Henderson's name.

'Will you arrange an interview then?' I asked.

He turned his head slowly towards me with exaggerated astonishment.

'You've got a fugging nerve, Trooper. I've got more important things to do than run around arranging interviews for the likes of you. And another thing, I'm *"Corporal"* to you.'

'Sorry, Corporal,' I mumbled. I'd swallowed so much pride by then, another mouthful wouldn't make any difference. But Baker didn't help us any further.

When we caught Booth-Henderson a couple of days later he looked troubled. 'I don't advise you to do anything rash,' he said. 'Think it over.'

'We've thought about it and we're quite certain, sir,' I said.

'Well, I'll look into it.' He hurried off.

A few days later our names appeared, with those of the other P.O.s, on Squadron Orders, for the C.O.'s interview. I asked Baker what we should do.

'You can read, can't you?'

'Yes, Corporal.'

'Well, what does it say?'

'It says that we're to parade for interview on Friday afternoon outside the C.O.'s office.'

'Well then, you fugging well parade. Jesus Christ! It couldn't be any clearer.'

'But we told you last week that we didn't want to be P.O.s any longer,' I explained patiently.

'Did you see Lieutenant Henderson?'

'Yes.'

'What did he say?'

'He said he'd see about it.'

'Well I don't know anything about it, and what's more I don't give a monkey's fugg. You'll have to explain it all to the C.O.'

The explanation of Baker's and Booth-Henderson's strangely evasive behaviour suddenly dawned on me. From their point of view it would not look good if two P.O.s in their charge withdrew their applications. Many are called but few are chosen, was the official attitude to a commission. Awkward questions might be asked if anyone proved indifferent to the call. Baker and Booth-Henderson were no doubt hoping that we would not have the nerve to announce our decision to the C.O. himself. In this they were wrong. We hadn't been in the Army long enough to acquire that awe-struck reverence which is the usual attitude towards a Commanding Officer.

Our determination gave great pleasure to Percy who, not long before, had been demoted from the status of P.O. on Baker's recommendation. At one point, indeed, it had seemed not impossible that he might be discharged from the Army altogether. This was not unknown. A mentally deficient in 'B' Squad, who had inexplicably been called up, was discharged after a couple of weeks. Mike and I met him one afternoon shambling down the road towards the camp entrance, dressed in civilian clothes and carrying a suitcase.

'Compassionate leave?' I asked.

'Naw. Got m' discharge. No more fugging Army for me.'

We tactfully refrained from asking him why he had been discharged, though I doubt if he understood himself. I doubt if he had understood anything that had happened to him in the Army, except that for two long weeks he had been harassed and bullied and laughed at and shouted at through some dreadful mistake which had now happily been rectified. We watched him depart with an ironical envy of his feeble, stunted mind.

Percy, however, despite his eccentricities and lack of co-ordination, was not mentally deficient. There were no grounds on which he could be discharged from the Army. After a second interview with the Personnel Officer he ceased to be a

P.O., and this was obviously a pathetic disappointment to him. 'Something to do with his family,' Mike explained to me. He was therefore pleased when Mike (particularly) and I told him that we were going to withdraw our applications.

By this time, however, Percy had already degenerated. A furtive, haunted look had come to fill the vacuum of innocent wonder in his eyes. The ribbing of the other soldiers was much milder than in his first days, but he was much more sensitive to it, often flying into childish fits of rage or lapsing into deep sulks. This of course only re-awakened in the others a desire to tease which might otherwise have remained dormant. I have a picture of Percy, white-faced and writhing with impotent anger, while Norman held him effortlessly at arm's length by his lapel. Sometimes Mike would intervene, but even he seemed to appreciate that Percy must not be too much protected if he were to survive. Sooner or later they would be separated.

Once Percy broke down and cried on the square. We had been sweating hard all the morning under a strong sun, striving to master the turn on the march, Baker was in a vile temper, and his venomous tongue flickered over the squad, leaving its poison to linger and bite under the skin. But, as usual, Percy came in for most of the abuse. Finally, at a particularly grotesque display on Percy's part, in which he tripped himself up and actually fell to the ground, Baker clapped his hand dramatically to his forehead and swore loud and long.

'Fugging Christ, Higgins,' he concluded. 'You march like a WRAC walking through these barracks—with her legs crossed!'

The rest of the squad guffawed mechanically. But when Percy slowly picked himself off the ground, he was crying. The squad looked at him with curiosity or pity.

'Eyes front!' snapped Baker.

We stared ahead listening to Percy's muffled sobs. Mike was directly in front of me, and I saw his neck glowing red.

'Higgins, I always knew you were a fool,' said Baker. 'But I didn't know you were a coward. Crying like a big baby, because the rude man shouted at you! Or did you hurt your tootsies when you fell over?'

Gasping for breath Percy replied:

'It's not—that at all. It's—because you—keep saying fugging—Christ.'

Even Baker was momentarily disconcerted. There was a breathless silence, abruptly and incongruously punctured by the chimes of a mobile ice-cream van which drove up to the side of the square.

'Smoke-break,' said Baker.

We broke up gratefully. Some drifted over to the van to buy ice-lollies. Mike and I loosened our webbing, and threw ourselves on to the grass which bordered the square. Mike tossed me a cigarette, and we smoked in silence for a while, inhaling hungrily. I was smoking quite heavily now. Mike glanced over at Percy, sitting alone and at some distance from everyone else. Guessing his thoughts I said:

'Perhaps we shouldn't have told him.'

'Perhaps not.'

We were both remembering the previous evening. The three of us had been sitting round a table in the Y.M.C.A. Canteen, delaying the moment when we would have to return to the hut and get on with our bulling. The canteen was a small, poorly furnished shack, but we preferred it to the institutional hygiene of the Naafi; and besides, the coffee was better. I was working on a poem—it was more of a gesture, a cultural nose-snook at the Army, than a serious attempt to write anything,— Mike was smoking and reading a tattered newspaper and Percy was brooding with his hands cupped round his beaker of coffee. Suddenly he broke the silence.

'What does "fugg" mean?'

The question startled us. I tittered nervously and looked round to see if anyone had heard. The word which had become as common to our ears as the definite article, sounded suddenly shocking on Percy's lips. Mike told him.

'And "c——t"?'

He went methodically through the list of Army obscenities, with Mike explaining as tactfully as possible. Then he said:

'How disgusting. How absolutely damnable.'

I believe 'damnable' was the strongest word I ever heard Percy use.

'Don't let it worry you, Percy,' said Mike gently. 'They don't really mean what they say.'

'Oh yes they do,' Percy replied quickly. 'They've got filthy, filthy minds.'

I felt relaxed, and almost light-hearted as I lined up with the other P.O.s on the veranda outside the C.O.'s office. The others fiddled nervously with their uniforms, rubbing their belt-brasses with handkerchiefs, and polishing their toe-caps on the inside of their trouser-legs. Fallowfield asked Mike if his cap-badge was in the middle of his forehead. 'Like Cyclops eye,' he assured him. Fallowfield seemed dubious, and checked his appearance in a nearby window-pane.

'I wish they'd hurry up,' he said.

'Why?' I asked. 'The longer it takes, the less drill we have this afternoon.'

'I don't mind drill,' he replied. 'But waiting makes me nervous.'

Our conversation was cut short by the appearance of the R.S.M., who brought us to attention and treated us to his professional, ill-tempered glare. We were marched in, one by one, to the usual accompaniment of rapidly-shouted orders, the Army's technique for instilling a sense of inferiority and insecurity in the private soldier when he appears before his commanding officer.

Eventually my turn came—before Mike's. I marched into the room, turned and saluted. Lieutenant-Colonel Lancing sat behind his desk, flanked by Captain James from the P.O. Wing, the Personnel Officer, and the Second-in-Command, reclining in chairs in indolent attitudes.

'Good afternoon, Browne,' said the C.O. civilly. 'Take a seat there.' I sat down on the seat he indicated.

'Uncross your legs, Browne,' said James. I did so. The C.O. grinned at James.

'Just a small point, Browne,' he said to me. 'But small points are important if you want to be an officer. Now I want you to tell me *why* you want to be an officer.' He smiled encouragingly.

'I feel in rather a false position at the moment, sir,' I replied.

'Because the fact is I don't want to be an officer.' The C.O.'s smile vanished abruptly. I continued: 'I told Lieutenant Booth-Henderson last week, but my name appeared on Orders for this interview, and Corporal Baker told me I should attend it.'

The C.O. turned to James.

'Did you know anything about this, Ronny?' he asked.

'No, sir,' said James,—and, to me: 'Why didn't you come and see me about this, Browne?'

'No one told me I should, sir.'

The C.O. turned to the Personnel Officer: 'This man *is* a P.O. I take it?'

'Yes, sir. He asked me to put him down as a P.O. when I interviewed him.'

This little exchange amused me. Confronted with the un-expected and possibly embarrassing situation, Lancing instinc-tively tried to detach himself from it, and to put the onus on his subordinates. However he recovered his self-possession quickly. I suppose he thought he would demonstrate the absurdity of my attitude.

'Well now, Browne, suppose you tell me why you have changed your mind?'

I thought I might as well enjoy myself while I was there.

'Well, sir, I'll be quite frank with you. I don't like the Army. I know I'm stuck with it for two years, but I'm sure I shall continue to dislike it. I don't see how I could possibly be an officer with that point of view. Don't you agree, sir?'

'What don't you like about the Army?'

'Almost everything, sir.'

The 2 IC smiled slightly, and looked at his shoes. The C.O. began to look rather angry.

'Now look here, I've been in the Army for twenty-five years. You've been in it for four weeks. I think you've got a lot of nerve to sit there and say the Army's all wrong.'

'I'm sorry, sir, I didn't mean to be impertinent. I quite understand that my position must seem inexplicable to you.' I began to get into my stride. 'I suppose it's my education. I've been encouraged to question everything, to form an indepen-dent judgment. In the Army one has to accept orders without

83

questioning them. I feel that if I were to hope to become an officer I would have to give up too many principles.'

'When you're older, Browne, you'll discover that there must be some sort of authority which is obeyed without question. But this is all beside the point. The point is that whether you like it or not you have been called up to serve your country for two years. I don't think you've got any reason to grumble about that. Your country has been pretty good to you up till now. It's given you a damn' fine education for one thing. Now are you, or are you not, going to make the best of it?'

'I don't think I've been given the opportunity of making the best of it,' I replied. 'I applied to go in the Education Corps, where I think I might have been of some use to the Army and to myself. In the R.A.C. I feel I'm wasting my time and the Army's.'

'Is there any chance of getting this man transferred to the Education Corps?' the 2 IC asked the Personnel Officer.

'None at all. I told you that before, Browne.'

'Well, Browne,' resumed the C.O., 'there's obviously no point in arguing with you, though I think you're making a great mistake. What do you want to do now. Train as a Signaller/Gunner? If you work hard you might become a tank-commander in time.'

He obviously hadn't understood a word I'd said.

'No, sir, I think I'd rather be a clerk.'

'Is that all right, Harold?'

The Personnel Officer nodded sourly.

'All right then. That's all, Browne.'

'Go over to the P.O. Wing and wait for me,' said Captain James. 'You'll have to sign a non-desirous statement.'

I saluted and left the room. Outside Mike was still waiting for his turn. I winked at him, and strolled over to the P.O. Wing. A little later he joined me.

'You were lucky to go in first,' he said. 'They were hopping mad. The C.O. said: "What is this, a conspiracy?" '

I laughed elatedly.

'We've got them worried, boy!' Then, 'Did you say you wanted to be a clerk?' I asked anxiously.

'Yes. No alternative,' he replied glumly.

The prospect of a warm, easy, sedentary occupation appealed to me, but filled Mike with dismay, Fortunately for me, he had no alternative. For Mike suffered from claustrophobia. On the afternoon when we had been taken to the tank park and allowed to clamber over the muddy monsters, he had emerged pale and trembling from the cabin. Therefore the tank trades were out of the question for him. I was never tempted by them. Tanks seemed to me to be ugly, noisy, dangerous, and quite absurdly obsolete in terms of modern war. Anyway, I was delighted by his news.

'Good. That means we'll do our Clerks' training together,' I said.

At this moment Captain James stalked past us into his office. We heard the clatter of a typewriter.

'This must be a rare case,' I murmured to Mike. 'He's having to type out a pro-forma.'

We were called in to sign the statements.

'I think you're a couple of insolent young fools,' he said. 'I hope you're satisfied. That's all.'

After the dramatic little scene on the barrack square, Baker perceptibly restrained his language. But unlike most N.C.O.s he did not rely exclusively on blasphemy or obscenity for his invective, and Percy's life was still a misery. Baker frequently threatened to back-squad him. I believe now that this was never a real possibility, for Baker prided himself on his ability to make a soldier of the most unpromising material. But with an Inquisitor's subtle cruelty he kept the threat dangling over Percy's head. Percy's dread of being back-squadded did not seem exaggerated to us. We were in a more or less permanent state of physical exhaustion and mental depression, and we longed for the end of Basic Training with an indescribable longing. We did not know what our Trade Training or our regimental life would be like, but we felt that it could not possibly be worse than Basic Training. To forfeit the precious seventy-two after the passing-out parade, and to begin Basic Training all over again, was unthinkable.

Two images rose persistently to the surface of one's mind during Basic Training at Catterick: one was prison, and the other was hell. The sense of being in prison was created by an accumulation of factors: the confinement to barracks, the bad food, the warder-like attitude of the N.C.O.s, the ugly denims, the shaved heads, the pervasive dreariness and discomfort of daily life. The photograph on my identity card, the haggard face and the cropped hair, with my Army number across my chest, irresistibly recalled a convict's dossier. The evening bull-sessions seemed as pointless and soul-destroying as sewing mailbags. Our weekly pay of one pound always seemed curiously unwarranted and unexpected when it was issued: one had no sense of earning money by service, only of being punished.

The feeling of being in prison was perhaps the dominant one, but there were times when life was touched by a quality of surrealism, of nightmarish unreason, and the prison-image gave way to one of hell. Not a real hell of course, but a kind of *opéra bouffe* hell, a macabre farce, one's response to which oscillated between hysterical laughter and a metaphysical despair.

An occasion when this impression was most forcefully made was when we were first ordered to prepare a full kit lay-out. With practice this becomes a relatively simple, though always tiresome operation. But to us the task seemed gigantic. Every single item of equipment had to be cleaned, polished or blancoed. All clothing had to be pressed to regulation measurements until it was no longer recognizable as clothing, but only as a number of flat, oblong shapes. There was one iron between fifteen of us. The official lights-out time was ignored by the N.C.O.s for, as they well knew, the task took us long into the night, and the early hours of the morning. I did not get to sleep until 3 a.m., and several others did not go to bed at all. When my travelling alarum clock woke me at five, they were still bent, red-eyed, over their boots as the grey light of dawn competed with the feeble electric light bulbs. I woke myself at five because to arrange the kit according to the complex regulation lay-out was itself a lengthy process. Little Barnes in fact laid out his kit at 2.45 a.m., and, wrapping himself in a blanket, lay down to sleep on the cold stone floor beside his bed. No one else adopted quite such a Spartan expedient, but several slept on the bare wire mesh of their bed-frames, their kit laid out on the mattress beside them, to be lifted on to the bed in the morning.

Everyone grumbled and swore, of course, but still we did it. And I can't really understand why we drove ourselves to such lengths. Fear of punishment? Perhaps, in some cases, but I doubt it. The punishment would only be abuse, and that would come however hard one worked. In any case, no punishment could be worse than the task itself. Pride in the work? There are a few chronic bullshitters in every squad, but this certainly didn't apply to most of us. Perhaps one has to admit, however grudgingly, that the Army's despotic authority does make itself felt on the most rebellious temperament, that very quickly one does become conditioned to respond automatically to any order, however absurd. Once you acknowledge this, it is very difficult to forgive the Army for it, and even more difficult to forgive yourself. It was with some half-conscious realization of this that Mike and I, while we flogged ourselves as remorselessly as the rest of the squad through that seemingly interminable night, tried to maintain an attitude of ironic detachment from the whole absurd affair. But it was not easy.

The rhythm of activity varied in tempo as the night dragged on. At about 10.30 a general melancholy fell upon the occupants of the hut. Someone began to hum *Unchained Melody*, a pop-song much in favour at that time, and the rest took it up, humming and singing. The tune was a plangent, melancholy series of cadences in a curiously repetitive form which, I suppose, accounted for its title. The words went something like this:

> *Oh, my love*
> *My darling,*
> *I've hungered for your kiss*
> *A long,*
> *Lonely*
> *Time.*
> *Time*
> *Goes by*
> *So slowly*
> *And time can do so much,*
> *Though you're*

Still mine.
I need your love,
God speed your love,
To me.

It is difficult, and embarrassing, to believe that one was ever moved by words so trite and meaningless. But at certain moments life out-manœuvres the defences of sophistication, lays one open to a shrewd flanking attack of cheap and vulgar sentiment.

It was not long before this mood of quiet melancholy was dispersed by Norman, starting up a rousing bawdy ballad, in his hoarse, dissonant voice:

Mary the maid of the mountain glen,
Shagged herself with a fountain pen,
They called the bastard Stephen,
They called the bastard Stephen
They called the bastard Stephen,
For that was the name of the ink!

Percy looked at us reproachfully, as Mike and I chuckled. I was constantly surprised by the wit and intelligence which obscenity seemed to reveal in the lower ranks of the Army who otherwise seemed scarcely literate. In the course of my service I was often handed a grubby piece of paper on which was typed some scurrilous doggerel, of stomach-turning obscenity, yet possessing an ingenuity and wit which Rochester would not have been ashamed to own.

As the night wore on, and p.m. changed unbelievably to a.m., weariness and desperation combined to produce a mood of hysteria in the hut. Instead of finishing off the task as quickly as possible, we snatched eagerly at every distraction and interruption. Brief, spontaneous fights broke out. Norman and his friends indulged in several 'riding' sorties against each other. One lad, who had abandoned his kit and was trying to sleep, cursed them for the noise they were making, and they retaliated by lifting the bed with its occupant into the air and carrying it round the hut shoulder high, finally tipping the unfortunate youth on to the ground in a heap of blankets.

At about 2 a.m. Norman decided to sweep his end of the hut. The floor was made of stone flags. Several were cracked and pieces were missing, leaving open cavities. Norman swept the refuse into the largest cavity to save the trouble of dumping it outside.

'Yer can't leave all that shit there, Norman,' protested someone. 'Pox and Faker'll 'ave somethink to say about that.' (Sergeant Box and Corporal Baker were known familiarly as 'Pox and Faker', 'Faker' lending itself to a further, obvious distortion.)

'Fuggit, I'll burn it then,' retorted Norman, and applied a match to the rubbish. There was quite a lot of newspaper and brown paper in the cavity, and the flames leapt up alarmingly, igniting a gleam of wicked, infantile pleasure in the eyes of the spectators. A few ran to feed the fire with more paper and rags.

Little Barnes sniffed the smell of burning in his sleep, and sat up bolt upright in his bed screaming 'Fire!' We howled with laughter at his panic, eyes running with tears, tears of laughter, tears provoked by the stinging smoke, tears that were at the same time *lachrymae rerum.*

Norman and two of his cronies commenced a grotesque ritual dance around the fire, roaring and whooping at the tops of their voices. Others drummed on their lockers with knives and forks. A demonic frenzy seemed to have seized everyone. and though I was only a spectator, I was completely absorbed in the spectacle, until I caught sight of Percy, crouched on his bed, his hands over his ears, white-faced and shivering as if in the grip of an ague.

'What's the matter, Percy?' I yelled to him; but he just looked at me and shook his head.

The flames quickly died away. but the density of the smoke increased. Someone shouted: 'For fugg's sake, Norman, put the fire out.'

'Give us some water then,' he growled hoarsely, lurching towards the ironing table where Joe Matthews, a sharp little Cockney, had a mug of water for pressing. Joe snatched up his mug.

'Get your own bleeding water, Norman.'

'Come on youth,' said Norman. 'Ah haven't got time to get any water. The whole bloody hut'll go up in flames in a minute.'

'Then piss on it.'

The suggestion appealed to Norman, and ripping open his flies, he emptied his capacious bladder on to the smouldering remnants of the fire.

'*Gulliver's Travels*,' I said to Mike, and he grinned in acknowledgement of the reference. His grin faded as he inhaled the foul-smelling steam which now mingled with the acrid smoke. Laughing and cursing, the others struggled to open the windows, or stampeded to the door, which parted from its one remaining hinge and fell outwards on to the ground. They stood on it, hooting and shouting into the hut, where Norman was trying to stamp out the fire.

'You vile bastard, Norman!'

'You silly c——t, Norman!'

'Wrap up or I'll ride ya!' he retorted.

Eventually the smoke cleared, the temporary exaltation faded, and we returned to our tasks, more exhausted than ever. Percy came over and sat at the end of my bed, prodding ineffectually at a boot.

'I can't get this toe-cap to shine,' he said hopelessly.

I inspected the boot. The toe-cap was marked by hundreds of minute scratches.

'The first thing you want is a new duster,' I said. 'That one must have some grit in it which is scratching the surface.'

'Here, borrow mine,' said Mike, tossing over his duster from the next bed. 'I've had enough for tonight.' He took off his boots and, without undressing further, got between the blankets, where he smoked his customary nicotine night-cap.

'Well,' he said, 'it won't be long before we've finished square-bashing.'

'It's all right for you,' said Percy. 'But I'll probably be back-squadded.'

'Baker won't back-squad you, Percy,' I said.

'Oh yes he will. He'll wait till the day before passing out, and then he'll tell me.'

'Well, if the worst comes to the worst,' I argued, trying to console him. 'At least you won't have Baker in charge of your new squad.'

'It's not just Baker,' he replied vehemently. 'Do you think I could bear to go through this again?' He swept out his arm, embracing the whole scene, the bleak, badly-lit hut, the glum soldiers hunched over their boots or groaning in their sleep, the lingering fumes of the fire and of Norman's urine. 'I'd rather die,' said Percy.

In fact Percy died on the Tuesday of the last week of Basic Training. That day we went out to the rifle range. It was raining, a fine, persistent drizzle, but there was a holiday atmosphere in the coach that took us out to the moors. We were tired, because the day before we had been doing various physical fitness tests. The standards required were not exacting, but since all the tests were held on one afternoon—the mile, the hundred yards, the high jump, the long jump, rope-climbing and several other items—the total expenditure of energy was pretty considerable. However, all that was behind us; passing-out and the seventy-two were before us; and the present, the expedition to the moors, was at least a novelty. The inside of the coach was warm and smoky; the radio was playing 'Housewives' Choice'; even Baker, sitting with the driver, seemed in a better humour than usual, and did not check the exuberance of the passengers, except to say 'Pipe down, c——t-struck,' when Norman bellowed like a bull in June at a couple of girls we passed.

We quickly left the camp behind, and drove through a lunar landscape of rugged moorland, torn and rutted by the tanks which crawled over it night and day like sluggish prehistoric monsters. Eventually we reached the rifle range, which was situated across a valley: on one side were the butts, on the other the firing points. There was no shelter, apart from an open-sided structure of corrugated iron, and a ramshackle latrine with no plumbing. The rain fell softly but unremittingly, and the prospect of spending a day in this bleak, inhospitable place began to look distinctly unattractive.

The party was divided into two parts: 'C' squad was detailed to man the butts, while the other two squads fired;

later, we would have our turn. We wrapped ourselves in our groundsheets and trudged across the squelching grass to the butts. The butts consisted of a wide concrete trench, partially flooded with rainwater, which protected us from the rifle fire. Each target was manned by two men. It was raised by a pulley to be fired at. Between each round we signalled a bull, 'inner', 'magpie', 'outer', or miss, with various flags. After five rounds had been fired we lowered the targets and pasted over the holes with appropriately coloured pieces of paper. It was a slow, tedious business. Each man's score was being recorded by frowning, pencil-licking N.C.O.s across the valley. Queries had to be answered by the antiquated field telephone. The novelty of the first few minutes, the temporary sense of danger as the bullets whined over our heads, soon gave way to damp boredom. Baker's good humour melted away in the rain with his trouser creases, to be replaced by one of his wickedest tempers. It was rarely profitable to seek an explanation of Baker's black moods, but I caught him stroking his cheek a few times, and a slight swelling there made me suspect toothache.

'I think Baker's got toothache,' I said to Mike, as we hoisted our target above the trench.

'Stop, you're breaking my heart,' he replied.

At half past twelve we ate our corned beef sandwiches with the hot sweet tea brought out by the Naafi van. At about half past two it was our turn to fire.

'Have you ever fired a rifle before?' Percy asked me, as we struggled across the valley, our sodden capes flapping round our knees.

'Apart from the ·202 the other day, no.' We should have had a practice at firing ·303s a few days before coming out to the range, but at the last moment there had proved to be a shortage of ammunition. So for the majority of us this was our first experience of firing a proper weapon. Yet we were supposed to attain a certain standard of accuracy before passing out.

'I hope I manage all right,' said Percy. 'I hope Baker doesn't watch me. It's just what he will do, of course. He'll put me off completely.'

'You'll be all right, Percy. But watch your right shoulder. I believe the recoil can give you a nasty bruise.'

'I'm left-handed,' he said.

'Well then, your left. What about you, Mike?' I asked, turning to him. 'You did pretty well at the small-bore range.'

'I've done a bit of shooting in Ireland,' he replied. 'But not with these clumsy great things. I thought they went out with the Boer War.'

'Higgins! Browne! Brady! not so much gab,' called Baker from behind. 'Get a bloody move on. We don't want to be here all night.' I glanced briefly over my shoulder. Baker was holding a khaki handkerchief to his jaw, and appeared to be in some pain.

When we reached the firing point, Baker curtly explained the procedure:

'When it's your turn to fire your name will be called. You go to Sergeant Box and he will give you a clip of five rounds. You will then take up your position ten paces behind one of those already preparing to fire. When he has finished you step forward and lie on the ground. On the command "Load!" you insert the clip into the magazine. On the command "Release Safety Catch!" you release your safety catch. At the command "Aim!" you aim your rifle at the bull of your target, taking care to align both sights. At the command "Fire!" you will fire one round and operate the bolt to eject the empty case. You will fire five rounds in this manner. Do *not* fire before the order is given. Do *not* fire more than one round at a time. When you have fired five rounds you will pick up the empty cases and return them immediately to Sergeant Box. Anyone who attempts to take away a live shell is liable to be court-martialled. Is that understood? Right. Let's get the fugging thing over as quickly as possible.'

The drizzle did not make for accurate shooting, and the general standard was low. Baker fretted and swore at the recumbent marksmen. We stood around on the wet hillside, awaiting our turn, fiddling apprehensively with the heavy rifles.

Mike and I were firing immediately after Percy, and we stood behind him, suffering with him. He was trembling with

93

nerves as he lowered himself to the ground. Immediately, he had trouble getting the ammunition into the magazine. He tried to force it, his hand slipped, and a red gash appeared on the back of his hand.

'For Christ's sake, Higgins, can't you even load the fugging thing?' yapped Baker; and snatching the rifle from Percy's nerveless fingers, he effortlessly pushed home the clip with the palm of his hand. He stood over Percy while the latter fumbled awkwardly with the safety catch which, as he was left-handed, was on the 'wrong' side for him.

'Is the target moving, Higgins?' Baker inquired sarcastically, as Percy took aim.

'No, Corporal.'

'Then what's your bloody barrel waving about for?'

Percy steadied his arm, and one could sense the determination and concentration in his rigid figure.

'Fire!'

The shots rattled out. After a pause the butts began to signal. Percy's target indicated a miss. A spasm of pain crossed Baker's face, and his hand went up to his jaw.

'Get your finger out, Higgins,' he said in a low, dangerous voice. 'I'm warning you.'

Percy went on firing. Each time the red and white flag waved sadly over his target. Baker grew more and more insensed. For the last time he ordered 'Fire!' As the shots began to rattle out a Regular came up to Baker with a message.

'Sergeant Box says the butts have rung up to say there are seven holes in number two target and what the fugginell are we playing at,' he said with a grin. Baker went white with anger. With his boot he rolled Percy on to his back.

'You stupid c——t, Higgins! You've been firing at the wrong target! That does it. I don't want to see you again, you horrible man. You're back-squadded. Some other poor fugger can try and make a soldier of you. I've had enough. Get out of my sight. Go on! Get out.'

Percy stumbled miserably between Mike and me, and we watched him dragging himself blindly up the hill through the rain. We couldn't follow him, because Baker called us forward to take up our firing positions.

'Jones!' Baker called to the Regular who had brought the message. 'Pick up that c——t's empty cases.'

Sprawling on my damp groundsheet, I tried to put Percy out of my mind and concentrate on shooting accurately. I didn't want to get back-squadded too. Jones, rooting in the grass at my side, was an irritating distraction.

'Come on, Jones,' called Baker.

'There's only four cases, Corporal,' the soldier replied.

'Oh Jesus! Go and get the——'

His words were cut short by a muffled explosion from behind us, followed by an anguished moan, terrifying because it seemed to come from a distance, and yet was clearly audible. There was a paralysed silence. Then Mike scrambled to his feet and, throwing down his rifle, began running like a stag up the hill.

'Brady! What the——' began Baker. But then he was running too, and we were all running.

We found Percy behind the foetid latrine, lying on his rifle, a horrible stain creeping swiftly through the turf around his body. Mike, with tears streaming down his cheeks, was lifting Percy's face from the wet grass.

'Act of Contrition, Percy,' he was saying urgently. 'Your Act of Contrition. "O my God, I am heartily sorry for all my sins . . ." '

I knew what Mike was afraid of: suicide. The unforgivable sin. And it seemed as if Percy understood too, for he tried to shake his head. He made no sound, but his eyes bulged from their sockets, as if he were astonished by so much pain. Mike looked up at Baker.

'You swine,' he said softly.

Baker had suddenly become old and yellow and crumpled.

'It was an accident,' he said dully.

Mike opened his mouth to reply, but suddenly Percy murmured:

'Accident.'

Baker straightened perceptibly. 'You heard that,—it was an accident,' he said in a dry, eager voice to the little group of terrified soldiers. 'Higgins said it was an accident. You're all witnesses to that.'

Percy opened his mouth to speak again, but all that came out was a gush of blood. I turned aside and, leaning against the latrine wall, my fingers digging into the rusting corrugated iron, I was violently sick. When I turned back Sergeant Box was ordering the soldiers away from the scene; two soldiers who had fainted were being slapped into consciousness; Baker was nursing his jaw; Mike was crossing himself; and Percy was dead.

Percy performed one last, ironic service for us by his death, for our Basic Training ended with it.

The firing, of course, was abandoned immediately, but no one seemed to know what to do. Harassed N.C.O.s flapped about like startled poultry. We saw Booth-Henderson, summoned by the field-telephone from the butts, running clumsily up the hill towards us. Eventually he drove off in a jeep to find a call-box. Soldiers loitered in the drizzle, sucking on damp cigarettes, casting scared, surreptitious glances at Percy's body, covered with a wet groundsheet.

'A soldier's death,' said Mike bitterly. 'A soldier's bloody death.' He didn't say anything more.

Booth-Henderson returned after about twenty minutes, and said that we were ordered back to camp. We were herded into the coaches, and jogged back to Catterick in a stunned silence. In the warmth of the bus a strange, sickly smell of rotting vegetation emanated from our damp khaki. We passed an ambulance and two police cars going in the opposite direction.

'There's an ambulance,' cried someone, as it passed. 'They're taking him to a hospital. Perhaps he's not dead after all.'

'Don't be so bloody daft, man,' retorted another. 'There has to be a post-mortem. He's dead all right, the poor bugger.'

The cleaning of rifles had been forgotten. We handed them back, still dirty and fouled, to the resentful armoury staff. Then we dispersed to our huts. Quietly, almost guiltily, the soldiers took their eating irons from their lockers and moved off to the cookhouse. I threw myself on my bed. The bout of vomiting had left me feeling weak and dizzy, and, callously, I was more concerned with my trivial distemper than with Percy's death.

Every time the image returned of the blood bubbling up in Percy's throat like a hot spring, I retched. It was painful retching on an empty stomach, but I could not face the evening meal. I tried not to think about Percy's death, standing like a stone-faced guard between my stomach and compassion. But, inevitably, Mike, who was lying beside me, broke his silence when we were left alone in the hut.

'Well, what do you think about it?'

'I don't know. It's a terrible thing. I've never seen death before. I feel sort of numb.'

'Oh I've seen death before. It runs in our family,' he replied, with grim, cracked humour. 'But I don't want to see a death like this again. It was like a murder. Baker killed Percy. He did everything but pull the trigger.'

'You think it was suicide?'

'No I don't. It was an accident. But it wouldn't have happened if Baker hadn't got Percy into such a state of nerves and misery that he didn't know what he was doing.'

'What makes you so sure it wasn't suicide?'

'Percy said it was an accident, for one thing.'

I pondered for a while, and then observed:

'But don't suicides often say that?—try to make their deaths appear to be accidental?'

Mike frowned. 'Yes, I know. My reasons for believing it was an accident probably won't mean much to you. It's simply that Percy was a Catholic. A convinced, practising Catholic. He knew that suicide is the ultimate sin of despair, that he would be risking his immortal soul. But I don't expect you to understand that.'

'I understand,' I replied, slightly nettled. Why did Catholics always assume that their theology was beyond anyone else's comprehension? Mike sat up and swung his legs to the floor.

'Look, Jon,' he said. 'In one sense I would be pleased if it *were* suicide. There might be some chance of getting Baker to answer for his crimes then. But it wasn't suicide. I'm convinced of that. And the only thing we can do for Percy now, is to make sure that the Coroner's Court doesn't bring in a verdict of suicide.'

'What on earth can we do about it?' I asked, surprised.

'We're key witnesses. Tomorrow probably, very soon anyway, the police or someone will be asking us questions and
taking evidence. We mustn't give any evidence that would
suggest suicide.'

'You're not suggesting that we perjure ourselves?'

'Of course not. It's just a question of emphasis. We mustn't
emphasize Baker's persecution of Percy. We must play down
any possible motives for suicide. It goes against the grain, I
know; I'd like to see Baker rot in Hell. But we must do it.'

'I don't know . . .' I muttered doubtfully. Mike's motives, as
far as I could follow them, seemed to derive from a curious
mixture of materialism and eschatology. 'I mean, I don't
see how whatever we do is going to affect Percy——'

'Of course not, from your point of view,' Mike cut in angrily.
'To you he's just dead.'

'No, I mean from *your* point of view. Surely, theologically,
whatever *we* decide happened won't affect his destiny in the
next world, if there is one.'

Mike fumbled impatiently with a packet of cigarettes. He
omitted to offer me one.

'The trouble with you Agnostics is that you regard theology
as a kind of cold mathematical science like economics. It's not
like that at all. First of all let me make it quite clear that I'm
not attempting to disguise a suicide. I don't believe Percy
committed suicide, though I think there's a considerable risk
that the law will reach that opinion. You say that wouldn't
affect Percy's eternal destiny. Well, in a way you're right. He'll
have to answer for his actions whatever we make of them. But
it isn't quite as simple as all that. Our Church is made up of
the Church militant, the Church suffering, and the Church
triumphant,—that is the faithful on earth, the faithful in
purgatory, and the faithful . . .'

'In Heaven. Yes. I do know a little about Christianity you
know.' Mike grinned, and relaxed a little. He tossed me a
cigarette.

'Well, all these three parts of the Church are very closely
connected by prayer and mutual help. We invoke the saints to
intercede for us; we offer up masses for the repose of the souls
of the faithful; and when *they* get to Heaven they intercede for

us. Now if a soul slips out of this system of prayer and mutual help it's a great pity. If Percy is stigmatized as a suicide, there'll be no requiem mass, no masses for the repose of his soul. He'll be buried in unconsecrated ground, without a prayer said over his body. He'll be regarded as a shameful chapter in the history of a very old and devout Catholic family. We have a great affection for our dead. It would be tragic if Percy were denied that affection.' He paused.

'Well,' I said, anxious to placate him. 'I don't really understand you, but I'll do what I can, short of lying.'

'Good man!' He got to his feet, and reached for his sodden cape.

'Where are you going?'

'To church.'

'Won't you need a pass?'

'Fugg the pass.'

It was the first, and the last time I heard him use the word. I recalled him explaining it to Percy. Throwing his cape round his shoulders he went out into the rain. I heard him squelching past the window.

The other occupants of the hut began to drift back from tea. Someone came round giving back the beer-money that had been collected for an eve-of-passing-out booze-up planned for the next evening. I decided to go over to the Y.M.C.A. Canteen for a cup of coffee. When I returned there were only a couple of incorrigible bullers at work. No one felt like sitting there polishing brass in the presence of Percy's empty bed, and already there was a rumour that the passing-out parade was cancelled. I was asleep before Mike came in.

The next morning's parade was later than usual. We hung about in the hut until 8.30, when Sergeant Box appeared, and hurried us on to the square. But there was no inspection. A number of names were called out, Mike and mine among them, and we were ordered to fall out and line up at the side of the square. We were marched off to the Orderly Room, while the rest of the squad were taken on a cross-country run by one of the P.T. instructors.

Baker was waiting outside the Orderly Room, looking tense

and pale. From the veranda the Adjutant explained to us that we were to be interviewed by the Coroner's Clerk in connection with the death of Trooper Higgins. Baker went in first, and was inside for a long time. We stood at ease on the veranda, the object of curious glances from passing soldiers. A small, bullet-headed lad under detention was picking up leaves by hand from the lawns and flower beds which, bordered with white-washed stones, encircled the Orderly Room. He edged his way up to the veranda.

'Got a fag, mate?' he whispered.

As Mike's hand went to his pocket the regimental policeman overseeing the prisoner rapped a command, and the prisoner shuffled off with a rueful grin.

Through the window on my right I saw two pretty short-hand typists making their mid-morning tea. Women look maddeningly desirable in an Army camp. Perhaps that is why they choose to work in such places: it must be exhilarating to know that you are being mentally raped a hundred times a day. It looked cosy in their office. The electric fire was glowing. One of the girls smoothed her skirt over her haunches as she sat down, like a cat licking itself contentedly. Standing on that narrow peninsula between the soft, well-cared-for typists, and the unfortunate soldier grubbing about in the dirt, I was struck by a sense of the injustices, the inequalities of life.

A few minutes later the prisoner was marched off, the police-man striding behind him rapping out the time at an absurd pace: 'Leftrightleftrightleftrightleft,' with the poor fellow straining grotesquely to keep in step. I found the whole business of Army discipline deeply shocking. Like the bad old penal code, it seemed to create crime in order to punish it. Crime and punishment, which were purely abstract ideas in civilian life, seemed to nudge me on every side in the Army. A small slip, a thoughtless action, the neglect of some trivial regulation, and you were suddenly a criminal, incarcerated, bullied, stigma-tized. With sub-intelligent soldiers the thing tended to snow-ball. One night at the end of their leave they didn't want to go back to camp, and so they sat by the fire until the last train had gone. The next morning, they were scared to return, they hid themselves. Soon they were deserters, hunted, there were footsteps in the street at night, loud knocks on the door, they were arrested, brought back to camp under escort, thrust into a cell.

Not only did the system degrade the prisoner; it degraded the policeman too. The regimental police at Amiens camp, in their black webbing, with the diagonal strap that distinguished them from ordinary soldiers, had an air of the Gestapo about them. Shouting and bullying was their trade, and yet most of them were National Servicemen like myself. The Army gave too many people too many opportunities of cultivating sadism.

At last Baker emerged, and walked away without a glance at us. The Coroner's Clerk dealt more rapidly with the next three soldiers, but Mike was in quite a long time. Then it was my turn.

The Coroner's Clerk had been loaned the 2 IC's office. He was a heavily-built, middle-aged man, with greying hair and a relaxed manner. When I entered he was plugging his pipe with tobacco.

'Close the door, will you? Thanks. Now you're Trooper Browne, aren't you? Sit down and make yourself comfortable. My name's Adams. You know who I am, I suppose? And what this is all about?'

'Yes, sir.'

He administered the oath, and asked me a few routine questions,—name, age, etc. Then:

'Were you a friend of Trooper Higgins?'

'In a way I suppose. I mean I saw quite a bit of him, but I wouldn't describe him as a friend exactly.'

'You didn't like him particularly?'

'Oh I liked him all right. It depends what you mean by "friend". We hadn't very much in common.'

'I see.' He exhaled a mouthful of smoke. 'Now, suppose you tell me in your own words what happened yesterday afternoon, from the time Trooper Higgins prepared to fire. I may have to ask you to go slowly, because I shall be taking down your evidence in longhand.'

I gave him a brief, factual account of the incident. From time to time he interrupted me to ask a question.

'Could you describe more exactly the position of the rifle, in relation to Higgins's body?'

'Yes, he was lying on the rifle, face downwards. Perhaps I could draw you a sketch?"

'That would be very helpful. Thank you.' He passed a pencil and paper over the desk. He studied my sketch and turned his mild, grey eyes on me.

'The butt of the rifle then, projected from his right side?'

'Yes. And as I said, his thumb seemed to be caught in the trigger guard.'

He nodded. 'Just a few more questions: did Higgins appear to be in an unusual frame of mind on Tuesday?'

'No, nothing that struck me.'

'Not nervous or tense?'

'He was always nervous and tense.'

'Why was that d'you think?'

'Well, he found life in the Army pretty unpleasant.' I searched my mind for more explanations: we were approaching the ground I had agreed with Mike to avoid. 'As you probably know he was going to be a priest before he came into the Army.'

'Yes, so I believe. Tell me, how do you account for his possession of the bullet that killed him?'

I thought for a moment. 'I suppose he didn't fire his last round. As I said, Trooper Jones came up with the message just as they started to fire. Possibly Percy—Trooper Higgins— was slow to fire because he was specially anxious to get his last shot in the target. Presumably Corporal Baker thought he had fired and missed again, when he ordered him away.'

'This "back-squadding" Corporal Baker threatened Higgins with. What does it mean exactly?'

I explained.

'Is it a very serious thing?'

'No . . . but it doesn't happen very often I think.'

'Did Higgins ever say or write anything about suicide to your knowledge?'

'No. He certainly didn't say anything. I didn't see anything he wrote. In fact I don't remember ever seeing him writing.'

'Not even letters?'

'Once or twice perhaps.'

'Did he receive many letters?'

'No, not many.'

'Did he have a girl-friend.'

I almost smiled. 'Percy? I should be very surprised if he had.'

Adams grunted, and tapped out the charred contents of his pipe.

'What was the first explanation of Higgins's death that occurred to you, Browne?'

'That it was an accident,' I replied. This was true. It was only when I realized what was in Mike's mind as he muttered the Act of Contrition that suicide entered my mind, and proved difficult to dislodge. And yet Mike claimed that he had never thought it was suicide: the Act of Contrition was what he would urge on any dying Catholic.

'Why did you think it was an accident?'

'I don't know exactly. I think it must have been because Percy was so clumsy, accident-prone I suppose you might say,—though it sounds rather flippant. He was always hurting himself unnecessarily. Why, he cut his hand just in trying to load his rifle.'

'Ah yes, there *was* a cut on his hand I believe. Now I'd just like you to read through this summary of your evidence . . .'

In the afternoon the whole intake was addressed by the C.O. As his comrades, he said, we must all be deeply shocked by the tragic misadventure of Trooper Higgins. We would be glad to know that a telegram had been dispatched to his relatives on behalf of the regiment, expressing profound regret and sympathy for them in their bereavement. A Coroner's inquest would be held in due course, and also a regimental inquiry, at both of which some of us would be required as witnesses. Meanwhile the incident should impress upon our minds for the rest of our service the great importance of exercising the utmost care when handling fire-arms and live ammunition. In the circumstances the passing-out parade scheduled for the following afternoon had been cancelled. He realized that this would come as a great disappointment to us and to our instructors after the hard work of the previous weeks, but he was afraid that it was unavoidable. We would therefore proceed on leave that afternoon, as soon as bedding and equipment had been handed in to the stores. A number of those soldiers who had been interviewed by the Coroner's Clerk that morning, however, would be required as witnesses at the inquest, and would be confined to the Garrison until the inquest had been held, after which they would get their leave. Their names were . . .

But I knew before my name was called that I was among the unlucky ones. To be disappointed, at the last moment, of the long-awaited leave, and of the extra day (for I was sure we would not get the extra day afforded to the others by the cancellation of the passing-out parade),—it completely overwhelmed any genuine grief I felt at Percy's death. Mike was kept back too, of course, but part of the bitterness of my disappointment was in the knowledge that I would have to conceal my feelings from him out of piety to Percy's memory. I could scarcely bring myself to speak to Mike, as we walked back to the hut, for fear of losing that status as Percy's friend which was now inextricably involved with my claims on Mike's friendship.

'I should have thought the C.O.'s speech was out of order,' he commented. 'That bit about handling fire-arms for instance: it suggested that it was an open and shut case of death by misadventure. It's pretty clear how *they* want the verdict to go. No nasty scandal in the Press, and questions asked in the House.'

'Well, that suits you doesn't it,' I replied irritably.

He shrugged his shoulders. 'I suppose so.'

'It's a nuisance about this leave,' I said, unable to hold my tongue any longer. But Mike appeared not to have heard.

There was a subdued elation in the hut. Mike and I sat on our beds and watched the other lads thrusting clothing into kitbags, to be deposited in the stores. I could just imagine how delighted I would be in the same position. Percy was more popular in his death than in his life. Someone began to whistle. Scouse Miller, a good-humoured and popular lad, called across to his mate.

'Hey, Albert!'

'Yeah?'

'Bit of luck i'n it eh? I'll be 'ome in time to take me tart to the pictures.'

'Yeah. Where will you go? Regal? Me mum wrote there's a good film on this week.'

'Dunno. It's no odds. I don't take 'er to the pictures to watch the bloody film.'

There was a general laugh.

'*Shut up!*'

Mike was on his feet, his face white and strained. 'Don't you know *why* you're going home tonight? Because a boy died. Yesterday. One of us. A boy you've all been so very kind to, from the first night he arrived. The least you can do is to keep a decent silence, instead of rubbing your hands over the women you're going to . . . Oh you make me *sick*.'

Miller flushed, and bridled.

'I know Percy was a mate of yours, Ginger. I'm sorry for the poor bloke. But *I* didn't kill 'im. There's no need to bite *my* 'ead off.'

Just as Mike began to relax, someone said :

'It's all right, Scouse. Didn't you know? Ginger's 'ad 'is leave cancelled. Fuggin' 'ard luck, i'n it?'

A premonitory shudder passed through me as I located the voice. It was Hardcastle, the Regular with whom Mike had clashed over Percy's kneeling figure that first evening. Ever since then he had maintained an attitude of sneering indifference to Percy and Mike. What devil, what stupidity, had prompted him to make his move *now*?

He was a big, rugged fellow, a formidable brawler, one would have said. But Mike carried into the fight a crusader's righteous indignation, and a ruthless intention to punish rather than conquer. He dominated the encounter, refusing to wrestle, and forcing Hardcastle to box, circling his victim, dodging the latter's clumsy blows and methodically battering at his face. The fight took place in a curious, shamefaced silence. Shamefaced because everyone else present realized that they were being punished in the person of Hardcastle, punished for not loving Percy. Eventually a number of the spectators intervened, and Hardcastle sank down on the nearest bed, dazed and speechless with pain. Mike stalked out of the hut in an embarrassed silence.

It was just as well that Mike had the opportunity of releasing his pent-up feelings of rage and pity on Hardcastle, because it probably permitted him to bear stoically the undisguised jubilation of the rest of the intake. Each squad had little or no contact with the others, and Percy's death touched 'A' and 'B' squads very little, except insofar as it had caused the passing-out parade to be cancelled, and the seventy-two to be extended. There was therefore much hilarity and joy in and around the huts as their occupants prepared to go on leave, and I was apprehensive that Mike would start another mêlée, in which I might feel obliged to go to his defence. But he appeared to ignore further provocations.

The others did not get away as quickly as they had expected. When we went to tea we saw them lining up outside the Squadron office to collect their leave passes, and it was a small satisfaction to know that Scouse Miller would not be taking his tart to the pictures that evening after all. But when we returned to the hut it was bleak and deserted: beds stripped of blankets and mattresses, doors hanging open on vacant lockers, dust and shreds of paper on the floor. We sat down on our beds and lit up.

'Well, it's nice to have a bit of privacy,' I remarked, with hollow cheerfulness. My voice rang in the empty room. At the same moment Sergeant Box poked his head round the door.

'Oh, 'ere you are. I've been chasing you two for the last hour. Where've you been?'

'Only to tea.'

'Well you've been a fuggin' long time about it. Anyway, get your kit packed up and your bedding. You're moving.'

'Where to, Sarge?'

'All witnesses are being moved to Waiting Wing until the inquest is over.'

'What will we do there?'

He gave a sadistic grin. 'Fatigues, I should think.'

Waiting Wing was a kind of Limbo, where soldiers who had finished their training were billeted while awaiting posting.

As Sergeant Box had prophesied, we were kept occupied by fatigues, shovelling coal and coke. It was a dreary, depressing existence,—only slightly less disagreeable than Basic Training in that there was no bulling, and morning inspections were perfunctory.

On the Saturday we went into Richmond and tasted the heady pleasures of the two cinemas, the '& chips' cafés, and the Naafi Club, where a dance was being held. The revolving doors spun round, feeding in a steady stream of unappetizing female flesh from Richmond and Darlington, to be snapped up by the soldiers who stooped like vultures along the walls of the vestibule. With a five-to-one majority of men, the women swiftly began to look like badly-mauled carrion.

The Naafi Club was scarcely a relaxing place. Women were not the only commodity in short supply. The TV Room overflowed. There was a queue for table tennis. There was a queue in the canteen. If you vacated a chair in the Quiet Room, somebody else was in it before you had straightened up; and a discarded newspaper scarcely reached the table before it was whisked away by another hand. But the Club was probably the warmest place in Catterick as an autumnal chill spread through the region, and we spent most evenings there. We discovered that there were baths (again only two between the thousands of troops), and from then onwards I ceased to use the draughty and erratic showers at Amiens camp.

The days passed slowly. The cancellation of our leave seemed totally unnecessary, as we were not interviewed again until after the rest of the intake had returned. This second interview was very brief. We were simply asked whether Percy was left-handed or right-handed. Even then we didn't catch on.

The Coroner cleared his throat and began his summing-up.

'Gentlemen of the jury: the death into which we are inquiring today presents many problems. The evidence you have heard is extremely complex, and it is my duty to try and reduce this evidence to order, and to help you to reach your verdict.

'First of all, I think you can rule out the possibility of

homicide. The bullet that killed Higgins was fired from his own rifle at point-blank range. There is no evidence that anyone else was near him at the time. Neither, I think, need you consider for very long a verdict of manslaughter. There is no doubt that, whatever the reason for Higgins's death, it would not have occurred if he had not been allowed to leave the firing point with a live bullet. There are strict military regulations, which have been described to you, to prevent such an eventuality. Clearly Corporal Baker, who was in charge of the firing at the time, was seriously negligent here; and you may feel that in other ways his conduct was not beyond reproach. He seems to have lost his temper with Higgins, though there was the extenuating circumstance that on this particular day Corporal Baker was suffering from toothache. However, the important point I wish to make is that in order to reach a verdict of manslalughter you must be convinced that the death was caused by someone's *criminal* negligence, wanton, deliberate disregard for human life; and if you did reach such a verdict the person concerned would face a very serious charge indeed. There has been negligence in this case, gentlemen, and no doubt the military authorities will conduct their own inquiries into the matter, and take appropriate disciplinary measures. But I do not think you can say there has been *criminal* negligence.

'The alternative explanations which suggest themselves in this case are that Higgins's rifle went off accidentally, or that he took his own life deliberately.

'Some of the evidence that you have heard would seem to support the first explanation,—that the rifle went off accidentally. The deceased himself is reported to have uttered the word "Accident" just before he died. Higgins has also been described as a person of poor physical co-ordination,—"accident-prone" is how one witness described him. On the other hand, it would be dangerous to place too much weight on the last words of the deceased. He might have a motive for wishing his death to appear accidental,—to conceal the fact that he had tried to kill himself, for instance. And you have heard Inspector Jordan explain and demonstrate that it would be extremely difficult to inflict this kind of wound on oneself accidentally while carrying a rifle in the way Higgins was last seen carrying it, or, indeed, while carrying it in any normal way.

'You must consider, then, the possibility of suicide. Higgins was a shy, sensitive boy, thrown into the rough-and-tumble of Army life, after a sheltered life at home and at school. The hardships of a raw recruit's training, which more robust young men take in their stride, might have acted on such a temperament in such a way as to drive him to suicide. But in this case you may feel that there is not very much concrete evidence to support such a conclusion, nothing but the general impressions, partly conflicting, of his comrades, N.C.O.s and officers. Second Lieutenant Booth-Henderson has said that he did not detect signs of undue stress in Higgins at any time. But recruits are rarely open with their officers, and Higgins's comrades have left me, at least, with little doubt that he was deeply depressed and unhappy in the Army. There is however, no concrete evidence that this depression and unhappiness had reached the point where he would seek escape in this terrible and tragic way. He left no note, no reference in any letter to such an idea, nor did he speak of it to anyone. The most weighty piece of evidence which suggests suicide is the fact that he was found with his thumb in the trigger-guard of his rifle; for a person aiming a rifle at his own body would find it easier to operate the trigger with his thumb than with his finger. Against the supposition of suicide you must weigh two further pieces of evidence. Firstly, Higgins was a devout Roman Catholic, to whom suicide would be a serious sin, perhaps the most serious of all. This in itself is not conclusive, but it deserves to be considered. You may be inclined to give more weight to the second piece of evidence: Higgins, as I said, was found with his thumb caught in the trigger-guard of the rifle—but it was the thumb of his *right* hand. And Higgins was *left*-handed. You may think that a left-handed person, about to shoot himself, would naturally use his left hand. What possible reason could Higgins have for pulling the trigger with the thumb of his right hand? The only explanation that I can think of is one that has no doubt occurred to you as you listened to the evidence: that Higgins intended to shoot his left hand, to shoot off his trigger finger.

'This kind of self-mutilation is of course not unknown in times of war. Soldiers on active service have been known to take this drastic step in order to be invalided out of the Army. Of course in actual combat it is possible to claim that the mutilation was in fact a wound, for self-mutilation is a serious military offence. Higgins may not have known this, or not thought about it; or perhaps he hoped to pass off the mutilation as an accident. Anyway, supposing that this was Higgins's intention, you have heard Inspector Jordon explain what might have happened. The rifle, which you have seen, is a long, heavy weapon. Higgins may have rested the butt on the ground, and stooped, or perhaps knelt, to get his thumb on the trigger, while holding his left hand outstretched in front of the barrel, or against the mouth of the barrel. Then, through nervousness, clumsiness, any one of a dozen causes, he may have slipped, overbalanced, or the rifle may have skidded on the wet grass so that when the weapon exploded, the barrel was pointing not at his finger, but at his body. This, perhaps, was the "accident" to which Higgins referred with his dying breath.

'How does such a hypothesis fit in with the rest of the evidence? We have a young man, deeply unhappy in the Army, and no doubt desperately anxious to escape from it. Not sufficiently desperate to contemplate suicide, perhaps, against which he would have religious, and ordinary human scruples. But still capable of seizing on any other expedient, however drastic. On the day of the rifle-practice his unhappiness reaches a climax. He fails humiliatingly at the rifle-firing. He is roughly reprimanded by his N.C.O. He is told that he will be "back-squadded"—that is, he will have to begin all over again the training he has hated so much. But at the same time he is left alone in possession of a weapon with a live round in it. It is unlikely, I think, that the idea of mutilating himself should have occurred to him out of the blue at that moment. But you have heard his friend, Trooper Brady, recall that he had casually mentioned self-mutilation in Higgins's presence. The reference was clearly made in jest: Brady and some other soldiers were joking about ways of getting out of the Army. But the suggestion may have lodged in Higgins's mind, with the tragic result that we know. If so, it is scarcely necessary to say that Trooper Brady has no cause to feel in any way responsible. Only a somewhat unbalanced mind could have taken his joke seriously.

'Well gentlemen, I have put to you the alternative explanations of Higgins's death as clearly as I can. You may feel that none of the explanations can be proved beyond reasonable doubt. In that case you would have to return an open verdict. . . .'

After retiring for three-quarters of an hour, the jury returned an open verdict. But neither Mike nor I had any doubt that Percy had met his death by trying to shoot off his trigger finger and, characteristically, had bungled the operation.

It was a shock to Mike, but to me merely a surprise. I was mildly piqued at not having perceived the significance of the fact that Percy was left-handed. The shrewd and careful investigation of the Coroner's Court drew from me a half-grudging respect for 'our British Institutions'. It had been an interesting experience, but I was glad that Percy's death, with all its attendant inconveniences, was over and done with. Or was it? I wondered, looking at Mike huddled in the corner of the truck that was taking us back to camp. In defiance of regulations he was smoking, frowning as he drew deeply on the cigarette. In the presence of the other soldiers who had been witnesses at the inquest, conversation was imprudent, but I guessed what he was brooding about: the probability, revealed to him for the first time as he stood in public view in the witness box, that his casual joke about shooting off one's trigger finger had suggested to Percy an escape route from his private military hell that led to his death. It was a remark that anyone might have made, and had I done so, my conscience would not have been troubled. But Mike's mind did not work like mine, and I had a feeling that behind that frown a guilt-complex was already in gestation.

But I was wrong; or at least Mike said I was wrong. We didn't have the opportunity to speak openly until we were in the train that took us from Richmond to Darlington, on our way to London for the long-delayed seventy-two. As it was a

Thursday evening there were few passengers in the train, and we had a compartment to ourselves. I said as casually as I could :

'You're not worrying about what you said to Percy, are you?'

'What I said to Percy?'

I couldn't decide whether he genuinely hadn't caught my meaning, but his answer when I was more specific was reassuring.

'Oh no. I'm not "blaming myself", if that's what you mean. If Percy was that desperate . . . it doesn't really matter where he got the idea from.'

'What's on your mind then? You don't look too happy. After all, they didn't come to a verdict of suicide. Isn't that what you wanted?'

'But don't you *see*?' he burst out, dragging off his beret, and running his fingers through his coarse red hair. 'Don't you see? Don't you see what fools we've been? By trying to protect Percy from a verdict of suicide, we had to protect Baker. But it was totally unnecessary. Baker was responsible for Percy's death ; without him Percy would never have tried to mutilate himself. Now he's going to get off scot-free.'

'I wouldn't be so sure. Remember what the Coroner said. And there's the regimental inquiry.'

Mike merely said : 'We'll see,' and relapsed into a moody silence. Then he said :

'The young fool.'

'Who?'

'Percy. What did he think he could gain by shooting off his finger? He'd have been court-martialled straight away. How was he going to explain it?'

I began to take an academic interest in the problem. 'Yes, he'd have been better advised to shoot off his big toe. I believe they used to do that in the War. It's easier to explain as an accident.'

Mike regarded me suspiciously, as if he thought I was being too detached. I continued hastily :

'The whole thing's full of tragic irony. After all, if there were seven holes in the other target, at least three of them must have been Percy's. He couldn't have been such a bad shot after all.'

Mike nodded gloomily. 'You'd think,' he said, 'that some of the other witnesses would have had the guts to tell the Coroner how beastly Baker was to Percy all along.'

This seemed so irrational, that I made no reply. The train trundled sluggishly through the dark, misty countryside. I was suddenly filled with impatience to get home.

'Will you get to Hastings tonight?' I asked.

'I'm not going home this week-end,' he replied. 'I couldn't face it.'

'But won't your family expect you?'

'I didn't tell them about the leave. I'm staying with some friends in London.'

'Oh,' I said, surprised. Then I added: 'What about meeting somewhere in London on Sunday, and coming back together?'

'Good idea.'

'Where then? And what time?'

'Have a drink with me on Sunday. Could you manage two o'clock?'

'Maybe,' I said doubtfully. I wanted very much to meet Mike, but I knew it would upset my parents if I missed the ritual of Sunday dinner.

'I'll be at O'Connell's Club. It's just off the Tottenham Court Road. Ask the doorman for me.'

'O.K., I'll try and make it. I might be a bit late.'

'I'll be there till about three.'

Darlington Station seemed more than ever like a frontier post: on the broad, busy platform where the London expresses pulled in, one inhaled liberty with the sulphurous air. It was a relief to see, for the first time in weeks, people who had no connection at all with the Army. But in another way this made one more keenly aware of one's exclusion from the free world. In our coarse, ill-fitting uniforms and clumsy boots, we lost the right to be considered as individuals; we were marked out as 'soldiers', an inferior species of humanity. The middle-aged woman in our compartment of the London train eyed us over her *Harper's Bazaar* with vague alarm, as if she expected to be raped at any moment. Her presence inhibited conversation, and in a way I was glad. Matching Mike's concern over Percy's death was becoming rather a strain. Lapped around by the warm upholstery and the fug, I surrendered to sleep.

I was surprised by my own excitement as we approached London. The northern suburbs flashed past, and then, more slowly, the dingy, sooty environs of King's Cross. I went into the corridor and put my head out of the window, watching the great engine picking its way delicately over the points. It seemed impossible that I had been away for only two months.

'Cor, ain't it bleeding marvellous to be back in the dear old Smoke,' said a Cockney soldier behind me.

It was.

FOUR

AFTER lunch I sat on my bed polishing brasses for the guard-duty. It was a hot day, and the other occupants of the hut lay prone on their beds, held back on the brink of sleep by the dance music from somebody's portable radio. At 1.45 the programme changed to 'Listen With Mother'. We listened solemnly to the nursery rhymes and tales of anthropomorphous railway engines.

In the afternoon I went round the camp with Roy Ludlow, checking the P.R.I. inventory. Panes of glass in the carpenters' shop; mowing machines in the gardeners' shed; vacuum cleaners in the technical museum; armchairs in the unit Quiet Room; heaps of broken electrical equipment in a deserted Nissen hut. . . . It was the busiest day I had had at Badmore for a long time.

When we got back to the 'A' Squadron Offices, Henry the barber was in action. He toured the camp every week, visiting a different section each day.

He was a sleek, dapper little man, with a neat, black moustache, and thin, black, oiled hair combed straight back from his widow's peak. The usual Army barber is a kind of half-tamed sheep-shearer, but Henry was a true representative of his ancient trade: I felt sure that somewhere in the case where he kept his scissors and combs, there was a razor and cupping-bowl. He really belonged to some marbled emporium, applying the mysterious arts of hot towels and vibro-massage, discreetly urging the beneficial effects of brightly-coloured and exotically-named hair lotions. His various working-places at Badmore could scarcely have been more different. He cut 'A' Squadron's hair, for instance, in the Unit Sports Store, which adjoined the Squadron Offices, surrounded by piles of mud-encrusted football jerseys, taking his equipment as he needed it from his battered case. His customers did not pay him personally: each man had sixpence per week stopped from his pay for one haircut per week, whether he wanted it or not. There was thus no incentive to Henry to give individual attention, and yet he did. Poised on the balls of his feet, he snipped deftly at our hair, delicately adjusting personal tastes to the exigencies of Army regulations; while from the corner of his mouth dribbled a constant stream of banter, gossip, innuendo and—to anyone above a lance-corporal—servile flattery. Since Henry was paid by the P.R.I. he was particularly deferential to me.

I deliberately left it late before going to get a haircut: I wanted to be Henry's last client. When I entered the Sports Store there were only two customers: Roy Ludlow was in the chair, and his pal Connolly was waiting. Henry was in the middle of one of his salacious anecdotes.

'. . . he was up and down, up and down, faster than a barmaid's knickers——'

Connolly, who hadn't heard the expression before, guffawed.

'Good afternoon, Corporal!' Henry greeted me. 'I didn't expect to see you again.'

'Neither did I, Henry. The bastards have put me on guard tonight.'

Henry clucked sympathetically. 'That's hard, that is; and you being released on Wednesday.'

'Go on, Henry,' said Ludlow, anxious to hear the rest of the story.

'No, I'm sorry,' said Henry firmly. 'Corporal Browne is a pure-minded young man. I wouldn't want to scandalize him.'

'Fugg off,' protested Connolly derisively.

'How old are you?' Henry asked him.

'Eighteen. Why?'

'Eighteen, and using language like that,' sighed Henry, shaking his head with every appearance of real concern. 'What would your mother say?'

'She don't know anythink about it. I don't swear when I'm at 'ome. 'Sa funny thing that,' he continued reflectively. 'In camp I'm fugging and blinding all day long, and when I'm at 'ome I don't say nothink except maybe "soddit", and me ma says that 'erself when she's burnt the joint or somethink.'

'Thanks, Henry.'

Ludlow got up from the chair, running a finger round the inside of his collar. 'See you,' he added to Connolly. As his heavy footsteps receded I pondered the truth of Connolly's observation. For us soldier-commuters 'home' and 'camp' were two disparate, self-contained worlds, with their own laws and customs; every week we passed from one to the other and back again, changing like chameleons to melt into the new environment. At home I drank tea without sugar; in camp I drank the common, intensely sweetened brew. They seemed like totally different drinks. The particular instance Connolly had stumbled on had more serious implications. I had been swearing more and more steadily as my military service lengthened and approached its end. At Catterick Mike and I had, by tacit agreement, abstained from using obscene language, as a kind of gesture, a way of signalling our resistance to the brutalizing forces of the Army. My present free use of obscenity was a measure of how far I had moved from those days of stubborn non-conformity.

'Now, Corporal,' said Henry, shaking Connolly's glossy curls from his cape.

I seated myself on the hard wooden chair, and Henry tucked the cape round my neck with his cool, moist fingers.

'Not too much off, Henry.'

'I know. Just enough to get past the inspection tonight. Who's Orderly Officer?'

'The Adjutant.'

'Hmm. I'd better take a bit off the sides then. He's a great one for having the sideboards level with the ears, is the Adjutant.'

'O.K., Henry, you know best. But remember, I'm released on Wednesday.'

'Trust me, Corporal. Nobody will know you've been in the Army.'

'I don't know about that. I shall feel like shouting it to everyone I meet.'

'Glad to get out eh? Well, it's not surprising. I won't say I didn't enjoy my time in the Army. But that was different. France and Belgium at the end of the war.'

'I shouldn't have thought that was very enjoyable. There were some pretty tough campaigns then, weren't there?'

'Oh I kept well out of that. I was batman to a captain on the general staff. We were in Paris after the liberation; then Brussels. Lovely. Those French women, they were so grateful they were fighting to sleep with you. Exhausting it was, in the end.'

'That reminds me, Henry,' I said, grasping the opportunity. 'I want some French letters off you.'

The snip-snap of the scissors behind my ears faltered momentarily. I was grateful that there was no mirror in which I would have to brazen out his surprise.

'Certainly, Corporal, certainly,' he murmured obsequiously, after a pause.

'Could you give them to me now?' I asked, alert for the sound of another customer approaching. Henry laid down his scissors and took a cardboard box from his case.

'How many, Corporal?'

'Oh, I don't know. Two? No, make it half a dozen.' How many times could you use them? I wondered vaguely.

'Plain or teat end?'

'Plain.'

I didn't stop to ask what the difference was. I was sweating slightly under the strain of appearing unconcerned. Henry gave me the packets, and I slipped them into the map pocket on my thigh, as it was the most accessible. It occurred to me that I had never used it before, for maps or anything else.

'How much do I owe you, Henry?'

'Forget it, Corporal.'

'No, Henry——'

'You've done me a few favours in the past, Corporal. Getting me my money early last Christmas. Have them on me. A little parting gift.'

There was no humour in his voice: rather an almost sentimental gravity. He continued to cut my hair in silence, while I gradually relaxed.

I trusted that the things were as easy to use as they seemed to be in theory. And that Pauline would have no objection. But my mind was fairly easy on that score. Hadn't she said once that Catholic teaching on marriage was 'squalid'? No doubt that had been one of the knottiest problems in her tangled relationship with Mike. When had she said that? It was a long time back. It must have been a time when Mike was still very much the link between us, when we anxiously talked and corresponded about him, like two watchers conferring at the bedside of someone gravely ill, our fingers straying imperceptibly towards each other in the darkness of the sick-room. One of those strangely tormented, bitter-sweet week-ends wrested from the serfdom of Catterick.

MY FIRST leave was inevitably a disappointment. Three short days in London could not fulfil the expectations that had been built on them in the preceding weeks. The more unfruitfully the priceless hours passed, the more exasperated I became, with myself and with others. It was, of course, foolish to have imagined that things would be different. The three days were not particularly important to my family or acquaintances. They did not realize that those three days constituted for me a precious parole, that I needed their co-operation to squeeze from that short time the essence of the free life, so that I could carry it back with me like a cordial, to warm myself with it in captivity. Somewhere in the back of my mind I had nourished the absurd expectation that everyone would greet me like a returned veteran, overflowing with sympathy and admiration, exerting themselves to give me a good time, and (girls) throwing themselves generously into my arms. Nothing of the sort happened of course. I knew no girls, and had few friends. I had left a dull, uneventful life to go into the Army, and I returned to find the same dull, uneventful life. It was not surprising that no one felt particularly sorry for me, because my pride prevented me from revealing how deeply miserable the Army had made me. Nevertheless, at the time, I was disappointed by what seemed to me the selfishness and callousness of other people.

The first evening, Thursday, was agreeable enough. I shed my uniform as soon as I got home, although it was late, The silky caress of my worsted trousers and poplin shirt, the savour of home cooking, and the resilience of my Dunlopillo mattress, made the evening and night pass in a trance of sensuous euphoria.

The next morning I visited my college: a mistake. Term

was only a few weeks old. The anxious, excited faces of the freshers, the self-absorbed assurance of the older students, the atmosphere of easy, casual self-indulgence, excited a mixture of aggravating emotions in me: envy, regret, nostalgia, impatience, loneliness. Once again I felt keenly my lack of friends. I dearly wanted to meet someone who would know me, who would come up and clap me on the back, congratulate me on my degree, and take me off for a coffee. But my own generation had left with me, and I knew few people outside that group. I tried smiling at a few people I recognized, but their acknowledgements were faint or puzzled, and I gave it up in embarrassment. I went over to the English department: there were few people there as it was a Friday, when there weren't many lectures. My professor, with whom I had hoped to discuss a research project, was away. I had a few desultory conversations with some members of the staff. They all thought I looked well, which infuriated me. The Senior Tutor, who had been asked for a testimonial by the War Office, asked me if I had got my commission yet, and seemed disgruntled when I told him I had withdrawn my application. I climbed the stairs to find Philip Meakin's room.

Meakin had been, I suppose, my closest friend at college. Our mutual lack of personal charm, and exclusive interest in study, had drawn us into a lukewarm friendship of the kind that exists between 'swots' at school, in which the strongest element was one of jealous rivalry. I had been very pleased when he had obtained an Upper Second instead of his expected First in Finals. Since then, however, his fortunes had improved. He had been exempted from military service on medical grounds, and the Prof. had offered him a Research Assistantship. This meant that he earned a small salary by doing a little tutoring in the department, while working for a higher degree.

There were a couple of female freshers giggling nervously outside Meakin's room. I gathered that he was their tutor, and that they were waiting to see him. The awe with which they appeared to regard him seemed absurd to me, and I was tempted to inform them of his total lack of qualifications to teach them anything useful. Instead I raised my fist to knock on the door.

'Mr Meakin's engaged,' said one of the girls reprovingly. I believe she thought I was another of Meakin's consultants. The idea of my consulting Meakin on anything made me smile. I knocked on the door, but at the same moment Meakin opened it to usher out another, very pretty girl.

'Thank you, Mr Meakin,' she said, fluttering her eyelashes.

'That's all right, Miss——' He goggled through his spectacles at me. 'Jonathan! What are *you* doing here? I thought you were in the Army.'

'Even the Army gives one a few days off from time to time,' I replied sourly. 'Can I come in?'

'Of course. No, just a minute. Would you mind if I saw these two students first? I've just got to give them a book-list.'

He kept me waiting for about ten minutes before the two girls emerged, their eyes lowered reverently as if they had just received an audience from T. S. Eliot. I barely restrained an urge to bawl 'Pity about your Upper Second' to Meakin while they were still in earshot.

'Well,' he said, when we had seated ourselves. 'How's life in the Army?'

'The expense of spirit in a waste of time.' I had been polishing this epigram for some time, but it was wasted on Meakin. 'You don't know how lucky you are,' I added.

'I expect you feel pretty peeved about chaps like me?'

'Oh no,' I lied. 'I've every respect for anyone who manages to wangle out of National Service.'

'I didn't wangle,' he protested. 'I've always been asthmatic.'

If my words were malicious, they were nothing to my thoughts. Tarring and feathering was too good for Meakin as far as I was concerned. I was seized by an overwhelming self-pity. It was *I* who should be occupying this book-lined study, soaking up the admiration of pretty freshers, not Meakin. I looked past him, through the window. It was damp and foggy outside, but warm and snug in the room. Meakin would go on being warm and snug, physically and spiritually insulated against the cruel outside world by his books, his status, and the old-fashioned central-heating which bubbled and clanked in the pipes. While *I* saw ahead of me nothing but a bleak prospect of windswept barracks, cold water in the early morning, the harsh cries of stupid authority, the dreary monotony of the slow-moving days. I wept dry, invisible tears of chagrin.

The shadow of Catterick lay over the rest of my leave. On Friday evening I saw a play, and on Saturday a film. But in the middle of a dramatic scene my mind would wander off into a brooding anticipation of the return to camp. Without a companion to talk to I was defenceless against these gloomy thoughts. By Sunday I was longing to see Mike. So, callously ignoring my parents' disappointment, I bolted down my roast beef, bade them a hurried farewell, and rushed, belching, out of the house at a quarter to two. Unfortunately I was obliged to wear my uniform, as I did not intend to return home again. I was hoping to hang on to Mike until we caught the 11.15 train from King's Cross.

O'Connell's was an Irish drinking club occupying a dingy basement in a narrow passage off the Tottenham Court Road. A man in shirt-sleeves and braces looked up from a newspaper called *The United Irishman* as I entered.

'Michael Brady? Aye, he's expecting you. Go on down.'

I descended the rickety staircase and peered into the saloon. The air was thick with cigarette smoke and the brogue. I saw Mike's crew-cut glowing like a red coal at a table near the bar. I shuffled through the crowd, rather self-conscious in my uniform, boots and gaiters, which attracted many curious looks. Mike was wearing an expensive-looking suède jacket, and the cleanest shirt I had ever seen him in. He was sitting with a couple of young men, one plump, curly-haired, with twinkling eyes, the other tall, thin and saturnine, with a cowslick of straight black hair across his forehead.

'Jon! It's good to see you,' Mike greeted me, standing up. 'Come and sit down. What will you have?'

'Could I have a coffee?' I asked.

'Ssh. Coffee's a dirty word round here,' said the plump one. 'Have a glass of porter.'

'What's porter?' I asked.

'*What's porter?*' He turned to Mike. 'What kind of a barbarian is this man of yours then?' Mike grinned, and the speaker continued: 'What's porter? What's nectar? I'll tell you what porter is. It's a particularly glorious form of Guinness, and it's specially imported from Ireland by O'Connell himself, and if you ask me what Guinness is I'll leave immediately.'

I laughed, and agreed to a porter, though I had never liked Guinness. Mike interrupted:

'Jon, let me introduce you: Jonathan Browne, Brendan Mahoney, Peter Nolan. They know who you are.'

Mike pushed his way to the bar, and I noticed with surprise that his resplendent dress terminated in army boots. While he was away, Brendan Mahoney, the tubby one, treated me to a disquisition on the properties and ingredients of Guinness. He seemed to be an expert on the subject, and laid special emphasis on the fact that the water used to make the drink came from one special well. Mike returned with, to my dismay, a pint tankard of the black, unappetizing fluid. He seemed to be in good spirits.

'Have a good leave?' I asked.

'Great,' he replied. 'And you?'

'Not bad. Quiet. Don't feel like going back to camp, do you?'

He grimaced, and swigged his drink. 'Don't talk about it.'

'I don't know how you stick it, Mike,' said Nolan, the tall one, speaking for the first time. 'They'd never get me in their bloody Army.'

'Knowing you, Peter, I don't think they would,' Mike agreed with a grin. He turned to me: 'You remember that Lane Bequest picture that was stolen from the Tate not so long ago?'

I did. An Irish student had coolly walked out of the Tate Gallery with the picture under his arm, in full view of the public and the gallery staff. His confederates had even tipped off a Press cameraman in advance, who photographed the student walking nonchalantly down the steps with the picture under his arm. The bare-faced cheek of the theft had caused a minor sensation in the Press, until the picture was traced to Ireland, and handed back.

'Well, tell it not in Gath, but Peter here was one of the

brains behind the operation,' said Mike. Nolan permitted himself a thin smile.

'I never really understood what it was all about,' I admitted; and immediately Nolan and Mahoney launched into an involved explanation of the legal history of the Lane Bequest, and the perfidy of the English interpreting the law to their own advantage.

'Why did you give the picture back then?' I asked finally.

'It wasn't my idea,' said Nolan darkly. 'I——'

'It was no use to us,' interposed Mahoney. 'There's only one place where it belongs: the Municipal Gallery in Dublin. It's all ready for the pictures. There's a room with "The Lane Bequest" written over the door. You go in, and there's nothing there except for Lane's portrait. The room is waiting for the pictures; and one day they'll come. We made people think by pinching that picture from the Tate.'

I sipped my porter slowly, and with distaste. I was beginning to find the noise, the smoke, and the Celtic fanaticism of Mike's companions rather wearing. I was glad when Mike got up to leave. We all shook hands. Nolan did not release Mike's hand at once.

'Remember, Mike, you can always count on us.'

'Sure, Peter,' said Mike. 'See you.'

'Where to now?' I asked, as we emerged into the fresh air, deliberately assuming that we were going to stay together.

'Would you like to come and have tea with a friend of mine?'

'Delighted. But do they expect me?'

'No, she doesn't. But it'll be all right.'

'She! It wouldn't be the one who's been sending you all those long, mauve envelopes by any chance?'

'The same.'

I looked forward to the meeting with interest.

'I didn't know you had a girl-friend, Mike,' I observed, as we walked towards the tube station.

'Why should you? I never told you. We've known each other for about a year.'

'What's her name?'

'Pauline Vickers. Ghastly, isn't it?'

'What is she,—a student?'

'Was. She's a librarian now. I met her at some hop. Have you got a girl-friend, Jon?'

'No one specially,' I said, unwilling for some reason to reveal my total lack of female acquaintance. 'You look smart,' I added, to change the subject.

'All borrowed,' he explained, 'Except the boots. Couldn't find a pair of shoes to fit me. I don't like this suède much though. It creaks.'

'I wish I weren't wearing this uniform,' I said. I was anxious to make a favourable impression on Mike's girl,—otherwise she might resent my presence. And khaki did not become me.

We took the Piccadilly line from Holborn, northbound, and got out at Turnpike Lane. As we left the station a group of young children turned to follow us along the pavement, chanting:

> *Ginger, you're barmy,*
> *You'll never join the Army.*

They scattered, shrieking, as Mike rounded on them. 'If only it were true,' he observed with a rueful grin. As we walked on, the children began again, from a safe distance.

> *Ginger, you're barmy,*
> *You'll never join the Army,*
> *You'll never be a scout,*
> *With your shirt hanging out,*
> *Ginger, you're barmy.*

Pauline occupied a bedsitter on the first floor of a large Victorian house honeycombed with small apartments. The first feeling I registered as she opened the door was one of surprise. She seemed too conventionally pretty and normal to attract or be attracted by Mike. She seemed a little put out to see me, but recovered herself quickly and put me at my ease. She appeared pleased to discover that I had been at college with Mike.

'It's a pleasure to meet a friend of Michael's who isn't from that dreadful Irish drinking club,' she said.

'Another word from you against the Irish, and I'll put you across my knee and spank you,' he replied. I glanced involuntarily at Pauline's neat round bottom. She stroked it as she sat down. It reminded me of the typist in the Orderly Room.

'Can I take my boots off?' demanded Mike.

'If you wash your feet first.'

'A good idea. I think I'll have a bath while I'm about it.'

'I'll get you a towel,' said Pauline. 'And don't make a mess in the bathroom, or Mrs Partridge will be after me. Do make yourself comfortable,' she added to me. 'Take your boots off. I'm sure *your* feet are clean.' She giggled and blushed.

'Oh it's quite all right,' I replied hurriedly.

While Mike was having his bath I had the chance to size up Pauline, and fill in her background with a few well-chosen questions. She is rather difficult to describe physically, for none of her features is particularly striking. She just makes a kind of blurred impression of well-distributed prettiness: softly-waved, light brown hair; a round, slightly asymmetrical face, unobtrusive nose and mouth; a modestly curved figure; unexceptional, unexceptionable legs, size five feet. Her dress that afternoon was attractive but not chic, the hem at least two inches below the fashionable length. She made a pleasant, eye-resting picture as she sat opposite me in one of the two armchairs that flanked the gas-fire. One thing I noticed, and liked, at once, was that she took full advantage of an armchair, instead of sitting perched on the edge like most women.

I learned that she had taken a Lower Second History degree at Westfield, a girl's college of London University, and subsequently a diploma in librarianship. Her people lived in Essex, but she preferred to live on her own in London. Her parents hadn't liked the idea at first, but she had talked them into accepting it.

The conversation turned to the Army.

'Michael never tells me anything, so you must.'

The invitation could not have been more welcome. This was the audience I had been seeking all the week-end. I described the miseries and inanities of army life, affecting a humorous and detached tone, but drawing exquisite sighs of dismay, incredulity and sympathy from my listener.

'Has Mike told you about Percy,—the young chap who was killed?'

She looked grave. 'Yes. It was terrible, wasn't it? But he didn't tell me much.'

A muffled gurgle of water from across the landing indicated that Mike had almost finished his ablutions.

'I think it would be best if we kept off the subject,' I said quietly. 'Mike is very upset about the whole thing. He was very attached to Percy. Percy was a Catholic, you see. Are you a Catholic?'

She frowned slightly. 'No. Are you?'

'No.'

Mike came into the room, red and glowing, with little beads of perspiration on his forehead. 'Phew! I'm limp,' he said, prostrating himself on Pauline's divan bed.

'You had it much too hot, Michael; you always do. Did you open the window?'

'I think I did.'

Pauline clucked her tongue, and went out to inspect the bathroom. Mike grinned at me.

'You look a bit more comfortable now.'

I was. Relaxing under Pauline's easy friendliness I had taken off my battledress blouse and loosened my collar. I now put myself finally at ease by taking off my boots.

The evening passed lazily and agreeably. We had tea, washed up, and listened to gramophone records. Pauline collected mainly L.P.s of musicals and Spanish folk-music. She had been to Spain that summer with her parents.

'I'd like to go again,' she said, 'But not on one of those ghastly coach tours.'

'We'll go together when I'm released from the Army,' said Mike.

'I don't know what Mummy and Daddy will have to say about that.'

'Oh you'll talk them into it.'

'Anyway, that won't be for two years. What am I going to do until then? I feel like a nun already.'

'A very good way to feel,' said Mike.

'Oh you just don't care,' pouted Pauline.

As far as I was concerned, there was only one fly in the soothing ointment of that evening: the nagging suspicion that

Mike and Pauline would naturally prefer to be alone together. I selfishly suppressed this thought until about ten o'clock, when Pauline was in the tiny kitchenette making some coffee.

'Look, Mike,' I said, 'I hope I haven't spoilt your last evening by staying on. I mean, two's company and all that. . . .'

'It's all right, Jon. I invited you on purpose. It's stopped her getting all upset before I go back. But perhaps if you could manage to nip off a few minutes before me. . . .'

So at about ten past ten I explained to Pauline that I had to phone my mother before leaving London, and that I would meet Mike at the tube station. She smiled gratefully; and when I saw the phone in the hall I realized that she had seen through the manœuvre. I was curiously pleased that she had done so. As I clumped down the empty Sunday-night street, the metal studs of my boots grating on the pavement, I cast a covetous glance back at the window of Pauline's room. The main light went off, leaving just the faint red glow of the gas-fire.

The tube station was quite busy, and among the travellers I noticed many of my own kind,—dispirited youths in ill-fitting uniforms, and soldiers of longer service who were permitted to wear civilian clothes on leave. The latter were chiefly distinguished by the small, cheap canvas grips which they carried, probably containing shaving kit, sandwiches against the journey, and a pair of socks which Mum had washed and darned over the week-end. Mike was a long time coming, and I was beginning to look anxiously at the clock and to contemplate leaving him behind, when he appeared, dressed in his uniform. This meant that he had kept it at Pauline's, and I wondered in a vaguely troubled way whether he had spent the last three nights there. But his religion, and Pauline's undemonstrative air of virginity, allowed me to dismiss the idea. Mike's mouth was set in a grim line, and he only grunted when I rallied him for being late. I had to urge him to run for a train, and we only just made it. Everything indicated that his parting from Pauline had been painful, and I maintained a tactful silence.

With each successive stop, the proportion of soldiers among

the passengers on the tube train became greater. King's Cross, that Sunday night, seemed to be swarming with them. They stood or sat about the platforms, waiting for their trains, clad in creased uniforms or rumpled suits, smoking, or playing the automatic vendors, or just shuffling their feet amongst the litter, staring out of numbed, hopeless eyes: disconsolate shades on the banks of the Styx waiting to be ferried across to Hades. Many were being seen off by their girl-friends, and for once I was glad that I was unattached, so wretched did the couples seem: joking unhappily, or holding hands in dumb misery, or striving to lose consciousness in a joyless kiss of parting. I watched one couple writhing in a passionate embrace up against the wall of the Gentlemen's lavatory; they separated abruptly, and the girl walked away without a word or a flicker of expression. With a slight shock I saw that they were both chewing gum. All over the station people were demonstrating their inability to say good-bye.

I had time to observe all this because we discovered that the train left at 11.30 instead of 11.15. Our miscalculation was advantageous; we secured an empty compartment at the front of the train, and pulled down the blinds on the corridor side. Our hearts sank as someone ruthlessly pulled back the door, but a shout from one of his mates drew him away. So we had the unusual good fortune of a compartment to ourselves. We were able to extinguish all the lights, except for the blue bulb which glowed dimly in the ceiling, imparting a weird purplish tinge to Mike's hair. As soon as the train was in motion we stretched out on the seats, munching a couple of apples from the food-bag my mother had thoughtfully slipped into my small pack.

The dim light, the metallic syncopation of the train wheels, and a mutual melancholy at being carried back to Catterick, encouraged me to risk an intimate question.

'Are you and Pauline engaged?'

He shook his head. 'Too many problems. Family, religion'— he bit deeply into his apple, munched, and swallowed,— 'Me . . .'

'Pauline isn't a Catholic,' I said, poising my intonation half-way between a question and a statement.

'No. I wanted her to receive instruction, but she's scared of it for some reason.'

I lapsed into meditation as Mike fell effortlessly asleep. I thought about the evening I had just spent. It had been both soothing and disturbing. Soothing because it had assuaged a hunger which had been a dull pain in my bowels for so long that I had come to live with it, almost ignoring it: woman starvation. It was not just sex,—though that too of course,—it was *femininity* that had wanted in my life.

I had gone up to college, young, pimply, diffident, but with my mind full of erotic poetry and my desires aimed at beautiful, shameless young women. There were plenty of those, both in college and on the streets around, but I was too callow to make any impression on the former, and too scared to approach the latter. This had such a humiliating effect on my ego that, rather than console myself with the normal, friendly, unsensational type of girl who could always be found with patience, I retired into an eremitical existence and devoted my energies to study. Although I lived at home, I found no compensation in my mother: the Oedipus complex seems to have missed me out somehow. My relationship with my mother since the 11-plus has been rather like that between a bachelor of fastidious tastes and the woman who 'does for' him.

So what soothed me that evening was not Pauline herself, but her femininity, which she exuded like an essence in which her whole environment had become steeped. The mingled perfumes from her dressing-table, the teddy-bear in which she kept her night-clothes (Mike had unzipped its belly to demonstrate), the prints of Degas's ballet dancers on the wall, the stockings and petticoats hung out to dry on the line in the kitchen,—all this was indescribably novel and delightful to me.

It was Pauline herself who was the disturbing element in the evening. I coveted her. I had not yet arrived at the stage of consciously desiring her; but I wanted very much to own her. I wanted to have her on my arm, to have her write me letters, to enjoy that easy familiarity and almost wifely solicitude which I had seen Mike enjoy. I am not an envious person in the ordinary sense. I am, I think, as conscious of my limitations as I am of my merits, and I do not waste time and energy coveting what is manifestly beyond my reach, whether it be an expensive car or an expensive woman. My envy is really an impatient sense of unfitness in the world around me, of some dislocation of the natural order of things. Thus, for instance, it seemed to me that it was not merely unfortunate, but *unjust* that Meakin should have the comfortable berth in the English Department, and not me. Mike's relationship with Pauline afflicted me with no emotions of erotic jealousy or envy. I simply recognized in it another example of inefficiency in the cosmic administrative machinery which had allowed them to become intimate before I had had a chance to intervene. For they were manifestly unsuited to each other, the neat, sensible Pauline and the wild, unconventional Mike; whereas she fitted *me* like a long-lost glove. I whiled away some of the long hours of that journey back to Catterick trying her on in my imagination. She fitted beautifully.

I woke from a troubled sleep at 6 a.m. The train had stopped. I lifted the corner of the blind and peered out. We were at York. I went out to the w.c., where a notice reminded me not to use the lavatory while the train was standing in a station. Waiting for it to move I leaned against the door, surveying the dismal furniture of the cramped room. Another notice said: '*Gentlemen lift the seat*'. Statement or imperative? I wondered. With a pencil I scrawled '*Officers &*' before the word '*Gentlemen*'.

When I returned to our compartment there was another soldier in it. Mike and I did not speak to the newcomer, nor to each other until we reached Darlington. The second train was full, and dawdled slowly through the damp countryside, stopping at every small station to deliver milk and mail. At the terminus lorries waited to cart us off to our respective units. We paid a penny for the transport. Although this was preferable to paying for a taxi or walking, the Army's thoughtfulness in providing the transport seemed slightly sinister, as if we were being rounded up into captivity as efficiently as possible. Standing in the back of the truck, swaying and stumbling as it swung round corners, the high-pitched whine of the four-wheel drive seemed the most melancholy sound in the world.

The personnel undergoing training in the Clerks' Training Wing at Amiens Camp were a curious collection. We were a concentration of misfits; all of us, for some reason, were unfitted for the normal pursuits of the R.A.C., and had either chosen to become clerks, or had been press-ganged into doing so, for there was always an alleged shortage of clerks in the R.A.C. The average IQ was startlingly high, because we included several ex-P.O.s who had failed Uzbee or Wozbee, some of whom were graduates. Of course the majority were only just literate, but there were better brains to be found among us than anywhere else in the unit, including the Officers' Mess. It was as if the authorities had determined to seed out from the intakes of new recruits anyone with a spark of intelligence or individuality, together with the odd moron or psychopath, and to subject us all to most farcical and futile form of training they could devise, just to teach us our place.

The training course lasted for a month. The first fortnight was devoted to learning a few simple facts about Army procedure which a bright schoolboy could have mastered in ten minutes. The second fortnight was occupied mainly by learning to type at the hair-raising speed of fifteen words a minute.

There were only three instructors: Sergeant Hamilton, Corporal Wilkinson, and Corporal Mason. Hamilton was a rather pathetic little man, with the ugliest countenance I had ever seen. His mouth was obscenely crowded with teeth,—when he drew back his melon-slice mouth to smile you could count hundreds of them,—and their luxuriant growth had given him a deformed jaw which projected into space like some craggy promontory. His words tended to lose themselves in this dental jungle, and to emerge in a strangely primitive guttural splutter, raining saliva on anyone within ten feet. Few people could resist grinning when he spoke, and that I managed to avoid doing so was the only explanation I could produce for his strangely benevolent attitude to me.

Hamilton, wisely, left most of the instructing to the two Corporals. Wilkinson was a spoilt, baby-faced sibling of the *petit-bourgeois*, who owed his two stripes to his ability as an opening batsman in the Brigade XI. Far more interesting was Corporal Mason, a Regular. I later had the opportunity to check on his age, and was astonished to find that he was only nineteen. He looked at least twenty-nine. He had a white, depraved face, with pale, bloodless lips, and cold, almost colourless eyes. I think he enjoyed his job. He liked the sense of power, and was of a speculative turn of mind. His first action when we clattered into the nissen hut which served as our classroom, was to order someone to stoke up the stove. (The room was always kept at a stifling temperature, with the windows tightly shut and streaming with condensation.) Then he would write something on the blackboard, which we copied into our exercise books. We spent the rest of the day 'learning' this, while Mason conducted a kind of Socratic dialogue with various members of the class. He would ask us personal questions with a calm presumption that his right to do so was unquestionable. The first thing he ever said to us, on our first morning in the classroom, was:

'How many of you are virgins? Come on, put your 'ands up.' He counted the hands, and observed to Wilkinson 'Three more than last time.' I think he was conducting a kind of amateur Kinsey report. He proceeded to interrogate everyone more closely concerning their sexual experience. I had noticed that Mike had not raised his hand, a fact of no small interest to me; but when Mason commented on this Mike replied angrily that he had refused to answer the question. I then wished I had not put my own hand up.

On another occasion Mason asked everyone what they had been doing before their call-up. Several of us said that we had been at a university. It was just the time of year when graduates were being drafted. Mason looked at Wilkinson.

'Fugg me, we've got a right lot 'ere. Shower of bleeding long-'airs.'

'What did you study?' he asked me.

'English, Corporal.'

'English? What you wanner study that for? It's your native fuggin language i'n it? What about you?'

The man now interrogated confessed to having read psychology at Manchester.

'Psychologist eh? I've always wanted to meet one of those queers. Reckon you know what everyone's thinking, don't you?' He brushed aside the psychologist's disclaimer. 'Know what I'm thinking now?'

'No, Corporal.'

'I'm thinking you're a fuggin lot of use if you don't know what I'm thinking.' He guffawed.

'I'm a psychologist, not a thought-reader,' said the other testily. But Mason was unperturbed.

' 'Ere, I bet when you're lying on a woman, you're working out why she's lying there. You never wonder why the fugg *you're* lying there.'

The kind of one-sided debate which Mason conducted could be irritating, and occasionally embarrassing, but we all co-operated out of sheer boredom with the paltry 'work' we were given. All, that is, except Mike, who remained sullen and resentful. I knew he loathed the whole set-up of the Clerks' Course, and observed him with some anxiety. I was afraid that he might do something desperate to escape, like changing his trade or volunteering for the paratroops. For myself, I counted the tedium and the humiliation a small price for the relief from the rigours of Basic Training.

Mason and Wilkinson occasionally enlivened proceedings by deliberately provoking one of the class to insolence, and then punishing him. Their favourite punishment consisted in making the victim stand at the end of the room, against the door, and throwing a tennis ball at him. Wilkinson, who was a good thrower, took a sadistic delight in this sport.

We had occasional 'evening classes'. These were imposed upon us with the object of bringing the Clerks' Course more into line with the Wireless and Driving Courses, which entailed night exercises. Our evening classes were of course absurdly unnecessary: no more teaching or learning was done than in the day classes. But Mason and Wilkinson rarely kept us for the full hour, and on Thursdays, pay day, there was no evening class at all if enough volunteers could be found to risk the Queen's pound in a poker-session with the two instructors.

A few days after we had commenced the course, we were astonished to find Norman in our midst. He had been thrown out of the Driving Course after having rammed a telephone kiosk with a Centurion tank, and the authorities, with inspired lunacy, had thought to make a clerk of him. At least he provided a diversion: to watch him entering notes in his exercise book, tightly grasping the pen-holder in his great fist as if it were a chisel, ink seeping slowly over his hands, wrists, uniform and face, was a memorable experience. He quickly adapted himself to the whimsical despotism of Mason and Wilkinson, and justified Mike's original description of him by playing Caliban to their Prospero and Ariel, by turns slave, clown and victim. It was Norman who laid and stoked the fire in the classroom, Norman who offered Mason and Wilkinson the most outrageous cheek, and Norman who usually ended the morning crucified against the door, roaring and bellowing with simulated pain as the tennis balls thudded into his thick torso.

If Basic Training invited traditional images of hell, the Clerks' course suggested more sophisticated versions, such as Sartre's in *Huis Clos*, its pains compounded of *ennui*, futility and a sense of time passing with unbearable slowness. This, multiplied by two years! I could never bring myself to do the sum.

It was perhaps because of the low state of my morale that Pauline took such a hold of my imagination. Loyalty to Mike should have made me put her out of my mind, and common sense too, for I could not persuade myself that I was likely to win her from him, even if I were prepared to forfeit his friendship in the attempt. But I could not force the memory of her vague prettiness, her insidious femininity, from my mind. Sleep, as I say, is the opium of the soldier, but I looked forward to bed for a special reason. Between the blankets, warm and comfortable at last, eyes shut against the squalid realities of my existence, I could indulge in weaving fantasies about myself and Pauline, fantasies which are embarrassing to recall. I can understand why the pure of heart are generally religious people. If you believed that there was a fanlight in your mind, through which an old man with a beard was perpetually peering, taking down notes, you would think twice about throwing orgies in there.

I had to discipline severely my constant desire to talk about Pauline with Mike, forcing myself always to let him introduce the subject. But he rarely did, even when he received one of those tantalizing, long mauve envelopes.

'Letter from Pauline?' I would say, as we walked away from the office where the post was distributed.

'Mm,' he would grunt, thrusting the letter into his breast pocket.

'Read it if you want to. Don't mind me.'

'It'll keep.'

I rejected the cheap comfort of supposing that their relationship wasn't proceeding smoothly (though such a hypothesis was useful when the curtain went up on my nightly fantasies); I thought it was more likely that Mike was still brooding on Percy.

During the first week of the Clerks' Course we were both called to give evidence at the regimental inquiry into Percy's death. Mike suggested that we should try now to shift attention to Baker's responsibility, but, although I vaguely agreed, I stuck to the same story I had given the Coroner's Court. It seemed to me that it would be dangerous to do otherwise. Mike emerged baffled and irritable from his session with the inquiry; I gathered that all his attempts to steer the discussion away from the particular circumstances of Percy's death, and on to Baker's general behaviour towards Percy, had been sharply checked as irrelevant. He regarded the whole inquiry as a put-up job aimed at saving the Army's face. No doubt this was true, but only, I think, on a subconscious level. No doubt the officers concerned were pre-disposed in Baker's favour, but only because of sheer ignorance of the possible effects of Basic Training on a sensibility like Percy's. At any rate, Baker was charged as a result of the inquiry.

'They couldn't avoid it,' commented Mike. 'After what the Coroner said. The point is, what has he been charged with. It ought to be a court-martial.'

We never found out precisely what Baker was charged with, but he did not appear before a court-martial. He appeared before the C.O. and lost one stripe as a result. To Mike this was disgustingly inadequate, an insult to the dead.

That evening he sat at the table in the middle of the hut, writing a letter, tearing up several drafts in the process. We were having a kit inspection the next morning, and all except Mike were busy mopping floors, polishing windows, and dusting lamp-shades. Sergeant Hamilton had told us that our next forty-eight depended on the appearance of the hut, and this was an incentive we all respected, however grudgingly. Mike's refusal to do his share was vocally resented, but he appeared oblivious to the taunts and complaints. I thought perhaps he was releasing his feelings in a letter to Pauline, but when he finished I noted he had sealed two envelopes. Then he went out.

He returned about ten minutes later, and threw himself zestfully, if belatedly, into cleaning operations. My hands were chapped and sore from mopping the floor, and I gladly resigned my rag to him. I sat down on a bed and lit a cigarette.

'I've just posted two letters,' he observed. The platitudinous remark reverberated with a certain elation.

'What's the hurry? They won't be collected till tomorrow morning.'

'I didn't want to have time for second thoughts. I've written to Percy's guardian and the *Times*.'

I gaped at him. 'What about, for God's sake?'

'Percy, of course. And this squalid regimental inquiry.'

I whistled. 'You've done it now. God knows how many regulations you've broken. Writing to the Press for a start.'

'I didn't sign that one,' said Mike with rather pathetic slyness.

I felt a certain relief. Almost certainly the *Times* wouldn't print it, and with luck Percy's guardian would ignore the other letter. I managed to laugh.

'Why the *Times* anyway? It's practically run by ex-Guards officers. You'd have had a better chance with the *Mirror*. It's right up their street.'

'D'you think so?' he said seriously. 'Perhaps I'll write another——'

'For God's sake don't,' I interrupted hastily. 'You'll spend the rest of your service in the glasshouse if you go on like this. If I were you I'd be at the post-box when it's emptied tomorrow morning, and try and get those letters back.'

'No, I won't,' he replied obstinately. 'Anyway, we'll be on parade then.' He wrung the water out of the rag and began wiping the floor furiously.

Our hut passed the inspection, and we got our forty-eight. My hopes of seeing Pauline again were dashed when Mike declared his intention of taking her to stay with his parents at Hastings. I spent a moody week-end devoid of all pleasure except a fleeting sense of escape at the beginning. On the Saturday evening I went to see the sexiest Continental film I could find, but the images of lust, always fading exasperatingly just before the act, only aggravated my frustration. Afterwards I wandered through Soho eyeing the prostitutes, but when one accosted me I fled to the bright lights of Shaftesbury Avenue, which was thronged with Scotsmen, maudlin drunk because their football team had lost. At home that night, I sat up late reading the last chapter of *Ulysses* for the dirt, which, in my morality, is a kind of mortal sin.

Sunday passed like a stifled scream. I realized with horror that I was almost impatient to get back to Catterick. When parole affords no pleasure there is nothing to distract one's mind from the misery of returning to prison, and one wants to get the painful business over as quickly as possible.

I was forty-five minutes early at King's Cross, and decided to secure a carriage for Mike and myself. To my surprise and some annoyance Gordon Kemp walked up to the window from which I was leaning, looking out for Mike. I had to invite him into the compartment. When I returned to the corridor, and leaned out of the window again, I saw Mike coming up the platform, holding Pauline's hand. I waved vigorously, and Mike acknowledged the signal with a listless gesture. They both looked unhappy. I saw Mike say something to Pauline, and she smiled vaguely in my direction. They threaded their way through heaps of parcels and mail-bags, and came abreast of the window. I surveyed Pauline hungrily. She seemed more desirable than ever, but less composed than when I had seen her before.

'Hallo, Jonathan,' she said. I liked her refusal to abbreviate names. We exchanged a few meaningless remarks, Mike oddly silent throughout. Then, reluctantly, I retired into the compartment to let them say goodbye.

Gordon was wearing a white flash on his shoulder-tab which indicated that he had passed Wozbee. He was still very thin, but looked less haggard than when I had seen him on that first evening in Catterick. 'Congratulations,' I said, dimly recognizing an echo of that same evening.

'Thanks,' he said, with a ready grin. He was understandably full of Wozbee, and seemed undiscouraged by my lack of interest in the subject.

'Mike'll miss the train if he doesn't hurry up,' I said, glancing at my watch, and making this an excuse to peer through the window. They were standing by one of those machines which imprint your name on a strip of metal for the modest sum of one penny. Mike was operating the lever with a kind of wilful violence and concentration, while Pauline looked sadly and silently on. Something is wrong, I thought, with guilty pleasure. Then Mike extracted the metal slip and gave it to Pauline. She read the inscription and smiled. The guard's whistle bleated. They kissed. Mike boarded the train as it began to move, and turned to lean out of the window. Pauline raised the metal strip to her mouth and kissed it to him. Then the train left her behind. Mike came in the compartment and lit a cigarette.

'Well, Gordon?' he said. 'I see you know how to use your knife and fork.' He nodded towards the white flash. Gordon grinned, unruffled. We soon gave up teasing him about his prospective commission. He was a decent, harmless sort of chap. He plainly regarded the commission as just another test in the long series he had been presented with since the primary school, and to all of which he had applied himself with the same dogged, unquestioning perseverance. The conversation became desultory. We all said we had enjoyed our leaves, but only Gordon, I suspected, was being truthful. I was eager to probe Mike about the week-end at Hastings, but Gordon's presence made it impossible. I occupied my mind with trying to analyse the kiss I had just witnessed, trying to distil from it the nature of Mike's relationship with Pauline. I could best define it by negatives: it had not been passionate, nor cool. It had not been a prolonged kiss, nor a brief one. It had not been awkward—they had kissed before; but it had not been characterized by that conscious display of technique which one observes in lovers of real physical intimacy. It had been, I decided, a tender, gentle kiss, between two people for whom a kiss had not yet been devalued by habit or excess. I wasn't sure whether this conclusion was consoling or not. But I reminded myself that no amount of cogitation was going to allay my tormented sense of hopeless attraction to Pauline, nothing except perhaps time and distance. I decided that I would try and get posted to the Far East, and fell into an uneasy sleep, dreaming of delicate, charming and unspeakably licentious geisha girls.

The farce of the Clerks' Course took a new direction that morning: we began the typing classes. These were presided over by a gentle, grey-haired elderly spinster, Miss Hargreaves, in an old house converted into classrooms. Both she and her teaching methods had a charming antique quality, reminiscent of Miss Beale and Miss Buss. Had I given any thought, before being called up, to my possible experiences in the Army, I could never have envisaged that one day I would be sitting in a stuffy classroom, with a motley collection of oafs, morons, and university graduates, clad in the uniform of a soldier, hunched over a typewriter, tapping out a series of letters in time to the wheezing tune from an old gramophone, obedient to Miss Hargreaves's tirelessly gay 'Carriage return', after every twelve bars. The novelty of the situation, however, soon evaporated, and most of the students were quickly bored, restraining their irritation only out of politeness to Miss Hargreaves. She was wonderfully patient and enthusiastic, but Norman nearly broke her spirit. He wrecked three typewriters in as many days, and on the fourth day managed to inflict a ghastly wound on his hand by thrusting it into the bowels of his machine and pressing the tabulator key. He swore vividly, and then put his bleeding hand to his mouth in clumsy, but somehow touching repentance for having offended Miss Hargreaves's ears. She looked at the blood, blenched, and hurriedly sat down.

'Trooper Norman,' she said, in a faint voice (when she had first asked Norman his name he had cheekily given her his Christian name, and had not disillusioned her when she took it to be his surname), 'Trooper Norman, I'm afraid you will have to go.'

So once again Norman was without a trade, and it was a question of some theoretical interest to us how the Army would contrive to employ him.

The Clerks' Course had at least one virtue,—it was shorter in duration by half than the other trade training courses. The days passed very slowly, but they passed, and sooner than I expected the end of the course, and separation from Mike when we were posted, hove in view. The prospect of parting with Mike (for it was unlikely that we would be posted to the same regiment), aroused ambiguous feelings in me. I could not deceive myself that our friendship had been deep and instinctive: it had been almost artificially forced by our mutual distaste for the Army. On the other hand I viewed with little enthusiasm life in the Army without Mike's moral support. I mean 'moral' literally. Mike's hostility to the Army seemed to have an essentially moral basis, which somehow sanctioned my more self-centred grievances. But it was becoming increasingly clear to me that Mike's 'morality' was an unreliable guide to conduct, and I did not wish to become involved in some wild, quixotic crusade against the Army. The deciding factor was Pauline: it would surely be better for me if I could disengage myself from both of them. In the last week of the course I went to see the officer responsible for postings, and put in a request for the Far East. He said that there were only two R.A.C. regiments in the Far East, and that he didn't think there were any vacancies for clerks, but he would see what he could do.

I was coming back from this interview when I saw Mike turning away from the notice board where Squadron Orders were displayed. He came up to me and announced:

'We're on guard on Thursday.'

I groaned. We had done one guard, and I had hoped that we would complete the Clerks' Course without doing another.

'Well, at least we're on together,' I said.

'Yes, and guess who's the N.C.O.?'

'Who?'

'Lance-Corporal Baker.'

I grimaced. 'Should be a jolly little party.'

We went over to the cookhouse for tea, and discovered that the meal was Shepherd's Pie. We had rashly eaten this before. Mike swore it was made from real shepherds. 'After all, this is Yorkshire,—sheep country,' he said. I lent Mike some money, and we went to the Y.M.C.A. instead. I had frequent cause for self-congratulation on having saved a useful sum from my State Scholarship, which enabled me to buy myself a certain amount of comfort in the way of food and cigarettes. I often lent money to Mike, but usually got it back promptly. I was certain that Pauline paid for his fares to London, and kept him in pocket money. This thought angered me intensely.

We were due for another forty-eight at the coming week-end, after taking our trade test on the Thursday. The number of forty-eights enjoyed by the clerks was a cause of considerable jealousy among the other trainees, but as Mason and Wilkinson were partial to forty-eights, they had to wangle them for us too. The only soldiers more favoured were the professional footballers, perhaps the most privileged group in the Service. They were pounced on by the training regiment as soon as they were called up, and their lives were only slightly affected by National Service: they played football for the Army all the week, and had a forty-eight every week-end to play for their clubs.

'Going to Hastings again this week-end?' I asked Mike, as we bit into our hot dogs.

'No,' he replied. 'It wasn't exactly a success the other week.'

'Why was that?'

'Mother doesn't approve of Pauline.'

'I should have thought she was a very presentable girl-friend,' I said carefully.

'The term "girl-friend" is meaningless to my mother,' he said wryly. 'There are no such things as girl-friends. Only potential wives.' He changed the subject abruptly by inviting me to go out with himself and Pauline at the week-end on the coming Saturday. I accepted with mixed feelings.

'What were you thinking of doing?' I inquired.

'Oh, I don't know . . . a dance or something.'

This didn't appeal to me for several reasons. I produced the most cogent:

'I can't dance.'

'Oh. Well, what d'you suggest?'

I suggested a play and a meal afterwards, and Mike agreed. I said I would get the tickets on Saturday morning. What plays had they seen? I asked him; and was surprised to learn that they rarely went to the theatre.

'I'm too lazy to organize it,' he explained. 'So we usually end up at a dance, or a cinema.'

On the way back from the canteen Mike dropped in at the unit Reading Room, run by the Education Corps, to check the correspondence colums of the *Times*; but his letter had not appeared of course. Nor had he heard from Percy's guardian.

Since it was a training regiment, guard duty at Amiens Camp was attended with considerable pomp and circumstance, deliberately designed to impress the raw recruit with a sense of awe and terror. The inspection was lengthy and meticulous, and the guard was called out for a second inspection at midnight. The possibility of being charged for an ill-polished button was never remote, and was particularly near on that Thursday evening when Mike and I presented ourselves at the guard-room. For the Orderly Officer was our old friend Second Lieutenant Booth-Henderson. Rumour had it that he had been caught entertaining a Darlington tart in his quarters; at any rate he had committed some delinquency, and the C.O. had punished him by making him Orderly Officer for ten consecutive nights. This was his seventh, and already he had acquired a considerable reputation for irascibility and the liberal preferment of charges.

I tugged nervously at my uniform and webbing, fearing that our forty-eight was in jeopardy. I glanced over my shoulder and looked straight into the eyes of Baker, who was watching my efforts to improve my appearance with a sardonic leer. I plunged my hands into the pockets of my greatcoat, tingling with humiliation and rage.

'Baker's over there,' I muttered to Mike, who was flicking

his boots with a handkerchief. He straightened up and looked across to Baker. The latter had quite recovered his poise. He stood effortlessly erect, spick as a recruiting poster. His single stripe, neatly painted with white blanco, stood out on his arm like a fresh scar. For a few moments it seemed that he and Mike were trying to stare each other out. Then the Orderly Sergeant summoned us to fall in. Baker spat with deliberation, and turned on his heel.

It was the first time I had seen him since the inquest, except for occasional glimpses. He was a very different man from the yellow-faced, swollen-jawed Baker shaking with fear and shock over Percy's corpse. His malevolence seemed to have returned: there had been something unmistakably hostile in the way he had looked at us. It occurred to me for the first time that perhaps he considered the loss of his stripe, which seemed to us a mere token punishment, to have been unduly severe, and that we, as chief witnesses, had been the cause of it. I did not look forward to the night's guard.

Booth-Henderson's inspection went according to expectation: it was full of malicious tricks. He made one soldier take off his belt, and charged him because the brass on the inside of his belt was not highly polished. Another soldier was charged because the back of his cap-badge was dirty. He nagged everyone petulantly,—everyone except Baker, that is.

Booth-Henderson drew level with me. I came to attention and gabbled off my name and number, hoping that he had forgotten me and our absurd interview during the Basic Training. He regarded me with a frown; drew back two paces and squinted at me with his head on one side; prowled round behind me; and suddenly tugged at the shoulders of my great-coat. I jumped.

''Shun!' yelped the Orderly Sergeant, to whom Booth-Henderson had communicated a nervous irascibility.

'Your great-coat doesn't fit,' said Booth-Henderson.

'No, sir.'

'Get it changed tomorrow.'

'I've tried to before, sir. Stores say they won't change it.'

'Sergeant!'

'Sir!'

'See this man gets a new great-coat tomorrow.'

'Sir.'

The Orderly Sergeant entered my name and number in his note-book, while I cursed inwardly. A new great-coat meant tarnished buttons to polish, and pleats to be pressed. Booth-Henderson passed on to Mike, who escaped with a lecture on the buckles of his gaiter straps.

Baker's job was to post the sentries, and ensure that they were performing their duty. He read the orders, issued us with bicycle lamps, whistles and pick-axe handles, and allocated the 'stags'. Guard duty was from 6.30 p.m. to 6.30 a.m.—two hours on, four hours off for each man. Mike and I were put on second stag, generally regarded as the least pleasant. Our duty was from 8.30–10.30 p.m., and from 2.30–4.30 a.m.

Time passed with indescribable slowness. When we came off our first stag I already felt exhausted. The supper which had been brought to the guard-room at nine was cooling and congealing in aluminium canisters. I forced down a few mouthfuls, lubricated with lukewarm tea, and then dropped on to the hard bunk. Baker, beside the stove, was reading *Tit-bits* with sober concentration,—somehow he made it last all night, —while the Sergeant was snoring under his great-coat. I found it difficult to sleep under the bright lights, wearing boots and gaiters, my high-waisted trousers uncomfortably tight about the crutch. When I did manage to fall asleep I was woken—immediately it seemed—by the order to fall in on the guard-room veranda, where Booth-Henderson inspected us again. After that it was impossible to sleep until 2.30 when Mike and I commenced our second stag.

2.30 a.m., on guard, was a physical and spiritual nadir. At no other time was one more overwhelmed by the meaninglessness of National Service. There we were, guarding nothing against nobody; or, if anyone had been insane enough to covet the nissen huts full of mouldering blanco and damp mattresses that we guarded, we were ludicrously ill-equipped to defend them. Soldiers of the modern Army, armed with wooden clubs a cave-man would have disdained.

It was November now, and bitterly cold, but we were too tired to restore our circulation by walking briskly. We moved slowly between the dark buildings, swaying slightly with weariness, dragging our pick-shafts along the ground. Painfully we climbed the hill that overlooked the camp, where some stores were situated, to check the padlocks. They were locked, though the moorings were rusty, and could have been pulled away with a sharp tug. Nearby was a derelict hut, its doors and windows missing. Inside we found two old chairs, one minus a leg, the other with its back wrenched off. We were both seized by an overwhelming desire to sit down. The hut smelled of sheep dirt, so we dragged the chairs to the doorway, and seated ourselves precariously. Mike took out a packet of cigarettes and offered me one.

'Suppose Baker or someone comes snooping round?' I said.

'It's all right. This is a good position. We can see anyone coming before they see us. First principle of military strategy: take the high ground.'

I accepted the cigarette, and we smoked in silence for a while, keeping the cigarettes in our lips so that we could warm our gloved hands in our pockets. The camp sprawled out beneath us, asleep. In the huts, smelling sourly of sweat and boot-polish, bodies groaned and stirred restlessly in their sticky dreams, while consciousness and the grey reality of another day in the Army stole noiselessly up on them from beneath the eastern horizon. In the cookhouse, where soon pasty-faced cooks would be warming up yesterday's sausages for breakfast, only the cockroaches disturbed the silence, scuttling across the greasy floors. I said aloud:

> *I should have been a pair of ragged claws*
> *Scuttling across the floors of silent seas.*

'What's that?' said Mike. 'Eliot, isn't it.'

'*The Swan-song of Trooper J. Alfred Prufrock*,' I confirmed. Mike repeated the lines meditatively.

'What does it mean?' he asked.

'I've no idea.'

'It's good. D'you ever feel that suddenly you don't know who you are or why you're here?'

'In the Army you mean? Frequently.'

'One day you're marching along to the typing class, or some

such stupid nonsense, and suddenly you don't know why on earth you're putting one foot in front of the other. There seems no reason why you shouldn't just stop, let the others cannon into you, or walk past.'

'The reason is you'd be put on a charge.'

'But that shouldn't make any difference. That's giving in. The fact that you'd be punished for not doing something you regard as purposeless is the very worst reason for doing it. I mean, I know I wasn't put on this earth to wear army boots and put one foot in front of the other just because somebody tells me to, and to stop because he tells me to.'

'What *were* you put on this earth for then?'

He paused before saying, in the curiously pedantic tone he reserved for such statements: 'To exercise my free will, and to save my soul.' After another pause he added, more conversationally: 'Now I've no free will, and my soul is drying up like a prune. The Army's evil, Jon. It's intolerable, isn't it, that pacifism is considered the only ground for conscientious objection. I don't object to war,—a just war. I object to conscription, to being forced into uniform and being made into an automaton so that I can be pushed into the front line when some politician decides that he's going to embark on a war which he may consider just but I may not.'

I vaguely murmured my agreement. I objected to conscription too, but not on these grounds. I objected to having my studies interrupted, my liberty curtailed, my comforts removed. I objected to being woken up at 5.30, being offered revolting food, being made to do menial tasks. The theoretical questions of war and conscience which Mike raised scarcely touched me. The possibility of having actually to *fight* in the Army seemed infinitely remote.

'We'd better move,' I said, getting stiffly to my feet, 'or we'll get frost-bite.'

We made our way down the hill, and resumed our futile perambulations. It was still dark. I looked at my watch. Only 3.25. More than an hour to go.

We were looking up the road towards the guard-room, when the door opened, and a man was silhouetted against the light from within. The door closed again.

'It's Baker,' I said. 'Coming to snoop. Lucky we saw him in time. We'd better separate.' (Guards were not supposed to patrol together.)

'Who's going to challenge him?' said Mike.

'You can,' I said. I could not trust myself to pronounce the challenge with proper seriousness. 'Who goes there, friend or foe?' sounded so archaic. And my voice might crack with nervousness, for I didn't like the idea of Baker stalking us in the shadows.

'What about laying a little trap for him?' said Mike. 'Giving him a little shock.'

'What do you mean?' I said apprehensively.

'Well, you walk up the road under the lamps so that he can see you, and then sidle off round the bedding store as if you're going for a smoke or a pee. He'll follow you, hoping to catch you napping. I'll wait in these shadows, and as he goes by I'll roar out a challenge that'll make him jump out of his boots.'

'I don't know,' I said doubtfully, 'isn't it a bit risky?'

There was a just perceptible curl to Mike's smile. Had he penetrated my mask of sardonic self-assurance, and perceived the timid, cautious soul beneath?

'*You* haven't got anything to worry about. All you've got to do is——'

'All right,' I agreed hastily. 'I'll go.'

I stepped out into the road and walked slowly down the middle of it. I restrained myself with difficulty from glancing over my shoulder, fearing that Baker, having eluded Mike, might at any moment hiss some sarcastic remark into my ear, or even grip me in a half-nelson. I turned the corner of the bedding store without any pretended furtiveness such as Mike had suggested. Then I wheeled round, and took up a stance facing the corner of the store, clenching my bicycle lamp and pick-shaft, my heart thudding absurdly. I could see nothing of course, and I could hear nothing. It suddenly occurred to me that Baker might have made a detour to come round behind me on the other side of the hut. I turned again and peered round the back of the store. It was like hide-and-seek, a game I had always detested in childhood. By this time my head was almost revolving on my shoulders, as I tried to look in two directions at once. I cursed Mike and his crazy schemes.

Suddenly the silence was broken. I heard a faint crack, and a thud. I stumbled to the corner of the stores and looked up the road. About fifty yards from me Mike was standing astride Baker's prostrate form, leaning on his pick-shaft like some primitive warrior surveying his vanquished enemy. He lifted his face towards me, white under the lamps. Then, deliberately, he shouted into the silence: 'Who goes there? Friend or foe?' After a brief pause he raised his whistle to his lips and blew three short blasts on it. I ran up the road towards him.

'Christ. What have you done?' I gasped.

'He didn't answer my challenge,' said Mike slowly.

'But you challenged him after you hit him!'

A light went on in the nearest store, and further up the road the door of the guardroom opened, spilling light on to the road. There was a noise of boots thudding on the boards of the veranda.

'No, Jon, you heard me give the challenge quite clearly, and *then* I hit him. Because he didn't answer.'

I lost my temper. 'Look, Mike, if you want to get yourself court-martialled, that's your business. I think you're a bloody fool, but I'm not getting myself dragged into it.'

Mike's lips curled openly now. 'I may not have the virtue of Christian prudence,' he said with deliberation, 'but God help me from the unchristian sort.'

We glared at each other in silence, in declared conflict at last. There was a shout of inquiry from the direction of the guard-room.

'Look, Mike,' I appealed desperately. 'What do you expect me to do? Be reasonable. . . .'

He gave a swift look over his shoulder. 'All right. All you need do is say that you saw nothing. Just that you heard me give the challenge. It'll be up to them to prove——'

He stopped as the door of the store opened, and the security man came out rubbing his eyes, a great-coat over his pyjamas and boots on his sockless feet.

'Wha's a' this?' he mumbled; and then, as he saw Baker's recumbent form, 'Christ!'

It was raining as I came out of Turnpike Lane station, and I pulled up the hood of my duffle coat. I looked down the toggles of the coat to my fawn Bedford cord trousers with satisfaction, and with satisfaction reminded myself that under the coat I was wearing my slate-blue corduroy jacket. I was glad that this time I would not be presenting myself to Pauline in the dung-coloured garb of a soldier.

As I left the main road, busy with Saturday-morning shoppers, and stepped, strangely light-footed in shoes, down the grey, gaunt street in which Pauline lived, I told myself severely that mine was not a mission of pleasure. To Pauline I would be either a bearer or a confirmer of bad news, depending on whether or not she had heard from Mike. Yet I could not suppress a certain feeling of exhilaration and excitement at the prospect of seeing her alone. However, I adjusted my face to an expression of suitable gravity as I pushed open the sagging gate, and walked up the tiled path. It was as well I did so, for, as I approached the porch, I glanced involuntarily up at Pauline's window, and met her startled eyes staring down at me, as she stood pressing a duster against the window, arrested in the act of cleaning it. I lifted my hand and smiled wanly. She disappeared from the window, and I waited for her to open the door.

When she did so I saw that she was dressed in trousers and an old, hand-knitted jumper,—both garments agreeably tight, as women's old clothes tend to be.

'Jonathan! What a surprise. Michael said in his letter that we were meeting you this evening . . .'

'What letter was this?' I asked.

'I got it on Wednesday. Why? Anyway, come in. You must excuse these awful clothes, but I'm doing some housework.'

I stepped into the hall and wiped my feet. 'Oh, I see. He's probably written again, but you haven't received it yet.' I was perversely pleased to be the one to break the news. As she led me up the stairs I said: 'I'm afraid Mike won't be coming this week-end.'

'Not coming. Why?' She stopped and turned on the staircase. Her face was suddenly pouchy with disappointment, making me feel simultaneously jealous and ashamed.

'Shall we go up first?' I said gently.

As soon as she had closed the door of the bed-sitting-room she asked anxiously:

'Michael is all right, isn't he? There hasn't been an accident or anything?'

'No, there hasn't been an accident. But Mike's not all right, I'm afraid. He's in trouble.'

'What sort of trouble?'

'He's under arrest for assaulting an N.C.O.,' I said, suddenly struggling to keep a straight face. For the first time, at the most inopportune time, I was struck by the essentially comic quality of Mike's action in clubbing Baker with a pick-shaft. Pauline cupped her face in her hands and sank down on the nearest chair.

'Oh *no*,' she murmured.

I told her briefly the events of Thursday night. I had considered very carefully what version I should give her of what I knew about the incident, and had decided to tell her what I should say when Mike was charged. My motives were, firstly, to rehearse the story properly, and secondly, to position myself as favourably as possible in relation to Pauline. This latter problem was by no means simple. If I told her the truth,—that I knew Mike had struck Baker first, and challenged him afterwards, but that I was going to say, for his sake, that I had only heard the challenge, and could not say whether it preceded or followed the blow,—I would certainly ingratiate myself with Pauline as Mike's defendant. But if I was willing to lie to that extent, she might argue, might I not as well go the whole hog and testify that I had definitely heard or seen the challenge precede the blow? The short answer to that was that if, as was highly probable, Mike was found guilty, I would, in such a case, lie under suspicion of perjury: but it was an answer that I could not give to Pauline without indicating some lack of real loyalty and concern for Mike. So I cut my losses, and told Pauline that I had only heard the challenge, and had no means of judging the sequence of events. I gained no glory from this, but I was in a strong position when Pauline later hinted that I might support Mike's claim that he had not recognized Baker, that he had challenged him and, as he had not answered, had struck him.

'I'm sorry, Pauline,' I said gravely. 'I'd do anything to help Mike . . . except perjury.'

She lowered her eyes and blushed charmingly.

'I'm sorry, Jonathan, I shouldn't have——'

'Forget it. I understand how you must feel.'

She got wearily to her feet, shaking her head. 'Oh dear, oh dear . . . what a fool that boy is . . . just a wild Irish boy that never grew up . . . not a scrap of common sense. . . . I'm sorry, Jonathan, I haven't even asked you to take off your coat. It must be wet. Do take it off, and I'll make a cup of coffee.'

'Let me make it,' I said solicitously, rising from my chair.

'No, I'll do it,—oh darn, the gas is going. Have you a shilling by any chance? I've run out.'

I rooted in my pocket. 'Yes, here's one. Where's the meter?'

'You'd better let me do it. It's terribly tricky unless you know how.'

She squatted down by the sideboard, and fumbled with the meter, which was awkwardly situated underneath. The broken zip at the side of her trousers gaped, displaying a segment of blue nylon pants. I felt that somehow it was not playing the game to enjoy this in the circumstances, and looked away. Then I thought, what the hell, I might as well look my fill while I've got the chance. But as I turned back the coin fell noisily into the meter, the gas-fire flared, and Pauline stood up. When she came back from the kitchenette with the coffee she said:

'What do *you* think, Jonathan? Do you think Michael hit this man deliberately? Why should he?'

'The man was Baker. I don't know if you remember hearing about him before.'

'Baker. Wasn't he the Corporal who was so beastly to both of you in Basic Training?'

'He was beastly to Percy Higgins. I think that was what Mike's motives might have been. Sort of revenge I suppose. Some crazy idea like that. Mike thought Baker had got off too lightly, I do know that.'

'So you think he did hit him deliberately?'

I paused cautiously before replying.

'Yes, Pauline, I'm afraid I do. I shan't say so to the Army

of course, but from his manner immediately afterwards, I would say he did. God knows what good he thought it would do.' Or when the idea came to him. Had he been waiting all along for an opportunity to avenge Percy, or did the temptation to split Baker's head open seize him irresistibly as he stood in the shadows and Baker passed him, falling neatly into our trap in his eagerness to catch us out? A thought struck me:

'Has Mike ever had a nervous breakdown, or anything like that?'

'No. Why?'

'I just thought it might be a possible defence.'

'No. He's always been a wild, wayward boy. Never did any work,—well you know that. Never had any money. Never any thought for the future. But no nervous breakdown, or anything like that.'

We sipped our coffee in silence for a few minutes. Pauline, untypically, sat hunched on the edge of her chair; but whether this was because of her perturbed state of mind, or because she felt self-conscious in her trousers, I couldn't decide. Her eyes fell on a heap of dirty linen; she scooped it up with an apology and took it out to the kitchenette. When she sat down again she asked me what would happen now.

'Well, Mike's under close arrest on suspicion of having assaulted Baker. I suppose they can't bring a charge until Baker recovers.

'*Recovers!*'

'Yes, he's got concussion.'

Suddenly Pauline began to cry, mumbling between sobs:

'He might have killed . . . what will they do to him? They'll put him in prison . . . for years . . . .'

I rejected the comforting arm around the shoulder as too corny a gambit. Instead I leaned forward towards her as far as I could without actually getting off my chair.

'Don't get upset, Pauline. It's not as bad as all that. Maybe I'm wrong. Maybe Baker didn't respond to the challenge. I didn't mean to upset you. I just thought you ought to be prepared for the worst. But in any case Mike stands a good chance of getting off. After all, it's only Baker's word against Mike's.'

'But they'll never believe Mike's word against a corporal's.'

'That's not necessarily true.' I spoke without conviction, but Pauline looked up hopefully at me. She took a wrinkled paper tissue from her pocket and blew her nose delicately. Then she treated me to an embarrassed half-smile.

'I'm terribly sorry to have made such a fool of myself.'

I murmured my dissent.

'I'm very fond of Michael you see.'

I said nothing. There was a long silence. I swallowed the cold dregs of my coffee and said I ought to be going. I didn't want to go, but I couldn't think of any pretext for staying.

'Yes, I'm sure you must be very busy. It was awfully kind of you to come and tell me everything.'

'I'm not busy,' I said hopefully, 'but I'm sure you are.'

'Well I've got to go to the launderette. If you can wait a moment, I'll walk down to the station with you. The launderette's just near there.'

It was still raining as we left the house. I carried the washing, and Pauline put up an umbrella. She held it awkwardly, trying to shelter us both without coming too close to me. I said that I didn't need the umbrella, and raised the hood of my duffle coat.

'Should Mike's parents be told about this?' I asked her. She looked suddenly cross.

'*You* can tell them if you like. I shan't.' Observing my surprise, she added: 'They'll probably blame me for it.'

I said:

'I gathered from Mike that you didn't quite hit it off with his parents. I must say I was surprised.'

She smiled. 'Why?'

'Well, as I said to Mike at the time, I should have thought you were a very presentable girl-friend.'

She laughed shyly, but I could see she was pleased.

'What are they like?' I asked

'Who? Mike's parents? Well they're both Irish of course. They've both got broad Irish accents, though none of the children have.'

'Mike has brothers and sisters then?'

'Oh yes, two brothers and three sisters. And two others died.

I've only met Sean,—he's a medical student,—and Dympna, she lives at home and works as her father's receptionist. He's a doctor, as you probably know. The other girls are married, and the eldest son's a teacher in Africa.'

'Mike is the youngest?'

'Yes, unfortunately.'

'Why "unfortunately"?'

'Oh, you know what mothers are like with their youngest sons. She worries about him all the time. Not without reason I must admit. Michael said to me once: "You know that deep furrow in my mother's forehead, just over her nose? Well that's my furrow." And it's true. He showed me the family album once. She never had it till he was born.'

We were now approaching the station. Pauline glanced up at a clock.

'Good heavens! It's ten to one. I had no idea . . . I'm terribly sorry. You'll probably be terribly late for your lunch.'

'It's all right. I'm not going home for lunch. I was thinking of going to Charing Cross Road this afternoon to browse in the bookshops. I'll get something to eat at a snack bar.'

Pauline had come to a halt in the middle of the pavement, frowning slightly, and obviously pondering whether to invite me back to lunch. I studiously avoided an expression of expectancy; looked away from her to the trolley-buses hissing on the wet tarmac; transferred the bag of washing to my other hand.

'Look, would you like to have lunch with me, Jonathan? I was expecting Michael, and I bought a big steak and kidney pie. I shan't be able to eat it all.'

After a token show of hesitation, I accepted. We entered the launderette, had the clothes weighed, and collected a little beaker of soap-powder. Pauline opened a machine, and began to stack the clothes neatly around the inside of the drum. I watched her deft, efficient movements admiringly. She pulled out a soiled brassière from the bag and put it back again.

'Jonathan, would you mind terribly getting me some frozen vegetables while I'm doing this? It will save time.'

When I returned from the errand she was sitting before the machine, staring into the little window behind which the clothes were revolving, as if it were a crystal ball that could tell her something about her future, or Mike's.

I ate Mike's portion of steak and kidney pie with relish. Pauline picked listlessly at her meal. There was only one topic of conversation. To talk about Mike seemed essential if my protracted visit was to be respectable. But I kept trying to nudge the conversation on to Pauline herself.

'So Mike's mother is the problem,' I said, as we were washing up.

'Yes. Mr Brady's all right. I get on with him quite well. A bit too well. He pinched me once.'

'Where?'

She blushed and said: 'The usual place.'

Laughing, I explained: 'I mean whereabouts. I mean, did Mrs Brady see him? It might explain her hostility.'

'No, she didn't see, thank goodness. It was on the landing. No, the trouble with Mrs Brady is that she's so pious. She goes to mass every morning before anyone's awake, and makes everyone else feel guilty at breakfast. Even *I* felt guilty.'

'And Mr Brady isn't religious?'

'Oh he's religious in a way. He goes to church on Sundays—the last mass always. But he doesn't make a show of it like Mrs Brady. In some ways he seems to dislike his religion. He's always making cracks against the parish priest over Sunday dinner, and Mrs Brady gets quite angry because she thinks he shouldn't say such things in the presence of a non-catholic.'

'Meaning you?'

'Meaning me.'

'Do you feel any attraction towards Catholicism yourself?'

'No, that's the trouble. If I did, everything would be all right. Mrs Brady would be pacified; and Michael would be delighted. He's always trying to convert me. And he got me to agree to have lessons,—instruction, they call it,—once.'

'What was it like?'

'I don't know. I got cold feet outside the priest's house, and refused to go in. We had an awful row.'

She hung up the wet dish-cloths, and we went back into the sitting-room. I offered her a cigarette, and for the first time she accepted one. She handled the cigarette without familiarity, closing her eyes as she blew out the smoke.

'Are you a Christian, Pauline?' I asked.

'No. Well, not really. My parents are C. of E. They go to church occasionally. I used to when I was younger. I still do at Christmas, just to please them, and because I like the carols. But I don't really *believe*. If I did, I think I'd go back to the Church of England. It's sort of sane and reasonable. It leaves you alone; it doesn't go prying into your mind like Catholicism. And it's so much simpler. I mean, Catholicism is so *complicated*. I mean, it's difficult enough to believe in God,— why make it more complicated with Transubstantiation and the Immaculate Conception and indulgences and all that? It's like algebra. And it eats into them, you know. They can't stop talking about it, Michael's family. And it's all mixed up with Irish politics, which makes it even more confusing. They keep teasing me because I'm English, and because the English were so beastly to the Irish, and really, sometimes I feel like asking them why they're all living in England if they despise us so much.'

I laughed sympathetically, recalling my experience at O'Connell's Club. We had a cup of tea, and then I had to go. I could think of no further excuse for staying, and Pauline made no attempt to keep me. She said she would write a letter to Mike that evening.

'But Jonathan,' she added, 'I don't suppose Michael will tell me anything in his letters, in case it would upset me. He never writes much anyway. So I rely on you to let me know if anything serious happens. Otherwise I'll only worry all the more. Would you mind?'

I promised to keep in touch.

'You wanted to see me, Sergeant?'

I had been told when I handed in my pass that Hamilton wanted to see me, and I stood now in his 'office', a stone-flagged annexe to the Clerks' classroom, containing only a wooden trestle table and a chair. The stove in the middle of the floor had only just been lit, and gave little warmth. Wisps of smoke escaped from the cracked chimney. Sergeant

Hamilton sat with his overcoat on, and wore fingerless mittens. He looked up.

'Thank Christ you're back, Browne. I nearly lost a stripe over you.'

'Why was that, Sergeant?'

'You weren't supposed to go on your forty-eight because of this Brady business. You're a witness.'

'I didn't see anything, Sergeant.'

Hamilton displayed his multitudinous teeth in a sly grin. 'That's you're story and you're sticking to it, eh?' I shuffled back half a pace, out of range of the fine spray of saliva which issued from his mouth. 'Well anyway, Brady's going to be charged. Baker came round in hospital on Saturday.'

'Is he all right?'

'Yes; lucky he had his beret on. Your friend might have killed him otherwise. As it is he'll get two years for this.'

Two years! It sent a shiver through me.

'Does it count towards your National Service, Sarge, the time you spend in the glasshouse?'

'Does it fugg. It's added on. When he comes out he'll start all over again.'

I was too numbed by this revelation to reply. Hamilton leafed through some papers on his desk. 'He was a rum character that Brady,' he continued. 'I could see he was heading for trouble. He even messed up his trade test.'

'He passed didn't he?' I asked. Surely not even Mike could have failed the trade test.

'Yes he passed,' replied Hamilton grudgingly, 'but only just. He spoilt his paper with a lot of silly jokes.' Hamilton pulled Mike's script from the pile of papers. 'Like the specimen charge sheet. He made it out for the C.O. and charged him with conduct to the prejudice of good order and military discipline in that his fly-buttons were undone on parade.'

I laughed.

'Of course he covered himself. He didn't write down Lieutenant-Colonel Algernon Lancing. He put Trooper A. Lancing. But it's obvious, isn't it?'

I agreed that it was. Hamilton drew out my own script, and smoothed it out on the desk.

'Well, Browne, you didn't mess *your* paper up. You came top with 100 per cent.

I mimicked an expression of mingled pride and modesty appropriate to a Nobel prize-winner. Hamilton seemed to expect it. 'Thank you, Sergeant,' I said.

'The Army needs more clerks, Browne, needs them very badly. With a little experience you should make a very good clerk.'

'Thank you, Sergeant,' I said again. What was this leading up to? I wondered: conferment of a degree? letters after my name? Trooper Jonathan Browne, B.A. Hons (Lond.), Clerk B III (Catt.)?

'How would you like an opportunity to gain some experience before you're posted?'

'What do you mean, Sergeant?'

'The Orderly Room is a bit over-worked at the moment. They've asked me if I can find a man who could help out temporarily. What do you say?'

There was something touching in Hamilton's naïveté. He really thought that I was keen on being a clerk in the Army. The incentive he offered was quite ridiculous, but I didn't hesitate to accept the offer. It would mean that I would avoid the boredom and fatigues of Waiting Wing. Instead of shovelling coal in the raw November air, I would be comfortably installed in a warm office.

My expectations were not disappointed. The Orderly Room was probably the most comfortable berth in Amiens Camp. Paradoxically, the nearer one gets to the hub of authority in the Army, the easier and idler is one's existence. Discipline was lax, nobody bothered about parades, one could wear shoes instead of boots, there were frequent cups of tea, and mild flirting with the shorthand typists. I was excluded from this last diversion, since the girls in question were uninterested in anyone with less than two stripes. But I was content to make myself as inconspicuous as possible, and to ride out my last weeks at Catterick in relative comfort.

I was placed in the Records Office to assist Lance-Corporal Gordon, a volatile Scot jubilantly in sight of his release date, the 15th of January. I bore patiently his gloating over our relative positions, and he soon tired of it. Why I had been co-opted into the Orderly Room remained something of a mystery, for Gordon did not seem over-worked. In fact there were many hours when we just sat about chatting, or reading the newspapers with an eye cocked on the door. I amused myself sometimes by looking up the record cards of various people in the unit and finding out their past histories. It was there that I discovered Mason's age, and read the Personnel Officer's comments on my first interview with him. I also discovered that I had failed at pistol shooting in my Basic Training, which seemed rather unfair, as I had never fired a pistol either before or since being called up.

I saw Mike again when he went before the C.O. It was bitterly cold. We were all on the veranda outside the C.O.'s office,—Mike, Baker and I, standing at ease in a curious, artificial silence. Baker had a thick white plaster round his head. I did not see him and Mike look at each other once. I caught Mike's eye and he smiled, but the Provost Sergeant who was escorting him told him to keep his eyes to the front. Mike's smile was produced with an effort, it seemed to me. He looked worried, scared even.

I was reminded of an incident at College, more than a year before. We had met by chance outside the room of one of the lecturers, where we had come to collect our sessional papers from the pile heaped on a chair in the corridor. We exchanged a nod and a muttered greeting. I flipped through my script, and noted the mark with satisfaction. I had narrowly beaten Meakin. As I made to move off Mike said to me: 'What did you get?' I felt a momentary embarrassment as I said 'Alpha minus'. He was bound to have done badly, and I felt obscurely that it was slightly improper for him to compare marks with me. I refrained from the customary return of the question, but he volunteered the information that he had got a Gamma minus. He stood turning over his paper with a puzzled, hurt expression, as if he had been hard done by. I was sorry for him, but I thought to myself: 'What did you expect, for God's sake? You told me yourself as we went into the examination hall that you hadn't done a stroke of work.' I made an excuse and hurried away, but somehow the incident had blunted the pleasure of my Alpha minus.

And now, as we stood on the veranda, eyes watering in the cold wind, our breath clouding the air, that feeling returned. Mike had got himself into this mess, it was nothing to do with me, and yet his misfortune gnawed at my sense of relative comfort and security like a worm of conscience. Two years in the glasshouse! And then two years of National Service to do! A kind of vicarious desolation swept through me every time I thought about it.

Of course I could no longer fend off the implications of Mike's possible imprisonment. It would, as they said, give me a clear field with Pauline. But would it? Best-friend-of-imprisoned-man-makes-love-to-his-girl cast me too melodramatically as the cad. And I suspected that persecution would only endear Mike to Pauline.

The C.O.'s car drew up, and he stalked past us as if we were invisible.

'Take your cap and belt off,' said the Provost Sergeant to Mike. For some reason accused soldiers had to remove their belts and berets when they appeared before an officer. Whether this was intended, with the rest of the ritual of shouting and stamping, to unnerve the accused, or whether it was, as some said, a precaution against the accused assaulting the C.O. with his belt, or his beret, using the badge as a cutting edge, I never established. It certainly made Mike look already a condemned convict. His hair was so short that one could see the bumps on his scalp.

Mike was remanded for Court Martial. I wrote to Pauline and told her that this was inevitable in the circumstances, and not necessarily a cause for despair. The more formal and public the proceedings, I argued, the better Mike's chances of getting off lightly (for I could not see him getting off completely). It was still Baker's word against Mike's, and although the court might be more disposed to believe Baker than Mike, there would still be, as far as the court was concerned, the puzzling absence of a motive, on Mike's part, for assault, unless someone in the old 'C' Squad leaked to an officer the truth about the triangular relationship between Baker, Mike and Percy.

It was clearly not in Baker's interest to do this himself, since it would revive the whole question of Percy's death.

A frequent visitor to the Records Office of the Orderly Room was Corporal Weston, the C.O.'s driver. He was a tall, handsome man, with a dashing moustache. His battle-dress blouse was garnished with the medals of many campaigns, and he wore a paratrooper's wings on his sleeve, although he was now, of course, in the R.T.R. His battle-dress was tailor-made, and he was the only man I ever encountered who looked smart in that curious garment. He was popular with the shorthand typists, who perceptibly protruded their buttocks as they passed him, unnecessarily inviting a pinch or slap. He spent long periods waiting for the C.O. in the offices of the Orderly Room, and mainly in ours. When he had finished the *Mirror*, he would regale us with anecdotes of his military service. These were exclusively of a sexual nature. He told us of the field-brothels set up in North Africa during the Second World War, and painted a vivid picture of soldiers stumbling out of their tents in the early morning for a 'blow-through' before breakfast, at sixpence a time. He told us of the curious habits of Korean prostitutes. He told us of the street in Hamburg with gates at each end, where female flesh was displayed in the windows of every house like butcher's meat. All this with a wealth of detail that put Lance-Corporal Gorman, who had spent his two years in England, beside himself with envy and frustration, and almost made him sign on for another year in the hope of going abroad. Only once did Weston go a little too far, even for Gorman: when he described how, in North Africa an Arab woman came up to him and offered him her ten-year-old daughter for a bar of chocolate.

'About this high she was,' he said, holding his hand about three and a half feet off the ground.

'You didn't, did you?' said Gorman.

'It didn't mean anything to her,' said Weston defensively. 'She wasn't even a virgin.'

'You vile bastard,' said Gorman. Then, curiosity winning over disgust: 'What was it like?'

For me Weston epitomized the paradox of military courage.

This was the man we had decorated for valour; the man to whom we owed our freedom. And yet what had carried him through innumerable bloody campaigns was a fundamental barbarism, an utter disregard for human life and human decencies. He was not even proud of his military achievements. He was just a fighting, rutting animal in uniform, a true descendant of the mercenaries of the ancient world. He was rather a rare type in the modern Army, and I found him perversely fascinating.

As the C.O.'s driver, Weston had considerable opportunities for overhearing conversations between the C.O. and other senior officers, and he was a mine of information on regimental matters. On the Friday morning of my first week in the Orderly Room he came into the office and, instead of taking out his *Mirror*, addressed himself to me.

'Did you say this bloke Brady was a mate of yours?'

'Yes,' I said. 'Why?'

'Only that you won't be seeing much of him for a few years,' replied Weston, with a cruel grin.

'Why?'

'Up for court-martial, isn't he? For assaulting Baker?'

'Yes. But he may get off.'

'Not now, he won't.'

'Why's that?' I asked, more calmly than I felt. To show curiosity or anxiety would only incite Weston to delay giving me the information he obviously possessed.

'Not that I blame him for belting Baker. He's a big-headed bastard, that one. And he's got fuggall to be proud of. Never seen any service. Any *real* service. I don't call chasing a lot of bloody wogs in Kenya service.'

I remained silent. Weston spoke to Gorman, indicating me with a jerk of his head.

'Not very worried about his mate, is he?'

'I'm just waiting to hear something new,' I said patiently.

'O.K., here it is: you remember that silly c——t who shot himself a few weeks back—what was his name?'

'Higgins.'

'That's right, Higgins. Well, it seems your mate wrote a letter to Higgins's old man.'

'Guardian,' I corrected mechanically. I knew what was coming. 'His father's dead.'

'Well guardian then. Well Brady wrote a letter to this guardian bloke saying that Baker was responsible for Higgins's shooting himself. And the old geezer has just sent it to the C.O.'

'How do you know?'

'Heard the C.O. say it himself this morning to the Adjutant. In the car.'

I turned away and looked out of the window. A squad trotted past at the double on their way to the gym, cold and wretched in their thin P.T. clothes. There was no hope for Mike now.

Weston was saying to Gorman: 'Brady picked the wrong bloke to write to. The old geezer was a captain in the cavalry in the First World War!' They laughed. I rounded on them.

'It's bloody funny isn't it?' I said with heavy sarcasm. 'I can't think of anything funnier than a bloke getting two years in the glasshouse.'

They seemed to agree, for they laughed more loudly than ever.

'You stupid, selfish bastards!' I shouted against their mounting laughter. ' "Fugg you Jack, I'm all right"—that's it isn't it? Well——'

At that moment the door opened, and the R.S.M. poked his flushed, irritable face round the door.

'What's all this bloody racket? Weston!'

'Sir?'

'You're wanted by the C.O. Look lively.'

'Sir.' Weston went out quickly, straightening his tie. The R.S.M. came into the room. Glaring at me he said:

'Who are you?'

'Trooper Browne, sir.'

'What are you doing here?'

'Sergeant Hamilton sent me here to help out, sir, while I'm waiting to be posted.'

'Well, you're not doing much helping by the look of it. And who said you could wear shoes?'

'I thought all clerks could wear shoes, sir.'

'You can when you're on the permanent staff. Until then you wear boots. Understand?'

'Yes, sir.'

He made to go out, then stopped.

'Done a guard this week?'

'No, sir.' My heart sank.

'Well you're doing one tomorrow. We're one man short. Main Guard Room, 2 p.m.'

'Yes, sir.'

The R.S.M. went out. A twenty-four hour guard. And I had hoped to slip off for another forty-eight, with Sergeant Hamilton's assistance.

'Fugg the Army,' I said. Gorman laughed heartlessly.

It was not until the following morning, when I was bulling my boots in preparation for the guard, that it occurred to me that the duty might give me an opportunity of seeing Mike, even perhaps of talking to him. I did not hesitate long before deciding to tell him Weston's gloomy news: he might as well be prepared to face the new evidence.

There were only two other soldiers in the hut; everyone else was in the Naafi or on week-end leave. One, like me, was bulling his boots, spitting into the polish and rubbing the toe-cap in small circles, and the other was writing to his girl-friend, biting the end of his Biro and staining his lips with ink.

'I can never think of a fuggin' thing to say to my bird,' he grunted at last.

'Tell her if she's going to chuck you up to do it when you're on leave,' said the other sombrely. 'It's fuggin' awful when they tell you in a letter.' It quickly came out that *his* girl had lately written such a letter to him. He took it out and read it aloud:

' "Dear Alan, Thank you for your last letter which I received yesterday. I'm afraid what is in this letter is going to come as a shock to you Alan, but I have to say it. You have taken an awful lot for granted, Alan . . ." '

She repeated this last remark several times, without explaining what she meant. Her overt reason for breaking off the relationship was: ' "I don't think we should be tied to each other for two years while you are in the Army".' But she twice suggested that they should continue to write as friends, and concluded by begging him to reply to her letter.

'Are you going to?' I asked.

'No. But when I get my next forty-eight I'll find out who she's knocking about with, and then I'll get my mates together and we'll do 'im.'

The other soldier told an anecdote about his elder brother who was in Malaya when his fiancée wrote to break off the engagement. He had handed the letter round to his mates and they had all (there were about thirty of them) written to the girl simultaneously and told her what they thought of her. Knowing the soldier's capacity for abuse, I shuddered sympathetically.

'Wasn't that a bit hard on the girl?' I asked. They looked at me uncomprehendingly.

'If a girl can't wait for you while you're in the Army,' said the one who had read the letter, spitting into his polish, 'she's no good. Nothing's too hard.'

I saw Mike as soon as I entered the guard-room. He was sweeping the floor and looked up and smiled at me. But the Provost Sergeant locked him into his cell at once, and so I had no opportunity to speak to him. There was only one other prisoner, a haggard-looking N.C.O. who, I learned, was awaiting court-martial on a charge of buggery, committed with a young recruit in his squad. Quite apart from my personal relationship with Mike, I found the proximity of these prisoners disturbing. A few of the younger soldiers on guard observed them with a sort of awed fascination, but the officer and N.C.O.s seemed to fall easily into the impersonal attitude of professional warders.

I found my first twenty-four-hour guard even worse than I had anticipated. Time crawled with painful slowness through the Saturday afternoon and evening. The food was revolting, but one had to eat it: I couldn't get the taste of slippery fried eggs, baked beans and sweet tea out of my mouth for days afterwards. As the guard wore on I became increasingly tired, and increasingly incapable of relieving my tiredness. I found it impossible to sleep in the four-hour breaks between stags.

The bunks were hard and uncomfortable, the lights always blazing, the corporal's portable radio always tuned relentlessly to Radio Luxemburg.

I came off my third stag at 4 a.m. on Sunday, almost faint with exhaustion. Mercifully the guard-room was peaceful. The sergeant was snoring, and the rest of the guards asleep. The corporal was out, posting another guard. I went over to the stove and poured myself a cup of well-stewed tea. I heard a whisper from Mike's cell.

'Jon.'

I walked over to the cell, keeping a nervous eye on the sergeant. It seemed impossible to prevent my hob-nailed boots from making a tremendous noise on the wooden floor. Mike's pale face appeared at the bars of his cell. He clasped them in his hands, as all prisoners seem to do. We spoke in whispers.

'Hallo, Jon. Got any cigarettes?'

I gave him half of my packet.

'Thanks. They only allow us three a day.'

In the adjacent cell Mike's neighbour groaned and muttered in his sleep. Mike's use of the first person plural struck me. He seemed to have already acquired the convict's sense of solidarity.

'How's life?' I asked.

'Pretty bloody. I'll be glad when the court-martial's over.'

'Mike. I've got some bad news for you.' His grip tightened on the bars.

'What?'

'That letter you sent to Percy's guardian. The old man sent it back to the C.O.' Mike bit his lip.

'Hell, that's bad.'

After a pause I said: 'I thought I ought to tell you.'

'Yes. Thanks.'

'I'm very sorry.'

'Yes.'

'But don't give up hope.'

'No.'

I heard the boots of the returning corporal and guard scrunching on the gravel path.

'They're coming back, Mike. I'll have to go.'

I got back to the stove just as they came in. I lay down on my bunk and closed my eyes, but could not sleep. I heard the rasp of a match from Mike's cell. Then, to my surprise I felt a tug on my shoulder and a voice said:

'Your stag, mate.'

When I returned at ten, everyone was awake and it seemed that I would not have another opportunity to speak to Mike. But as I was filling my mug from the tea-pot on the stove I heard Mike's voice say:

'Can I have a cup of tea, Sarge?'

'Give 'im a cup of tea,' said the sergeant from behind his *News of the World*.

I went over to Mike's cell, and he handed me his mug.

'Wash it out for me, mate,' he said.

I looked into the mug and saw at the bottom a folded envelope.

'What d'you think this is, a bleeding 'otel?' said the sergeant.

'Don't be like that, Sarge,' said Mike. I sensed the anxiety beneath the humorous, placatory phrase. I carried the mug into the lavatory and took out the envelope, stuffing it at once into my pocket. Then I rinsed the mug in the wash-basin, although it was already clean. As I gave Mike his tea he said:

'Thanks, mate.'

I didn't look at the envelope until long after the guard was dismissed at two. I was sure it contained some message for me, and I wanted to read it in private. I took a bus into the Camp Centre and went to the Naafi Club for a bath. While the water was running I took the envelope from my pocket and unfolded it. It was not addressed to me but, mysteriously, to 'Gordiano Bruno' at an address in Camden Town. It puzzled me. I had never heard Mike mention an Italian friend. And why had he been at such pains to smuggle it out? As far as I knew he was allowed to write letters. After my bath I stamped and posted the letter. Then I went to the Quiet Room and wrote a letter to Pauline.

Later I was eating in the canteen when Fallowfield, Peterson and Gordon Kemp came in. They were wearing civilian clothes, a privilege for Potential Officers who had passed

Wozbee. Their clothes seemed curiously significant and revealing after the anonymity of khaki in which one had become accustomed to seeing them. Peterson wore a superbly tailored hacking-jacket and tapered cavalry-twill trousers, Fallowfield a navy-blue blazer and charcoal-grey trousers, and Gordon a Burton tweed sports-jacket and shiny light-grey flannels. I didn't particularly want to talk to them, but Gordon, in his friendly way, led them, bearing trays of food, to my table.

'Hallo,' I said. 'Wearing "mufti" I see?'

'Yes,' replied Fallowfield, oblivious to my sarcastic emphasis on the word, 'It's a jolly useful concession. Means you don't mess up your best B.D. at week-ends. Particularly on leave.'

'You don't mean to say,' I asked, 'that you had any scruples about wearing civvies on leave before? Did you two?'

Gordon, who was eating voraciously, shook his head. 'Not me, old boy,' said Peterson, 'I can't stand battle-dress. Makes me want to scratch all the time.'

'Well, it won't be long before you can wear that nice, smooth officers' gaberdine,' I observed.

'It's not a question of scruples,' said Fallowfield, slightly nettled. 'It's a question of obeying an order when there's no one to check up on you, just as you would if there were someone to check up on you.'

'That's what I call a scruple,' I replied.

After a pause, Fallowfield started a conversation with Peterson about a recent map-reading exercise. Gordon said to me:

'How's Mike, Jon? Have you seen him lately?'

'I saw him last night as a matter of fact. On guard. It's obviously a strain.'

'It must be. I was very sorry when I heard about it. What are his chances, d'you think?'

'Not too bright.'

'What really happened that night, Jon? You were on guard with him weren't you?'

Fallowfield and Peterson stopped talking and pricked up their ears.

'I'd rather not go into it now, Gordon, if you don't mind. After all, it is *sub judice* and so on.'

'Who's having scruples now?' said Fallowfield.

'All right. Put it another way. I don't particularly want to give other people an opportunity of gloating over Mike's troubles.'

'I wouldn't gloat,' said Gordon.

'I know you wouldn't, Gordon,' I replied, pushing back my chair. 'Well I must be going. I'd hate to interrupt a fascinating conversation about map-reading. So long.'

At the door Gordon caught up with me.

'Jon . . . I was wondering whether there was anything we could do for Mike.'

'What *can* we do?'

'I was wondering . . . perhaps the Prof. would write a letter on his behalf. . . .'

'My dear Gordon, you know Mike wasn't exactly the Prof.'s blue-eyed boy. This will only confirm his opinion.'

'Yes . . . well . . . I suppose we must just hope for the best.'

'Yes.'

There was a brief, awkward silence between us. Then Gordon said:

'You know, Jon, I reckon you made the right choice. I mean about refusing a commission.'

'It wasn't quite as grand as that, Gordon. I refused to *go in* for a commission.'

'Yes . . . well . . . anyway, I'm getting pretty sick of it in the P.O. Wing. They're a frightfully snobbish lot. And half of them are queer. When I came in late the other night, two of them were in bed together.'

'Not Fallowfield!' I exclaimed. 'Surely nobody of either sex would get into bed with Fallowfield.'

'No, not Fallowfield,' said Gordon grinning. 'He's all right really, you know.'

'Yes, he's all right; he's just a pig-headed, pompous idiot, that's all. If it's all so ghastly, why don't you chuck it?'

'Oh I don't know. Now I've got this far . . . and my parents wouldn't understand. Though I'll probably be thrown out of Mons anyway.'

I patted him on the arm. 'You'll be all right, Gordon. They won't chuck you out. When do you go?'

'Next week.'

'Well, the best of luck.'

'Yes. Same to you.'

We parted. I was beginning to feel the effects of the guard, and looked forward to an early night. Outside the Club I saw the red M.G. in which Peterson had brought Fallowfield and Gordon. Gordon was a decent chap. Why had he gone out of his way to tell me that I had 'made the right choice'? Did he think I envied him?

On the following Thursday morning Weston came into the Records Office with that smug expression on his face which denoted that he had another morsel of news. As he opened his mouth to speak I forestalled him.

'Yes, we know. He escaped last night.'

That evening I made a trunk call to Pauline. A woman, probably the landlady, answered the phone, and went to fetch Pauline. There was a long pause. Then, very faintly, I heard Pauline's voice. It broke in the middle of 'Hallo', and she repeated the word.

'Hallo, Pauline?'

'Yes?'

'This is Jonathan.'

'Who?'

'Jonathan. Jonathan Browne.'

'Oh.' A nervous, almost hysterical laugh followed. The receiver clattered on to a table. I caught a mutter of voices. Men's voices. What the hell was going on? Then a gruff voice spoke to me.

'Hallo, this is the Military Police here. Who is speaking please.'

'My name's Browne. I——'

'I understand you are a soldier. Rank and number please.'

'53174979 Trooper Jonathan Browne. With an "e".'

'Five three . . .?'

'Five three, one seven——'

'One seven . . .'

'Four nine, seven nine. Look——'

'Four nine seven nine. Trooper Browne. With an "e".
Regiment?'

'Twenty-first R.T.R. Look this call is costing me money. I
want to speak to Miss Vickers.'

At that moment the pips sounded.

'All right. Just a minute. Operator!'

After a long wrangle the M.P. managed to get the operator
to extend the call, and charge it to the Army. Then he came
back to me.

'Are you acquainted with Trooper Michael Brady?'

'Yes I am. That's what I want to speak to Miss Vickers
about.'

'You know where he is?'

'No, I don't.'

After some more questions I was put on to Pauline.

'Hallo, Pauline. It seems you know all about Mike already.'

'Yes. I thought it was him when you phoned. . . . It's
terrible . . . what . . .'

'Sorry, I didn't catch that.'

'What will happen to him?'

'I don't know. I should think they'll pick him up pretty soon.
The sooner the better. He's only making things worse for
himself.'

'What will happen to him?' she repeated, as if she had not
heard me. I caught sight of my face in the mirror of the call-
box, contorted with the effort to hear and communicate.

'I thought it was him,' she went on. 'They made me promise
to try and find out where he was.'

'The swine. Why don't you chuck them out?'

'Pardon?'

'It doesn't matter. Look, we can't talk properly over the
telephone. Shall I come and see you this week-end?'

'Yes please, Jonathan.'

'Saturday? I'll give *you* lunch this time.'

'Yes, that would be nice.'

'Well, good-bye till Saturday then.'

'Yes, good-bye, Jonathan.'

I waited for her to put the receiver down, but she didn't. So
I said 'Good-bye, and don't worry,' and put down my receiver.

The next morning I went to see Sergeant Hamilton to get a leave pass for a forty-eight. As I was filling it in he said:

'So your mate has scarpered.'

'Yes.'

'Silly man. Assaulting an N.C.O. Desertion while under arrest. He's up to his eyes in trouble. They'll pick him up of course.'

'I suppose so.'

'Where d'you think he'll make for?'

'I haven't the faintest idea.'

'He made a neat getaway, I'll say that for him. Taking the roof of the guard-room to pieces. Nobody thought of that before.'

'Perhaps they won't find him so easy to catch then.'

'Oh they'll catch him. Some time.'

I completed the leave form and handed it to him.

'You'll have to get it initialled by the Chief Clerk first.'

'O.K., Sarge, I'll do that now.' As I was moving towards the door he said:

'How do you like it in the Orderly Room?'

'Oh, it's all right.' I added, with an effort: 'It's quite interesting really.'

'Your posting hasn't come through yet, has it?'

'No.'

'Any preferences?'

'I've put in for the Far East.'

He sighed. 'Why is it all you blokes want to go to the Far East? Bet you think it's all beer and brothels, don't you. Well, it is—for about two weeks of the year, on your annual leave. The rest of the time it's flies and heat and patrols and dysentery.'

'Well, I don't suppose I'll get there anyway. Some God-forsaken hole in Germany most likely.'

Hamilton searched amongst the papers on his desk. 'I've just had a letter from an old friend of mine,' he said. 'The Chief Clerk at Badmore,—the R.A.C. Special Training Establishment. He needs a new clerk, and he's asked me to send him a good one. Would you be interested in going there?'

'Where is this place?'

'Hampshire, Dorset,—somewhere round there.' He paused before adding slyly: 'About a hundred miles from London.'

About a hundred miles from London. That was a comfortable distance for forty-eights, and not too bad for thirty-sixes, if the travel was reasonable.

'You'd probably be put in the R.T.R., unattached to any particular battalion. Well, anyway, think it over.'

'There's no need, Sergeant. I'd like to go, if you can fix it.'

'I can fix it,' he replied. 'Let's go round to the Postings office now. You won't regret this.'

Walking to the Posting office we passed Baker. His eyes met mine for a second, glittering with hate. I was sure that all along he had hated me more than Percy or Mike, and yet it was them, and not me, that he had driven out into the wilderness.

FIVE

By the end of the afternoon the sky had clouded, curving like a dull, metallic lid over the camp. It became hotter rather than cooler, prophesying a storm. Reluctantly I exchanged my working trousers, worn smooth and threadbare, for my best trousers, thick and itchy with their pristine nap intact. When I rolled down my shirt-sleeves and buttoned up the battle-dress blouse I began to sweat. I transferred Henry's parting gift from the map-pocket of the discarded trousers to my wallet.

I stepped out of my cubicle to inspect my appearance in the long mirror, and glanced enviously at a group playing cards round someone's bed: they were coolly dressed in jeans and light cotton shirts. A little shower of chaff was tossed casually in my direction.

'All bulled up, Corp?'

'Don't wake us too early tomorrow.'

'That's a shit-hot pair of boots you've got there.'

'Jock Gordonstone does 'em for 'im. Never bulls 'is own boots, the lazy sod.'

'Watch your language, Trooper,' I said, stamping my feet to get my trousers to fall neatly over the gaiters.

'Want some weights, Corp?' It was a common, though illegal practice, to put lead weights, or lengths of bicycle chain in one's trouser legs, which pulled the latter over the gaiters and kept the creases taut.

'No thanks.'

' 'Ere, Corporal. What size are them boots?'

'Eights.'

'That's my size. What about swapping them before you go?'

'Not likely. Stores wouldn't accept your boots. They look as if a Centurion ran over them.'

'No, me *best* boots, Corporal.'

'I *mean* your best boots.' The rest of the group cackled.

I had become accustomed to the image that confronted me in the mirror, but it still bothered me with a sense of the ridiculous. I never wore the uniform—it seemed to wear me, with a sheepish sense of failure. The khaki imparted a sallow, unhealthy hue to my skin, and the over-large beret sat uneasily on my forehead, making the face beneath look pinched and wizened. Pauline said that when she first saw me I looked like a refugee who had been hastily clothed by a liberating army in whatever came to hand. I never presented myself to her in uniform if I could possibly help it. I was turning away from the mirror when I realized that I had forgotten to transfer my shoulder flashes from my second-best battle-dress. I got them from the cubicle, and slipped them on to my shoulder-tabs. Brown, red and green stripes. 'Through mud and blood to green fields beyond,' as the regimental motto had it. Through boredom and discontent to blessed civvy street beyond. The thought of release was reviving.

'Well, this is the last guard I shall push,' I observed to the card-players, as I picked up my grip containing blanket, thermos flask, book, and cigarettes.

Chalky White was waiting outside the Montgomery guard-room when I arrived.

'What are you doing here, Chalky?'

'Same as you. I'm doing a guard for Nobby Clarke, and he's doing mine on Friday. I want a forty-eight next week-end,' he explained. 'The group's got a job on Saturday, starts early.' He added : 'Put me on first stag tonight, Jon, will you?'

'O.K., Chalky.'

Other soldiers began to appear, moving slowly and un-willlingly toward the guard-room.

'There's a bullshitting bastard,' muttered Chalky, as an immaculately turned-out R.E.M.E. craftsman approached us. 'Bet he gets stick.'

Chalky was referring to the quaint ritual of the 'Command-ing Officer's Stick', a non-existent object which was sym-bolically awarded to the best-turned out trooper at the inspection of the guard. The recipient was then excused the guard duty.

'I wouldn't mind getting stick myself tonight,' Chalky added, yawning. 'I always feel shagged on Mondays, after the week-end.'

I yawned also, and murmured my agreement. The short sleep of the previous night would soon begin to tell, and the next day I would feel dead. Fortunately a corporal's lot on guard was easier than a trooper's. And by 6 a.m. I should be a happy man, my last irksome duty completed, only one full day between me and liberty.

Suddenly I saw Sergeant-Major Fotherby approaching us from the direction of the Sergeants' Mess, wearing a sash.

'Good God! Don't tell me Fotherby's Orderly N.C.O. tonight?'

'Don't you ever read orders?' Chalky inquired.

'I didn't bother. Everybody else was so bloody eager to tell me what was on them.'

I made an effort to retain my self-possession as Fotherby drew nearer; in retrospect, my appeal to him that morning must have seemed to him more impertinent than ever.

Fotherby was accompanied by Sergeant Earnshaw and Sergeant Mayhew, the N.C.O.s in charge of Montgomery and Vehicle Park guard-rooms respectively. Earnshaw was a stupid, lazy, but not ill-willed man who could be relied on to steer us through the duty with the minimum of effort by all concerned. Fotherby glanced at his wrist-watch and told us to fall in. We spread out across the square, and formed up facing the guard-room. The Vehicle Park guard was the largest, since three men were required on each stag to patrol the hangars and tank parks. Montgomery Guard only required one man at a time to patrol the camp entrance. Therefore, besides myself, there were only three troopers in Earnshaw's file: Chalky, the resplendent R.E.M.E. craftsman, and an unhappy-looking little trooper from 'B' Squadron, whose name I did not know.

Behind us were the Armed Picket, supposed to be able to defend the camp from attack by the I.R.A., who had brought the Army into derision about a year before by a series of successful raids on regimental armouries in the North. This scare had long since passed, but the Armed Picket continued in existence, following a familiar military law by which measures designed to meet emergencies are never revoked, but absorbed into the ritual of the unit, more and more rules accumulating about them as their original significance fades into the past. The Armed Picket slept, fully clothed and with its boots on, in a hut near the Montgomery guard-room, from which it could be alerted by means of an electric bell. After the guard had been inspected the picket loaded its rifles, which were then locked into a wall-rack. On hearing the bell the N.C.O. in charge unlocked the rack, distributed the rifles, and led his men out to combat. That, at least, was the theory. In fact, the picket was a more real menace to itself and to the rest of us, than to any potential aggressor. The soldiers of Badmore were not used to handling fire-arms, and were easily flustered when they were alerted for practice purposes. Such occasions rarely passed without a rifle going off by accident, and one man had already been shot in the foot and invalided out of the Army, to his great delight.

As we stood at ease, waiting for Fotherby to make his preliminary inspection, Sergeant Earnshaw said to me:

'Aren't we one short, Corporal? There are usually four on this guard for inspection.'

He was correct. The fourth man would replace whoever got stick, unless he got it himself.

'You're right, Sergeant. But I don't know who's missing.'

'Sounds like him now.'

There was a sound of heavy footfalls, and round the corner of the bedding store lumbered a familiar uncouth shape: Norman.

'Get your finger out, Trooper,' cried Fotherby. He looked regretfully at his watch. 'Another ten seconds and you'd have been on a charge.'

Norman panted up, winked at me, and took his place at the end of the file. Fotherby began his inspection.

Since Badmore was the R.A.C.'s waste-paper basket, where troublesome or defective personnel could be conveniently disposed of, it had been no surprise to me when Norman had turned up there about a year before. At Badmore he realized himself at last. 'There's a place for you in the Regular Army,' the recruiting posters had told him when he enlisted; and at last, at Badmore, he had found that place. He was in charge of the unit piggery. Tanks and typewriters were things that went suddenly, disastrously wrong in Norman's hands; but pigs,—not even Norman could damage pigs. Indeed there was a certain *rapport* between them. There was a real gleam of affection in Norman's eyes as he heaved a bucket of swill into a trough and watched his charges guzzling an obscene cold stew of cabbage, potatoes, mince, suet pudding, gravy and custard, the left-overs from the troops' dinner. Norman, the product of an industrial slum, had become quite agricultural. He was to be seen occasionally with a straw in his mouth, and talked of 'going into pigs' when his three years were up.

Fotherby took longer than was customary over his inspection. In his own regiment he had probably been used to the Orderly Officer's duty, but there was a plethora of officers at Badmore, and most of the Warrant Officers had to be content with being Orderly N.C.O. He returned to the guard-room veranda, and we stood at ease under the dull, stifling sky, waiting for the Adjutant. A trooper in a red singlet and jeans, with a towel round his neck, emerged from a hut and made his way to the wash-house, whistling shrilly. His whistling faltered and died away as his glance met the silent, expressionless ranks facing him. A faint odour of pigs was wafted from my left where Norman stood, still breathing heavily.

The muffled growl of a powerful engine announced the approach of the Adjutant's Jaguar, changing down as it entered the camp. A touch on the throttle brought the low, green car to the steps of the guard-room in a single pounce. The driver stopped the car, and ostentatiously revved the engine before switching off the ignition. Captain Gresley emerged from his car, and stood erect in all the bizarre glory of his dress uniform: dark green hat, with a gold band and a glossy peak, deep maroon jacket, dark green trousers narrower than any Teddy-boy ever dreamt of in the wildest excesses of his sartorial imagination, with a broad gold stripe down the sides. Silver chain-mail had settled like snow on his shoulders, and silver spurs were screwed to the heels of his boots. He jingled faintly as he walked towards Fotherby, whom he greeted with a smile, for they were both in the same cavalry regiment.

'Ain't he gorgeous?' whispered Chalky.

'What must they all look like on mess-nights?' I replied. 'A commissionaires' conference.'

As Chalky had prophesied, the R.E.M.E. craftsman got stick. The unhappy-looking little trooper from 'B' Squadron, whose name proved to be Hobson, received a thorough grilling from Gresley and Fotherby, from which he emerged looking unhappier than ever. It was his misfortune to belong to the same regiment as them. He had never been with the regiment, knew nothing about it, and I imagine he fervently hoped that he would never have the opportunity to extend his knowledge. The inspection passed without further incident; we marched off the square; the duty truck bore the V.P. guard away to the other guard-room. I took the soiled mill-board on which the guard's orders were pasted, and intoned them to my oddly-assorted trio. I gave Chalky the first stag, Hobson the second, and Norman the third.

The guard-room was hot and stuffy. Gresley stalked about the room, elaborately checking that everything was in order. There were no prisoners in the cells. He pressed the alarm bell button, and we heard the bell ringing shrilly in the Armed Picket hut. Then he and Fotherby left. We began to settle down for the night.

Sergeant Earnshaw seated himself at the high desk, and began laboriously to fill in the guard report. Norman produced a tattered paper-backed novel entitled *Hell Beach*. A snarling Marine leapt from the cover, with a sub-machine-gun blazing from his hip. It was a not insignificant irony, I reflected, that the favourite form of escape literature among soldiers of the modern Army was not pornography, not Westerns, but war-books. I took out of my grip Empson's *Seven Types of Ambiguity*. Hobson sat on his bunk staring vacantly before him. He had not provided himself with reading matter. Or perhaps he couldn't read. Suddenly he said to me:

'Eh, Corporal: will it be dark on second stag?'

'Dark? I suppose so. It's pretty dark already. I should think there'll be a storm. Why?'

After a brooding silence he said:

'I don't like this bloody guard.'

'Neither do I as a matter of fact. But it's the last one I'll be pushing.'

'Getting released soon?' asked Norman.

'Wednesday.'

'Chuffed eh?'

'What do you think?'

We resumed reading.

'It's that bloody *tank*,' said Hobson suddenly.

'Eh?'

'That tank. That German tank. I don't like being near that tank when it's dark.'

'Oh I get you. The ghost. Norman, this lad's frightened of the ghost. Will you hold his hand on second stag?'

'I'm not so bloody keen on that tank myself,' he muttered darkly.

'What's all this about a tank?' inquired Earnshaw from his desk.

'Haven't you heard about it, Sarge? It's supposed to be haunted by the ghost of a German soldier.'

'All burned, his face is,' said Hobson, in a half-frightened, half-gloating voice.

'Ghost!' spat out Earnshaw scornfully. 'Never heard such a load of crap. Nervous as a lot of virgins, you nigs are.'

Silence returned, disturbed only by the ticking of the clock, and the tread of Chalky's boots as he paced his beat round the guard-room, the bedding stores, the armoury, the Armed Picket hut, the garage for the C.O.'s car. Round and round he went, like a satellite circling a dying planet. I read on into Empson, admiring the way he delicately dismantled a metaphysical lyric, laying out the components for inspection; then deftly reassembled them, shaking the mechanism into motion, holding it up triumphantly to your ear. The intellectual exercise of following him was flattering, and brought with it a comfortable premonition of the life that awaited me: the warm library at nightfall, the feel of new books, the smell of old ones, the pleasantries and vanities of footnotes and acknowledgments. I sniggered as Empson flicked the last remnants of his bard's robe off another eminent nineteenth-century poet.

'What yer reading?' said Earnshaw, who had left his desk. To avoid the labour of an explanation, I passed him the book. He glanced at the title on the spine, and began to read where I had left the book open, his brows knitted.

'What's it about then?'

'Literature.'

'Yer, but what's it about. Anything 'ot in it, like?'

'It's not a story. It's literary criticism. It's——'

'Wodjer wanner read that sort of crap for?' he interrupted, handing back the book.

'I happen to be interested in it.'

'Won't do you any good, will it?'

'As a matter of fact it will, though that's not why I'm reading it.'

'Why, what good will it do yer?'

'I hope to make the study of literature my career.'

'Gerna be a teacher I s'pose. But what *good* will it do yer? Or the kids yer teach. What *use* is lit'rature?'

I opened my mouth to launch into a defence of the study of literature . . . *getting to know, on all the matters which most concern us, the best which has been thought and said* . . . and then closed my mouth. I was not eager to return to the university because I thought my research would be of any use, to myself, or to others. All human activity was useless, but some kinds were more pleasant than others. The Army had taught me that much philosophy. There was no such thing as communication operating over the whole of society. In fact, there was no such thing as society: just a collection of little self-contained boxes, roped untidily together and set adrift to float aimlessly on the waters of time, the occupants of each box convinced that theirs was the most important box, heedless of the claims of the rest. Success did not consist in getting into the box where most power was exercised: there were many people who were powerful and unhappy. Success consisted in determining which box would be most pleasant for you, and getting into it. If you were forced to inhabit an unpleasant box for a time, then you could make it as comfortable as possible until you could get out. Luck or cunning were the most effective attributes in this world, and cunning, though it worked more slowly, was the more reliable.

'What's it mean, anyhow, the name?' asked Earnshaw from the desk to which he had returned.

'What name?'

'That book. Seven types of whatever it is.'

'Oh, "ambiguity". It means a word or statement which can have more than one meaning.'

Earnshaw laughed incredulously.

'You're a queer bugger and no mistake,' he said.

Luck or cunning. And if you didn't have either, you were like Mike, at home in no box, vainly trying to ignore the existence of boxes, tossed and buffeted by the pitiless winds that blew outside them. For it was better to be in the most uncomfortable box than outside, in the confusion of the elements.

' 'Ere, if you're so clever,' said Earnshaw, coming back to my bunk. 'See if you can do this.' He spread out six pennies in a triangle and challenged me to put them in a straight line in two moves. His conviction that my education had been useless seemed to be confirmed by my inability to solve the puzzle. There was a low rumble in the distance.

'Thunder. There'll be a storm soon,' said Earnshaw, sweeping the pennies into his palm. But the storm receded, or was circling. The hours passed without relief from the close, oppressive atmosphere.

At ten Earnshaw said he would have a sleep for a few hours.

'Wake me at two, then you can have a kip. And keep your ears pricked for the Adjutant. He's a keen bastard,—and so is Fotherby. They're likely to try and catch us napping.'

'O.K., Sergeant.'

I seated myself at the desk, and poured a cup of coffee from the flask I had brought with me. The darkness outside was lit occasionally by a flicker of sheet lightning on the horizon. Hobson's boots shuffled on the path outside. He was not moving very far from the guard-room. I went to the window and called out unkindly: 'You're supposed to patrol this whole block, you know. Don't stay up this end all the time.' He gave me a scared, reproachful look, and moved off in the direction of the tank.

Chalky was telling Norman about a Scotsman in his hut who talked in his sleep about his sexual adventures. I strained my ears to catch his words.

' "Are ye cold," he says—he must have had this tart in a ditch or something—"Are ye cold, Jenny? Och, your poor wee tits are cold, Jenny, let me warm them for ye,"—no, I'm not kidding, just like that, you can ask anyone in the hut. "Keep your head down, Jenny, there's someone coming," he says. We were all round the bed, pissing ourselves trying not to laugh out loud and wake him up. Then Nobby Clarke put his helmet in Jock's hands, and he ran his hands over it, smooth like, and "Och, you've a lovely arse on you, Jenny," he says . . .'

It was the hour for lubricious dreams. I wondered idly in what circumstances I would learn the last secrets of Pauline's clean-smelling body, and find that mental anaesthesia which I looked for between her smooth white thighs. In the hotel bedroom at siesta time perhaps, the strong Mediterranean sunlight broken up by the venetian blinds into golden bars that burned into her naked torso. Or as we rubbed each other dry and glowing with rough towels after a midnight swim; her skin would taste of salt . . .

There was a noise of someone running towards the guard-room, and a frenzied knocking on the door. Sergeant Earnshaw threw off his blanket and leapt to his feet, cursing under his breath.

'Go and see who it is,' he said to me, buckling on his belt.

When I opened the door Hobson almost fell across the threshold, pale and quivering with fright. His mouth opened, but nothing came out.

'Well?' said Earnshaw.

'I've seen the ghost!' blurted out Hobson.

Earnshaw flung down his belt in disgust.

'For fuggsake, is that what you woke me up for. I've a good mind to put you on a charge.'

Hobson turned pleadingly to me. 'It's true, Corporal. I saw 'im, by the tank. There was a flash of lightning, and I saw 'im.

'E 'ad one of them long German coats on, like you see in the pictures.'

'Why didn't you challenge him?' demanded Earnshaw.

Hobson stared blankly: 'Because 'e was a ghost, Sarge.'

Earnshaw stepped over to Hobson, grasped the lapels of his battle-dress, and lifted the unfortunate youth on to his toes. 'Now listen to me,' he bellowed. 'There is no bleeding ghost. Get back to your post in ten seconds from now, or I'll have you in the guard-room so fast your feet won't touch.' The formula came out before the speaker realized that he was already in the guard-room, but the words had their effect. Hobson stumbled miserably out into the dark. Earnshaw turned to me.

'You'd better go out and have a look. Someone may be snooping around.'

I picked up a flashlight, and stepped out on to the veranda. The heavy warm air seemed to part in front of me, and close behind, like water.

'Let's go and have a look,' I said to Hobson, who was cowering against a wall.

He kept close to me as we approached the tank, and his pace faltered as another flash of lightning on the horizon silhouetted the antique outline of the vehicle. Never having been troubled by fears of the supernatural, I enjoyed a sense of superiority over the terrified trooper as we came up to the tank. It was just a shell, the disembowelled carcass of a prehistoric animal. The back had been removed so that one could climb into it. I did so, and flashed my torch round, illuminating nothing but a few cigarette stubs and a small heap of dog's excrement. It was difficult to believe that this narrow evil-smelling room had ever churned through the mud of Flanders field, crunching the bones of dying men, bullets rattling like hail on its thin plate. Tanks, 'mobile coffins' as Mike had described them once. It was easier to imagine that this had been the fiery grave of a German soldier. It had the look, and the smell, of a vacated tomb.

The ground outside was hard, and yielded no clues.

'You must have been dreaming,' I said to Hobson as we walked away.

'I wasn't, Corporal, honest.' Then, abandoning the attempt

to convince me, he added with more urgency: 'Don't make me stay out here any longer.'

I glanced at my watch. 'It's nearly half past ten anyway. Stay near the guard-room for a few minutes, and I'll send the next man out to relieve you.'

Ten to one. 'The still point of the turning world.' I sat perched on a high stool behind the high desk, under the glare of the electric light. Chalky's footsteps slowly approached, passed, receded, beginning another circle. Earnshaw and Norman snored, irritatingly at different tempos. For a time they would snore alternately, then Norman would slowly begin to overtake Earnshaw, draw level with him, then pass him. Hobson, his blanket drawn over his head to keep out the light, or the ghost, sighed and whimpered in his sleep. Empson's words danced before my blood-shot eyes. I pushed the book aside, and picked up a newspaper which Earnshaw had brought with him. I flipped idly through the crumpled pages: gossip column, woman's page, film starlet stooping to reveal her breasts, competitions. *Win a new Aston Martin or £3000, cash.* Whoever chose the cars in these competitions, I wondered. And if nobody, why not just offer the cash? *Suddenly! A new way of life.* An advertisement showed a young couple in a luxurious bed, watching a television set placed on a shelf at their feet. 'George! Take your hand away. It's *Wagon Train* next.' Well, what odds, if they found it pleasant? An editorial drew my attention.

The Minister for Defence announced in the Commons yesterday that the Government hopes to bring conscription to an end within four years.

The nation is proud of its National Servicemen. They have fought bravely, shoulder to shoulder, with their Regular comrades in Korea, Malaya, Cyprus, Suez. Industry in booming Britain will welcome the labour released by the ending of conscription. Mothers will sleep easier at night.

But this last thought prompts another. National Service has done much to teach the younger generation independence, initiative, responsibility,—qualities which have stood this country in good stead in two World Wars. We must not send the youth of Britain from the barrack-square to the street-corner. Some substitute must be found which will have the same beneficial effects of character-training as National Service . . .

Mentally I phrased a reply: 'I think it will be difficult to find a substitute which will inculcate bad habits, bad language, idleness, slothfulness, drunkenness, and the amiable philosophy of "I'm all right Jack" half so successfully as National Service . . .' But the ignorance of newspapers was invincible. Journalism was another useless, self-compensating activity, like literary research, like soldiering itself.

The leader-writer went on to suggest that an extension of the Outward Bound schools would be the answer. I had nothing against the Outward Bound schools. If people enjoyed impressing the Duke of Edinburgh by scrambling over mountains and sleeping in the open, I would not wish to stop them. Evidently they found it pleasant. But the suggestion that such activities bore any resemblance to National Service struck me as ludicrous. I had never slept in the open, or under canvas, in the whole of my two years; nor, for that matter, had I taken part in any tactical exercise, nor fired a rifle more than twice, not indeed done or learned anything that might have made me the slightest bit more use in time of war than I had been when I first caught the train from King's Cross to Catterick. I had long ceased to feel any resentment about this, but I did rather resent suggestions that anything else was the case.

Yes, I had long since ceased to feel any resentment about National Service. Once one had accepted the fact that the whole thing was pointless and futile, it was easy enough to accommodate oneself to its trivial demands, and to make oneself reasonably comfortable. And yet, if it *was* quite meaningless, why in these last few days did my thoughts revert so insistently to my first weeks at Catterick, as if from them, and their contrast with my existence at Badmore, I hoped to tease out a meaning?

Perhaps it was just the insidious flattery of time, which persuades us that what is about to come to an end must have meant something, must have been significant. Who has left a hospital, in which he has suffered misery, pain and embarrassment, without a sudden, treacherous pang of regret, an irrational surge of affection for the fellow patients who kept him awake with their selfish groans, for the nurses who only got the hypo in properly at the third attempt, for the surgeon who let his wound get infected? I suppose even released convicts feel the same as the prison doors close behind them; and perhaps, too, even the souls winging their way through the gates of purgatory when their time is up.

National Service was like a very long, very tedious journey on the Inner Circle. You boarded the train with a lot of others, and for a while it was very crowded, very uncomfortable; but after a while the crowd thinned, you got a seat, new faces got in, old faces got out; the slogans on the advertisements got tiresomely familiar, but you sat on, until, after a very long time, you got out yourself, at the station where you had originally boarded the train, and were borne by the escalator back into the light and air. It was natural, then, that as you approached your destination, you should try to connect the end of your journey with the beginning, try to recall all the shapes and forms of humanity that had shoved and jostled and brawled and snored in the narrow, swaying compartment. Fallowfield, more like a seminarian than a cadet, Peterson with his Old Etonian smile, Gordon Kemp, good-humoured and generous; Hardcastle squaring up to Mike's bare white torso over Percy's kneeling form; little Barnes recommending *The Lady Of The Lake*; Baker, his face contorted by a rictus of anger; Mason, conducting his sexual seminars in the overheated classroom. Many were nameless: the mentally deficient shambling happily out of Amiens Camp in civilian clothes, the youth reading out the letter from the girl who had jilted him, the soldier—Jones, was it?—searching fruitlessly in the sodden grass at my side for the fifth shell-case. An endless succession of figures, many blurred by time, rose up and passed across my mind like the ghosts in *Macbeth*. Where were they all now? One of them was snoring only ten feet away. But Norman, oddly enough, provided no link between my first and last days in the Army. Norman at Badmore was a different creature from Norman at Catterick—like a strange, sinister shape in a child's darkened bedroom, which the morning light reveals as a harmless, if ugly piece of furniture. Where were the rest now? All, like me, awaiting release, polishing their boots for the last time, pushing their last guard, gloating over their comrades?

No, not all. Some would not be released. Percy would not be released. Gordon Kemp, shot in the back as he walked down a sun-lit street in Cyprus, would not be released. And Fallowfield had already been released: the strain of the officer cadet course had been too much for him; he had taken an over-dose of aspirin, but they had found him in time, and he had been medically discharged. Ironic, that he, of all people, should have gained his freedom, the freedom he did not want. As for the rest, where were they now?

I did not really care. They had no importance for me, except that at one time they had formed fragments of a mosaic in which a particular experience of my own had been delineated. Now I stooped to wipe away the dust of two years, and reveal the forgotten faces; but as the years passed I would tread over them again, more and more indifferent to the picture that was slowly disappearing beneath my feet. There was only one visage that would take some time and effort to efface, that stared up at me like a gaunt Byzantine saint, and would continue to stare. It would be difficult to lay that ghost.

The telephone rang. A routine call from V.P. guard-room. I walked slowly across the room to answer it.

'Montgomery guard-room. Corporal Browne speaking.'

The voice that replied was breathless and excited. 'This is Sergeant Mayhew, V.P. guard-room. Someone's just got away with a truck.'

'What?'

'A truck. Somebody's just stolen a bloody truck. They got into the hangars, and drove it past the guards.'

'Who did?'

'How do I know for Christ's sake. You'd better send up the Armed Picket.'

'Hold on a minute.' I went over to Earnshaw and shook his shoulder. He surfaced grudgingly from sleep.

'Whatisit?'

'V.P. is on the phone. Someone's stolen a truck. They want us to send up the Armed Picket.' He stared at me for a moment, then leapt to his feet.

'Well, don't just stand there. Press the bloody bell.'

He ran across the room to press the bell himself. We listened, but heard nothing.

'Bloody thing must have broken. Go and wake them up. And be quick about it.' He seized the phone and began talking excitedly to Mayhew. I ran out of the guard-room to the Armed Picket hut. I switched on the light and hammered on a tin locker with my fist.

'Wake up, wake up!'

Some of them sat up in their beds, blinking in the light and rubbing their eyes. I located the N.C.O. with some difficulty, and woke him up.

'This is a bloody game,' he grumbled, pulling on his boots.

'It's no game. Somebody's stolen a truck from V.P.'

'What are we supposed to do about it? They may be half way to Salisbury by now.'

'I don't know, but you'd better get cracking.'

For fifteen minutes confusion reigned. Most of the soldiers had taken their boots off, and fumbled awkwardly with boot-laces. The N.C.O. couldn't find the key to the rack in which the rifles were locked, and in the end we had to break it open. At last the rifles were distributed, and the Armed Picket drove off in the duty truck. Lightning flickered, and there was a loud thunderclap. Running back to the guard-room I bumped into Chalky.

'What's up?'

'Truck pinched from V.P.'

'Blimey! Somebody's gernna be in trouble. 'Ere, 'ave you got a ground-sheet? It's gernna rain.'

'Haven't time.' I ran on.

Earnshaw was still on the phone when I re-entered the guard-room. 'I'm trying to get the Adjutant,' he said. 'But he doesn't seem to be at the Mess.'

'The Armed Picket's gone off.'

'Took enough bloody time didn't they?' Still holding the phone to his ear, he turned towards Norman and Hobson, who, strangely, were still asleep.

'Wake those lazy sods up.'

As I moved towards them there was a knock on the door.

'That's probably the Adjutant. Let him in.'

I opened the door. There was nothing there except my shadow, thrown forward across the veranda. I stepped over the threshold, and an arm hit me in the throat like an iron bar, throttling me and dragging me sideways. A gag was wound round my face, and the voice of the Adjutant whispered in my ear, 'Relax, Corporal.'

The Adjutant and Fotherby stood together in the middle of the guard-room, wearing sweaters and plimsolls. They were breathing heavily, and their blackened faces were runnelled with sweat, but they radiated cocky triumph. The Adjutant was trying to look stern, but he kept grinning at Fotherby. Chalky and I stood together nursing our throats and mouths. Norman and Hobson were trying to button up their uniforms as unobtrusively as possible. Sergeant Earnshaw was sitting on the end of a bed, looking sick.

'Feel all right, Sergeant?' asked the Adjutant.

Earnshaw muttered something about his heart.

'You put up a good fight, anyway, Sergeant. Not like some of the other so-called soldiers in this unit.' He swept the rest of us with a contemptuous glance. 'You, Corporal, for instance,' he said to me. 'Do you usually open the guard-room door without finding out who's outside?'

I could not trust myself to reply.

'Anyone would think you were playing Postman's Knock.' Fotherby sniggered. The Adjutant turned to Chalky. 'And you, Trooper. We watched you for several minutes, and you didn't look to your right or your left. As for you two——' Norman hung his head and Hobson quaked—'We might have taken over the whole bloody camp without waking *you* up.' He began to strut up and down the guard-room. 'Well, I'm twenty pounds richer now. I bet the C.O. that with one man,—from my own regiment of course' (he grinned at Fotherby), 'I could steal a truck from V.P. and capture the Montgomery guard-room; and I have. I shouldn't think he'll be in a very good mood when you all see him tomorrow morning.'

There was a vivid flash of lightning, followed by a resounding thunderclap; then the sky burst over our heads like a swollen paper bag. The rain dinned on the roof, and hissed on the concrete outside the guard-room. Almost at once it searched out a leak in the roof, and water began to drip on to the floor. For some moments we were all struck dumb by the deluge. Then, as the intensity of the torrent diminished slightly, Earnshaw said anxiously:

'You're not charging us, sir?'

'I shan't charge *you*, Sergeant, since you put up such a good show. But the guards who let us get away with the truck, you Trooper'—he nodded to Chalky, and I froze as he turned to me—'and you, Corporal: you were all negligent, and you'll have to answer for it. The security in this unit is disgraceful, and I shouldn't be surprised if there were a regimental inquiry into this business.'

I struggled to control the questions, expostulations and protests which seethed within me. Exasperation at the humiliation and absurdity of the whole affair struggled with anxiety, rapidly turning to dread, about the effects it might have on my release. My timetable was tight. If I did not get away on Wednesday Pauline and I would miss the charter flight early on Thursday morning, and there was no other flight. My mind wandered off into calculations of possible alternatives, whether the airline would rebate the fares, if so, at what notice. Angrily I recalled my thoughts to the main issue. What would be the result of this stupid prank of the Adjutant's? Probably I would lose a stripe. That wouldn't worry me, and shouldn't delay me unduly. It might be all over tomorrow. But it might not. And there was that ominous reference to a regimental inquiry. Would they keep me back for it? Could they keep me back for it? In any event they might easily keep me back till Thursday, which was the statutory day for release. I could not keep silent any longer. The Adjutant was on the phone, trying to get the operator.

'Excuse me, sir,' I said.

'Well?'

'I'm due for release on Wednesday, sir. Will this affect it? You see, I've booked——'

'I really couldn't say, Corporal.' He turned back to the phone, tapping the receiver-rest impatiently. Fotherby was looking at me with undisguised delight. The Adjutant said:

'This phone seems to be dead, Sergeant Earnshaw.'

'It was all right a few minutes ago, sir.'

'Must be the storm. Corporal, will you cut along to the Orderly Room and use the phone there, if it's working. Ring up V.P. guard-room, and explain the situation. Tell Sergeant Mayhew to round up the Armed Picket, and send them back here. I want to see the N.C.O. in charge.' He turned to Fotherby. 'How long did they take to get out, Sergeant-Major?'

'Well, we were down here a good ten minutes before they left, sir. So I should say about twenty minutes altogether.'

'Disgraceful.'

'The alarm bell wasn't working, sir,' put in Earnshaw. 'Corporal Browne had to go and wake them up.'

'It was working earlier this evening. Anyway, that's no excuse. It could only have made a couple of minutes' difference. All right, Corporal, that's all.'

A curtain of water confronted me as I closed the guard-room door. I had no cape, but I stepped heedlessly into the deluge. The rain was as warm as blood. The great blunt drops bruised my face, ran down my neck, soaked into my khaki as if it were blotting-paper, boiled and bubbled at my feet. I splashed my way mechanically towards the Orderly Room, brooding on the sudden blow to my plans. It was not, however, the particular problems which had arisen which chafed me most: it was the general sense that the machinery which had been silkily responsive to my touch for so long had suddenly run amok. I had looked forward with pleasurable expectation to my last days at Badmore: I would leave the Army in a mood of relaxed enjoyment, my finger-tips on the controls until the last moment. It would be a ceremony, a ritual, trivial in its forms perhaps, but highly significant in its import, for its climax would be the transubstantiation of the soldier into the free man. But now I knew that whatever happened, even if I did contrive to get away in time to catch the plane, my last hours at Badmore would not be spent in the serene enjoyment of this ceremony. They would be spent in anxiety, and doubt, and helplessness,—emotions I had thought I had left behind me at Catterick.

I had to knock several times on the Orderly Room door: the duty clerk, incredibly, seemed to have slept through the storm. Eventually he opened the door. Yawning and rubbing his eyes he asked me foolishly:

'Is it raining?'

I stood in the doorway in my sodden uniform, a puddle spreading rapidly at my feet.

'No, someone's pissing off the roof,' I replied. 'I want to use your phone. The guard-room one's packed up.'

I squeezed past the camp-bed which was set up in the middle of the office.

' 'Ere, mind me sheets.'

Ignoring his protests, I sat down on the end of the bed to make the phone-call. V.P. guard-room was still in a state of considerable perturbation, increased by their inability to communicate with the Montgomery guard-room. It took me some time to explain the situation to Sergeant Mayhew, to answer his questions, and to listen to his oaths.

'The Armed Picket's out on the moors,' he said. 'It'll take me some time to round them up.'

'O.K. I'll tell the Adjutant.'

'I'm going to get fuggin' soaked looking for them.'

'You won't be the only one.'

' 'Ere, you've left a bloody great wet patch on my bed,' said the duty clerk, as I put down the phone, and rose to my feet. Then, curiosity winning over his sense of grievance, he pestered me about the night's events. I gave him a few short, surly answers, and left.

As I approached the guard-room my scepticism about supernatural phenomena received a severe jolt. A flash of lightning revealed through the sheeting rain a figure in a long, belted coat, that answered disconcertingly to Hobson's description of the ghost. I halted, my heart pounding as loudly as the thunder. I stood peering through the darkness. Lightning flickered again, but the figure had vanished. A few more steps, however, took me in sight of the guard-room, and I saw through its windows a tableau that taxed my credulity more than any ghost. The Adjutant and Fotherby had their backs to me, and their hands up. Between them I could see a masked man by the door, holding a Sten gun.

I was congratulated for the coolness with which I acted subsequently, but no one knows how much that coolness was due to the simple desire to understand what was happening. The events of that one night had been more bizarre and dramatic than all my nights at Badmore put together. I was too numbed to act impulsively.

Cautiously I skirted the guard-room, and reached the veranda of the Q.M.'s offices, which faced one side of it. Hidden in the shadows, I stared into the guard-room. The rain, drumming on the veranda roof, prevented any sound which might have carried through the windows of the guard-room from reaching me. It was rather like watching a film when the sound-track has broken down: violence enacted and emotions registered in a comical silence. They were all there as I had left them in the guard-room, with one addition, a figure in pyjamas whom I identified as the security man from the armoury. A raid was in progress, in earnest this time; and the raiders had struck a most lucky moment, with the Armed Picket dispersed over the water-logged moors a mile away, and the telephone out of action,—but this last must be their doing, I realized, and the failure of the alarm bell. The ghost too, he must have been one of them.

Another man, also with a scarf round his face, came into the guard-room and seemed to say something to the man with the Sten gun. The latter nodded, and motioned the Adjutant and the rest towards the cells. His companion took the keys, neatly labelled for his convenience, from the rack on the wall, and proceeded to lock the captives in the cells.

I deliberated as to what I should do. (It was only much later that I wondered why I had assumed that I ought to do something.) There were soldiers sleeping within fifty yards of me, but what use would they be, unarmed and fuddled with sleep, even if I managed to wake them in time? There was a phone in the Q.M.'s office, but the door was locked. The nearest accessible phone was the one in the Orderly Room, but by the time I got there they would be gone.

I slipped off my gaiters and boots, and padded along the veranda until I was out of sight of the interior of the guard-room. Then I scuttled quickly across the space between the Q.M.'s offices and the armoury. Between the armoury and the bedding store there was a narrow, noisome passage. I squeezed my way to the end, lowered myself reluctantly into the mud, and peered round. I saw the dim shapes of a Bedford van and, beside it, a Ford Consul. Noises of heavy objects being loaded came from the rear of the van. The light outside the armoury had been turned off, but a flash of lightning illuminated the vehicles. I shrank back into the passage. The Bedford van was grey, the Consul black. I protruded my head again like a tortoise. The thunder rumbled. I waited impatiently for another flash of lightning, and when it came glimpsed the number plate of the Bedford: MUP 5—I had not seen any more. I waited for another flash, but the door of the van was slammed, and I heard voices and hurried footsteps. I withdrew into the passage, and slithered backwards until I judged it safe to stand up and turn round. The engines started, and the vehicles moved off. I ran back to the Q.M.'s veranda from the end of which I could see the camp entrance. The Bedford turned left, the Ford right, and both accelerated out of sight.

I ran back to the Orderly Room in my socks, muttering to myself: 'MUP 5, MUP 5 . . .'

'For fuggsake, you again?' protested the clerk. 'Where are your boots?' he added in astonishment, as I squelched past him and seized the phone.

'Get me the C.O.'s home telephone number,' I said.

First I phoned the police, then Brigade, then the C.O. The C.O. said he would be round right away.

I padded slowly back to the guard-room. The rain was easing. My mind, which had been suspended through the time of action, began to function reflectively again. The agreeable thought came to me that I might gain some credit for what I had done, sufficient to gloss over the unfortunate incident earlier in the night, and to facilitate my prompt release from the Army. In any case the minor matter would be submerged in the major, and the Adjutant was unlikely to proceed with his threatened charge. He would have quite a lot of explaining to do himself, in fact, when the C.O. arrived and found him locked in a cell with Norman and Hobson, his face blackened, and dressed in civilian clothes.

I went first to the Q.M.'s veranda, where I took off my socks, wrung them out, put them on again, and donned my boots. I heard the C.O.'s car approaching.

'Well, Corporal Browne, you did a fine job of work for the Army in your last week. The police had no difficulty in tracing those cars with the description you gave them. And you did well to observe the directions they took. In fact you acted with remarkable initiative if I may say so, remarkable initiative.'

I smiled modestly back at the C.O., and murmured something deprecatory. The writers of the schoolboys' stories I had read in childhood had done their work well; I could think of no other reason why I should experience such pleasure at being the hero of the hour. It satisfied an appetite I had not known I possessed. The morning sun shone brightly into the C.O.'s office, bleaching the carpet and the drawn face of the Adjutant. It had been a trying night for him. The raiders had taken away the keys to the cells and it had been two hours before the duplicates had been found.

'When are you due for release, Corporal?'

'Tomorrow, sir.'

'Hmm. Trouble is you'll probably be required by the police in connection with this business.'

I started worrying again.

'I hope not, sir. I've arranged to go on holiday to Majorca on Thursday. My plane leaves early on Thursday morning.'

'Oh. Well, we can't let this interfere with your holiday, can we. How long will you be away?'

'A fortnight, sir.'

'Hmm. Just a minute.'

He picked up the phone and asked the operator to get him the Chief Constable of the county, whom he addressed as

'Fred'. I began to relax as the conversation proceeded, and the C.O. put down the receiver with a triumphant smile.

'Well that's fixed, Corporal. You won't be needed in person until after you come back. In the meantime I've arranged for you to make a statement to the police this afternoon in the town. My driver will run you down there this afternoon. You'll be able to get off in good time tomorrow morning.'

'Thank you, sir. I'm most grateful.'

'It's a pleasure, Corporal. Badmore would have been the laughing stock of the Army if those I.R.A. blighters had got away. Isn't that right, Geoffrey?'

The Adjutant nodded sourly. I saluted, and turned. As I crossed the room to the door the C.O. said:

'I think this is your line of country, Geoffrey. One of the blighters was a deserter apparently. The police want to know what——'

I turned slowly back to face them.

'Excuse me, sir.'

'Yes, Corporal?'

'The deserter you mentioned. . . . Do you know his name by any chance?'

'Er, Brady I think. Yes, that's right, Brady.'

'Not Michael Brady?'

'Yes that's right, Michael Brady. Why what's the matter man? You're white as a sheet!'

'I'm all right, sir. It's just that I knew him once.'

'Who, Brady? I hope he's no friend of yours. He's in a lot of trouble.'

'No, not what you might call a friend, sir. I'm sorry, sir. Excuse me.'

I saluted weakly and left the room under their curious gaze. As I negotiated the corridors leading to the 'A' Squadron offices, a hand touched me on the shoulder. I jumped.

'Take it easy! Got a guilty conscience or somethink?' The Post Corporal was grinning at me. 'Letter for you. Blimey, you do look queer.'

'I'm all right.'

He held the long mauve envelope under his nose before passing it to me.

'Smells nice. Some people 'ave all the luck.'

Instead of returning to my office I went to the lavatory, and sat in a cool, smelly closet to think. Already my mind had instinctively connected certain facts to form a picture of Mike's progress since he had deserted. Somehow he had got to Ireland, no doubt with the aid of that mysterious Italian to whom I had posted Mike's letter. At this moment it flashed upon me that 'Gordiano Bruno' was a pseudonym for Peter Nolan, the Irishman at O'Connell's. Bruno of Nola! It was a favourite pun of Joyce's. And Nolan was just the type to be associated with the I.R.A., probably a member of it. Mike had been smuggled across to Ireland, and there had become involved with the I.R.A. Why? There was his family background of militant nationalism. But surely anyone of Mike's intelligence could see that nowadays the I.R.A. was nothing but a bad joke,—and a criminally dangerous one at that? Was he still, then, bent on revenging Percy's death, accepting the I.R.A. as a convenient tool, as the Jacobean revenger employed the trivial squabbles of the rest of society to encompass his own obsessive ends?

These queries were forced to the perimeter of my mind by the increasing pressure of another thought. I stared with horrified fascination at the fact that I, of all people, had un- wittingly betrayed Mike, in the one act of my military career that had exceeded the minimal performance of duty. Some malicious providence had thrust me, with a powerful hand in the small of the back, into a double treachery: to Mike him- self, and to that code of contempt for the Army which we had once shared. Or was it merely the working-out of a treachery I had practised ever since Mike had deserted, in my subtle conquest of Pauline, and my easy self-adjustment to Badmore?

I still held Pauline's letter in my hand. I opened the envelope, and read the neat, round handwriting.

My Dearest Jonathan,

I thought I had to write, although I shall be seeing you so soon, just to tell you that you really mustn't be jealous about Mike, because honestly I never think of him at all. He was my first boy- friend, and if I'd been more experienced I'd have known that we could never get on together, and I'd have stopped the thing before it got started. In fact it never got very far, although it dragged on a long time. As far as I'm concerned, he's gone out of my life, and I don't particularly want to see him again. I thought I would write and get this off my chest because I think that there's been a certain strain between us about him. I've noticed that once or twice when the conversation seemed to be moving in that direction, you suddenly stopped talking. So it's perhaps a good job that we've had it out, and it can be forgotten. Don't let's talk about it any more.

I'm so looking forward to Wednesday, and of course I'm terribly excited about our holiday. I never thought Mummy and Daddy would agree, but they trust you! What do you think? I've bought a bikini! Well it's not really a bikini, but it's a two-piece, and rather daring for me. I hope you like it. Anyway, I'll try it on for you on Wednesday night and you can tell me if you think it's decent, I believe the Spaniards are a bit prudish . . .

I crumpled the letter in my fist and dropped it absently between my legs into the w.c. bowl.

After a long wrangle the Inspector said:

'Well, all right, Corporal. It's all against regulations, but I'll give you five minutes. Sergeant, take him down will you?'

'Yes, sir.'

'I will be alone with him, won't I?'

'Absolutely out of the question, Corporal. I'm permitting more than I should already.'

'Yes, I know. I'm very grateful. All right then.'

The Visitors' Room was a cross between a confessional and a Post Office. I sat facing the wire grille and waited for Mike. After all my efforts to see him, now I could not think what I would say. I heard footsteps approaching the door behind the grille.

I had asked the Sergeant to give Mike my name, so that time would not be wasted while he recovered from the surprise. But his face still wore an expression of astonishment as he entered the room.

'Jon! What are you doing here? I——'

The sergeant broke in with some formula about speaking clearly and other regulations, but I scarcely heard him. I too was taken by surprise,—by Mike's appearance. His hair was black, and he wore a heavy black moustache, like a French workman's, which obscured his upper lip. It made him look much older. Foolishly, the first question I asked him was:

'What happened to your hair?'

'Dyed. But what on earth are you doing here, Jon? How did you know . . . ?'

'I was at the camp you raided last night. I was on guard.'

He whistled softly.

'We knew there should have been another N.C.O. I was prowling round looking for him. My God, Jon, I might have coshed you.'

'It would have been better for you if you had. I was watching all the time. I contacted the police at once. But I didn't know you were one of them.'

There was a pause while Mike took it in.

'It's all right, Jon. You were only doing your duty.'

'Oh fugg my duty.'

The sergeant stirred restively on his seat a few yards away.

'I see you've got a couple of stripes,' said Mike. 'You must be getting near the end of your time mustn't you?'

'Yes. Tomorrow.'

'Tomorrow?' He was silent. What was going on behind those pale blue eyes? It was too painful to speculate.

'Mike, I must know, if you can tell me,'—I shot a glance at the sergeant. 'Why did you get mixed up with that lot?'

'The Irish Republican Army?' He rolled the syllables with ironic unction. 'It's a long story. They got me out of England, as you probably realized. They hid me in a convent for some time,—that's another long story. I was sort of automatically enlisted. There wasn't much else I could do. Funny really: out of one Army and into another. There's not much to choose between them, I can tell you. Mind you, as long as it was just a matter of breaking into armouries, and making the Army look silly, I didn't mind. But a few weeks ago some fools blew up a telephone booth in Armagh, and some people were hurt. That was enough for me. We made a deal, that if I helped them with this raid, they'd get me to South America. The rest you know.'

'Your time's up,' said the Sergeant. Mike stood up.

'Jon.'

'Yes?

'You haven't seen Pauline lately, have you?'

'Yes. I see her quite a lot actually.'

'How is she?'

'She's fine.'

'Give her my . . . best wishes. I'm sorry I haven't been able to write. It was too risky. Perhaps I'll write now.'

'Come along,' said the sergeant.

'I shouldn't do that, Mike. It might upset her.'

He looked at me for a moment, then said gently:

'All right, Jon. You know best.'

'I'll write and explain,' I exclaimed desperately, as the sergeant took him away. 'I'll come and see you again.'

As the door closed he lifted his hand in a gesture of . . .

. . . of what? Reassurance? Dismissal? Benediction? Would I ever know?

I leaned from the corridor window, and took my last look at Badmore. The guard's whistle blew, and the wooden platform of the halt began to slide backwards. A mile away the huts of the camp clung to the side of a hill. Behind them, tanks crawled like sleepy bugs over the moors.

A train had carried me into the Army, and a train was bearing me away. In the compartments behind me tweedy middle-aged travellers listlessly turned the pages of their magazines, yawned, nibbled chocolate, checked the progress of the train by their watches. For them it was a dull, unimportant journey to London. How could they know how momentous it was to me, how strange it felt to be travelling at all on a Wednesday morning, wearing civilian clothes . . .

But I had no enthusiasm to pursue these ideas. I had looked forward to this journey for two years, but I could not conceal from myself that I was not enjoying it; and the reason was not hard to seek. Reassurance? Dismissal? Benediction?

The train gathered speed. I thrust my head into the blast,

and looked back along the foreshortened line of carriages. The camp was still visible, low, black and ugly in the August sunshine. Beyond, the spires of the county town came into view. Beneath them my friend was immured.

'Ginger, you're barmy,' I murmured into the slipstream, which tore the syllables from my lips, carried them away with a paper bag that fluttered from a distant window. The train had reached a bend, and the curving carriages elbowed Badmore and the town out of sight. I withdrew my head into the corridor.

My friend. 'No, not what you might call a friend, sir.' For what friendship could exist between two people whose temperaments and destinies were so opposed? My temperament was prudence and my destiny success, as surely as Mike's were foolhardiness and failure. The Army had revealed our disparity with the precision of litmus.

'Excuse me, sir,' said an obsequious voice.

I pressed back to allow the restaurant-car attendant to pass. 'Morning coffee now being served!' he called out.

Mike still retained the knack of draining the sap of my own self-satisfaction: I had no zest for the journey, and the successful life that awaited me at the terminus seemed as heavy a sentence as that which awaited Mike. But I checked myself: was that not a mere sentimental hyperbole? For success was bound to be more *pleasant* than detention in a military prison. My own philosophy barred me from expiation. Even the wild idea of renouncing Pauline had to be rejected as soon as it occurred; for Pauline wanted *me*, not Mike. And one could not blame her. Mike was no hero, he was barmy, and there was no place for him. The most that could be said for him was that he was 'innocent', as they called barmy people once; and if the supernatural paraphernalia of his faith turned out to be true, and we found ourselves standing together at the bar of judgment, I knew who would blink and squint most in that dazzling light. If that happened, would Mike feel the same discomfort on my account as I did on his? Was Lazarus distressed because he could not moisten the parched tongue of Dives with a single drop of water?

Questions, questions . . . one could not forbear to ask them, tossing the pennies in the air, crying 'Heads' or 'Tails'; but they all fell behind a wall that could only be climbed in one direction. Meanwhile there was the coffee to be sipped in the quaint Edwardian comfort of the Pullman car, the cigarette to be savoured as the familiar landmarks between London and Badmore flashed past in the preferred order, Pauline to be greeted with an easy kiss at Waterloo, the mild dissipations of a Mediterranean holiday to be enjoyed, another degree to be acquired, a middle-class wedding to be arranged, a semi-detached house to be purchased, a carefully-planned family to be raised . . .

Before taking a seat in the restaurant car, I went to the w.c. and flushed Henry's parting gift down the plug.

EPILOGUE

I REMEMBER revising that penultimate paragraph, that vision of my future with its curious mixture of smugness and guilt, a few hours before Pauline shattered it beyond repair with the news that she was pregnant. That was about two months after our return from Majorca, two months spent in absorbed contemplation and revision of my story. Curious, how intricately that story is woven into the texture of my life,—not only in the experiences it records, but in itself. Michael, for instance, sitting on his pot beside me as I write, owes his existence to it in a way.

Almost as soon as we arrived in Majorca, Pauline was stricken with severe food poisoning, and confined to bed for several days. Three times a day I visited her darkened room, where she lay beneath a single sheet, looking wan and grey, her hair streaky with perspiration. She confided, with a feeble attempt at coquetry, that she had nothing on beneath the sheet, but I found myself unmoved by the information. Between these visits to the sick-room I was left to my own devices. I did not enjoy myself very much. The diversions of the beach soon palled: I am not a good swimmer, and a rash exposure of my white body to the sun resulted in a painful sun-burn. It was too hot to walk for long, and in order to sit down in the shade it seemed necessary to buy an unwanted drink at a café. Pauline spoke a little Spanish, but I had none; and I found my inability to communicate a constant embarrassment and irritation.

I tried to will myself into enjoying the long-awaited holiday by reminding myself that I was free; but I felt less at ease in the glaring gaudy, hedonistic resort than I had been in the Army. The dusty offices of Badmore, the gloomy huts of Catterick, tugged at my thoughts with a strength like nostalgia. And at the core of my un-easiness was of course Mike, silently reproaching me from his cell in the county gaol.

I had postponed telling Pauline about Mike, fearing that it might spoil our holiday. It became more and more difficult to tell her as the days passed, though the pressure of my unshared thoughts on the subject increased at a swifter rate. On the fourth day I bought a notebook and began to write. I covered fifty pages and completely forgot to visit Pauline at the usual hour.

She emerged from her sick-room to find a very different escort from the one who had brought her to Majorca; or rather, no escort at all. I told her vaguely that I was writing a novel about National Service, and at first she was impressed and intrigued. But when I declined to answer her inquiries, and more particularly when she realized that the book took precedence over her and her entertainment, she displayed a natural resentment. She was panting to make up for the lost days of her holiday, and though I obediently followed her from *pension* to beach, and from beach to café, the soiled, dog-eared notebook always accompanied us, arousing as much venomous jealousy in Pauline as if it had been another woman.

'I don't know why you bothered to come on holiday with me,' she would complain sulkily. 'Why didn't you stay at home with your old book?'

On such occasions I would relent, put aside my manuscript, and cajole her back into a good humour by taking a boat trip or fooling around in the tepid water. But before long I would relapse into abstracted silence, as some detail I had been searching for came welling up from the memory, and my fingers would be itching to curl themselves round a pen again. Poor Pauline! What a rotten holiday she had,—and the last Continental holiday she'll have for a long time too. On our last evening in Majorca she burst into tears and said it was the worst holiday she had ever had, and I don't think she was exaggerating.

It happened that I had just brought the book to a tentative conclusion that very afternoon, and was experiencing that euphoric state of relaxation and relief which follows literary creation: the intelligence and imagination are exhausted, but the other faculties and senses awaken, and one feels benevolent to the rest of the world. I took Pauline to a sort of night-club and blued the remainder of my pesetas on the best dinner and champagne that the place could provide. I even shuffled round the floor in a tipsy imitation of the other couples, and became demonstratively amorous as we walked back to the *pension* along the beach, where palm-trees, moonlight and gentle waves belatedly exerted the romantic charm about which I had heard and read so much. Pauline, demoralized and disarmed by my erratic behaviour, responded with starved eagerness, and I ended the night in her bed. There, after much effort and with little pleasure, I succeeded in rupturing her hymen, and planted in her the sperm which became the small boy now emitting such an offensive odour at my feet. Afterwards as we lay together, sticky, limp and dissatisfied, I chain-smoked and told her all about Mike. I left her silently weeping; but whether this was because of Mike, or the loss of her maidenhead, or just physical pain, I did not discover.

The next morning she had rallied, and I was the unhappy one, brooding on the possible consequences of the previous night, and cursing the impulse that had deprived me of the security of Henry's parting gift. But Pauline said that the date was all right; and once back in England I became immersed in the revision of my book, an occupation which pushed Pauline, and all thoughts of the future, to the rim of my mind.

Pauline's announcement that she was pregnant induced in me what most people would call a nervous breakdown, and some perhaps a spiritual crisis. The neurotic symptoms I developed were, I realize now, merely defensive mechanisms designed to postpone action. The only possible course of action was to abandon my postgraduate research, marry Pauline, and get a job. I did not want to do any of these things. Then Mike's long-delayed trial came up.

My relationship with Mike had been a fuse laid in the bed-rock of my self-complacency, which had been smouldering for two years, occasionally disturbing me as I sniffed its acrid smoke. Now it detonated, and with explosive force the possibility presented itself to me, for the first time in my life, of doing something positive and un-selfish. Looking at Mike in the dock, gaunt and wild-eyed, as he listened to the judge's ominous summing-up, I wondered despairingly what would become of him. Whatever sentence he received, it would no doubt be lengthened by many insubordinations. Perhaps he would even try to escape again. He would never find rest or peace. Because he was barmy. Then my idea came to me, and I smiled broadly at him. He must have thought *I* was barmy at that moment.

I married Pauline hastily—a quiet, off-white wedding at her parish church,—and as soon as I discovered which prison Mike had been sent to, we moved down here and rented this narrow cottage. The local secondary modern was glad to take me on, since teachers are not attracted to this damp, isolated place, where the local industry is a prison. On the first Sunday of every month for the past three years, I have visited Mike—except for one or two occasions recently, when I managed to persuade Mrs Brady to resume relations with her black-sheep son. Mr Brady, who is secretly rather proud of his son's criminal record, had made the long journey from Hastings a few times before, to visit Mike with me; but when he brought his wife I had to yield up my place, as only two visitors are allowed. I was strangely miserable on those two Sundays when I missed seeing Mike.

Crash! Another plate has bit the stone flags in the scullery. Being pregnant again makes Pauline clumsy, but she's nervous too at the prospect of entertaining Mike to lunch. For she has not seen him for nearly five years. She always made the baby the excuse for not accompanying me to the prison; but her reasons must surely lie deeper. Perhaps she thinks Mike is still in love with her. But I cannot very well tell her that he is not, still less that he is unlikely to fall in love again when he sees her as she is now. Another crash! But then I'm nervous too. I began and abandoned three books this morning before I unearthed this manuscript from a drawer. In only twenty minutes Mike will be standing outside the prison gates in his cheap new suit, inhaling the sweet smell of freedom. He didn't want me to meet him.

I hope Mike will agree to stay with us for a while. He has been the focal point of my life for so long that I am curiously jealous of the rest of the world with whom he will shortly resume contact. Also I feel a certain panic when I reflect that he will no longer need my support. It is not a question of what he will do without me, but of what I will do without him. Now he is free, and I am shackled,—by a wife and family I do not greatly love, and by a career that I find no more than tolerable.

I had always assumed that we would move back to London when my 'mission' was completed, and that I would pick up my research on the justly neglected eighteenth-century antiquarian and bibliographer whom I chose as my thesis topic. But now I am not so sure. It seems to me that the decision which I must make now is at least as important as the one that brought me here three years ago. The effort of combining a full-time teaching job with part-time research would be merely another excuse (Mike's welfare is the current one) for fulfilling no more than the statutory requirements of a husband

and father. Pauline, absorbed and distracted by maternity, does not seem aware of any lack in our marriage, but she will be eventually. I must forestall her. Somehow I must learn to love her. And it seems to me that it will be easier to do so here, than in London.

And besides, I have become strangely attached to this place, where the fogs come down in October, and scarcely disperse until Spring. In this remote community, besieged by nature for half the year, I feel I could build a life of modest usefulness. The lectures I gave at the prison have aroused my interest in remedial work. Since Mike began to study externally for his degree the idea has caught on, and several of the prisoners are preparing to sit for the G.C.E. Mike was fortunate to be tried by the civil authorities, and to be sent to a prison with so enlightened a governor.

It will be difficult to explain to Pauline why I want to stay here; but if, as seems likely, they offer me the deputy headship of the school next year, we might be able to afford a house with a bathroom and indoor lavatory, two amenities that would bribe Pauline to do almost anything.

Twelve o'clock striking. I must put a clean nappy on Michael, lay the table, and get out the cider. And the Guinness.

AFTERWORD

A QUESTION that novelists are frequently asked is: how does the idea
for a novel arise—in what shape or form does it begin? As far as I am
concerned, it begins with an intuition that some segment of my own
experience has a kind of thematic unity, and a more than private
significance, which might be explored through a fictional story. The
novel, in other words, begins as a short answer to the question that will
eventually be asked of it, as of every novel: what is it *about*?

Ginger, You're Barmy is a very straightforward case in point. It is
'about' peacetime National Service, as an institution and as an
experience—one which most young men born between, say, 1928 and
1941, underwent. Considering how common an experience it was, it
is perhaps surprising how few postwar novels dealt directly with
National Service, especially if you discount those set in places where
conscript soldiers were involved in actual combat, such as Malaya,
Korea, Suez. Such novels belong to the literature of war. For the
vast majority of National Servicemen, the likelihood of actually
fighting for one's country seemed infinitely remote, and the day-to-
day routine of military life, empty for the most part of any useful
occupation, did not inspire one with a sense of urgent readiness for
patriotic duty. This was why most National Servicemen resented,
with varying degrees of bitterness, the confiscation of their freedom
for two of the best years of their lives. The Services, and successive
governments, failed abysmally to give any kind of positive or con-
structive meaning to National Service. Those of us who did it felt,
not that we were being trained to be useful in a national emergency
(what training we received could have been accomplished in three
months or less), but that we were being maintained as a cheap
standing army, occupied with futile and demeaning tasks.

Of course, not everybody took so jaundiced a view. For many,
National Service was a chance to get away from home, see foreign
countries, and indulge in dissipation, at a period when such things

were harder to accomplish than they are today. For those qualified to become officers, and prepared to compete for the privilege, a National Service commission could be a useful addition to one's *curriculum vitae*. But for the vast majority National Service was an irksome suspension of freedom, rather like being forcibly compelled, as an adult, to go back to school—a particularly bad type of boarding school, staffed by brutal, snobbish, cynical and incompetent masters.

The majority of National Servicemen had, in fact, not long been out of school, and many came straight from it, so they adjusted without too much difficulty to being treated by officers and N.C.O.s with bullying condescension. Those, however, who had deferred National Service in order to do a university degree, and were called up at the age of twenty-plus, having achieved a certain amount of intellectual maturity and independence of mind, were more likely to feel outrage at the indignities of Basic Training and despair at the prospect of two years' servitude stretching beyond it—especially if, for one reason or another, the prospect of securing some creature comforts by means of a commission was closed to them. *Ginger, You're Barmy* presents National Service from precisely this perspective, for it was my own.

Like my narrator, Jonathan Browne, I was drafted into the Royal Armoured Corps shortly after obtaining my B.A. in English Language and Literature at London University (in August, 1955 to be precise). I received my Basic Training, and Trade Training, at Catterick Camp, and was subsequently posted to the permanent staff of the R.A.C.'s Driving and Maintenance School at Bovington Camp, Dorset, where I worked as a clerk until my release in August 1957, by which time I had attained the rank of Acting Corporal. In the interests of authenticity (and whatever weaknesses the novel may have, I do not think it can be faulted on that score) *Ginger, You're Barmy* cleaves very closely to the contours of my own military service. Although the story of the three main characters is fictional, there is scarcely a minor character or illustrative incident or detail of setting that is not drawn from the life.

The need for a fictional story was self-evident, since my own military experience was almost totally devoid of narrative interest. My response to the Army shifted from an indignant moral resistance to its values (I initiated, for instance, a renunciation of Potential Officer status by several graduate conscripts in my intake during

Basic Training) to a pragmatic determination to make myself as comfortable as possible and to use my time as profitably as possible (at Bovington I wangled myself the right to occupy a small security 'bunk' in an isolated office block, which gave me the privacy, peace and quiet in which to read and write: I wrote much of my first novel, *The Picturegoers*, there). For the purpose of *Ginger*, I split these reactions into two characters, and set them interacting. To heighten the contrast between them I gave the rebel an Irish Catholic republican background (and flaming red hair) and made the conforming pragmatist an agnostic. And to give additional interest to the see-saw of their fortunes, I put a girl between them.

The narrator, Jonathan Browne, is the agnostic, but in most other respects he is more like myself than the reckless, impulsive and wayward Mike 'Ginger' Brady, and I did not hesitate to choose the former rather than the latter as the lens through which to describe National Service. *Ginger, You're Barmy* is the only one of my novels, to date, in which I have used a 'first-person' narrator. It seemed, at the time, the obvious and natural way to register the impact of military life upon a sensibility unprepared for, and ill-adapted to it. To avoid the temptations of self-pity and self-justification that attend the use of quasi-autobiographical narrators, I made Jonathan betray some unamiable traits—envy, selfishness, conceit—which are meant to imply some detachment of author from character, but risk merely alienating the reader's sympathy. To mitigate this effect I bracketed the main narrative with a prologue and epilogue in which Jonathan shows some inclination to moral self-appraisal and self-renewal, but I am not sure, now, whether this was not a failure of nerve. And in the twenty years since the novel was written Jonathan has acquired some new vices that neither he nor his creator had heard of—sexism, for instance. It strikes me that several of his observations would now earn their place in the *Guardian*'s 'Naked Ape' column. This is hardly surprising: conscription, being sexually discriminatory, encouraged sexist attitudes.

Another problem was the treatment of time. Both in reality and in my germinating plot, most of the drama of National Service was concentrated in the first few months, yet the banal tedium of the rest of it was also an essential element of what the novel was 'about'. A linear, chronological structure would risk falling into the anticlimax and boredom which it sought to imitate. The best solution to this problem seemed to be a systematic flashback technique, whereby Jonathan's recall of his, and his friend's, induction into the Army is framed by his record of his last few days of service, and an evocation of the reasonably comfortable niche he has carved out for himself in the meantime.

Much later, after the novel had been published, I realized that this structure had been borrowed, subliminally, from *The Quiet American* by Graham Greene, a writer who influenced me deeply in the formative years of adolescence and early adulthood, and whose work I had studied closely in the course of postgraduate research between leaving the army and writing *Ginger*. I had been influenced, I think, not merely by the elaborate use of flashback in *The Quiet American*, but also by the relationship between Fowler, its cynical, sceptical narrator, and Pyle, the naive, dangerous enthusiast, who unsettles Fowler's complacency and leaves him, though ultimately successful in their sexual rivalry, troubled with guilt and self-reproach. Perhaps, too, Maurice Bendrix, the agnostic narrator of Greene's powerful religious novel *The End of the Affair*, whose obsessive probing of his own jealousy is also in some sense a spiritual quest, contributed something. There is a sentence in the first paragraph of *Ginger* which strikes me now as quintessentially Greenian in its relishing of the paradoxes of the moral life, its cadenced syntax and resonant abstractions: 'I could never again write so unflattering an account of myself as the following, because it would open up so many awful possibilities of amendment.'

If Graham Greene's influence on *Ginger* was not immediately apparent, even to its author, at the time of writing (the name of the narrator, Browne with an 'e', was perhaps an unconscious acknowledgement of the debt) this may have been because it has more obvious affinities with a kind of novel being written in the nineteen-fifties by novelists a generation younger than Mr Greene, writers tagged, rather unsatisfactorily, as 'Angry Young Men'. The original of this new culture hero was of course Jimmy Porter in John Osborne's play *Look Back in Anger*, first produced in 1956. I went to see it at the Royal Court during a weekend leave, and remember well the delight and exhilaration its anti-establishment rhetoric afforded me, and the exactness with which it matched my own mood at that juncture in my life.

The attraction of the phrase, 'Angry Young Man' to literary journalists was that it could be applied equally well to fictional characters and to their authors. Novels that were often discussed in this context included John Wain's *Hurry on Down*, John Braine's *Room at the Top*, Alan Sillitoe's *Saturday Night and Sunday Morning*, Stan Barstow's *A Kind of Loving*, and in the comic mode, Kingsley Amis's *Lucky Jim* and Keith Waterhouse's *Billy Liar*. Though they are far from uniform, there is a kind of family resemblance between these novels made up of the following features: gritty realism, exact observation of class and regional differences in British society, a lower-middle or working-class perspective, anti-establishment attitudes, hostility to all forms of cant and pretentiousness, a fondness for first-person, confessional narrative technique. When *Ginger, You're Barmy* was published in America, one of the epithets the blurb writer applied to it was 'angry'.

What were the Angry Young Men angry about? Nothing that could be formulated in political or ideological terms, as their subsequent development has made very clear. Fundamentally, I believe, they were angry at the slow rate of change in British society. Structurally, things had altered irrevocably as a result of the 'People's War' and the institution of the Welfare State by the 1945 Labour Government. The old rigid class society, in which inherited privilege was unquestioned by the vast majority of the population, had been, or should have been, swept away by egalitarian social, economic and educational policies. Evelyn Waugh, for example, thought this was inevitable following the Labour victory of 1945, and made a characteristically double-edged proposal that the county of Gloucestershire, in which he himself then lived, should be made into a kind of game reserve in which the aristocracy and gentry would be preserved in their natural state for the edification and entertainment of future generations of proles. Yet the British Establishment proved doggedly tenacious of power and privilege. The rising meritocrats produced by free grammar schools and free university education were apt to find that the old-boy network, the lines of power and influence that connected London, Oxbridge and the public schools, the possession of the right accent, manners and style, still protected the interests of the hereditary upper-middle class. Nowhere was this more evident than in the peacetime Army, where the rigid demarcation between Officers, Sergeants and Other Ranks was based on, and preserved, the class-distinctions of pre-war British society; and nowhere *within* the Army was it more evident than in the Royal Armoured Corps, which incorporated all the traditionally 'élite' regiments of cavalry. The anger behind *Ginger, You're Barmy* is, then, the anger of a bright, no doubt bumptious young man, who, having sensed exciting possibilities of personal self-fulfilment via education, found his progress rudely interrupted for two years by compulsory enlistment in an institution which he could neither identify with nor defeat. But if the novel is, to that extent, a personal settling of scores, I hope its anger is controlled, for I deliberately delayed writing it for some years after completing my National Service.

I began *Ginger, You're Barmy* in 1960, and completed it in the summer of 1961. It was published late the following year by MacGibbon & Kee, the publishers (now defunct) of my previous and first novel, *The Picturegoers*. 1961 was, of course, the year of the *Lady Chatterley* trial, the result of which was to have a profound effect upon the conventions of literary discourse in this country. After the acquittal of Penguin Books, there was no successful prosecution for obscenity of a novel with serious literary pretensions.

Within a few years of the trial, writers and their publishers felt free to describe sexual acts as explicitly as they wished, and to print the so-called four-letter words in full. This development was, however, too late to affect the form of *Ginger, You're Barmy*. Not that I was much concerned with the description of sexual acts in this novel, but the accurate representation of the monotonous obscenity of most spoken discourse in the army, especially in the ranks, was very much part of my purpose. Working within the conventions of the day, I adopted Norman Mailer's expedient, in *The Naked and the Dead*, of representing the most common of the four-letter words as 'fugg'; and I inscribed the vulgar term for the female pudenda with a dash between its first and last letters. (This dash was curiously elongated by MacGibbon & Kee's copy-editor or printer, perhaps to prevent the innocent reader from guessing the actual word, which was made to look more like an eight-letter than a four-letter one.) Even so, I felt it necessary to preface the book with a cautionary note in the following terms:

The coarseness of soldiers' speech and behaviour is a well-known fact, the representation of which I found necessary to my purpose in this novel. Readers likely to find such representation disturbing or distasteful are warned.

Some years later, in 1970, when Panther issued a second paperback edition of the novel, this note looked exceedingly quaint. I deleted it, and took the opportunity of a new printing to revise the text so that the obscene language was represented in full. It was a strange experience to sit down with a copy of my own novel and, like some conscientious vandal of the public libraries, write obscene expletives in the margin of nearly every page.

The present re-issue of *Ginger, You're Barmy* reproduces the mildly bowdlerized text of the first edition, which is perhaps appropriate to a novel that now seems very much a period piece—of the fifties rather than the sixties. The last National Servicemen were called up in 1960. The nation's youth entered upon a decade of unprecedented affluence, liberty and licence, unthreatened by what Jonathan Browne described as 'the bleak prospect of windswept barracks, cold water in the early morning, the harsh cries of stupid authority, the dreary monotony of the slow-moving days.' The dominant youth culture of the sixties—the music, the clothes, the hair, the experiments with sex and drugs and life-styles—would hardly have been possible without the ending of conscription. I hope my novel still has some interest as a reminder—or revelation—of the years before that deluge.

DAVID LODGE
December 1981

www.vintage-books.co.uk